DANCE AND SKYLARK

By the Same Author

THE BLUE FIELD

BRENSHAM VILLAGE

PORTRAIT OF ELMBURY

DANCE
and
SKYLARK

A Novel by

John Moore

THE REPRINT SOCIETY
LONDON

FIRST PUBLISHED 1951
THIS EDITION PUBLISHED BY THE REPRINT SOCIETY LTD.
BY ARRANGEMENT WITH WM. COLLINS SONS & CO. LTD.
1952

TO
MY GOOD FRIEND
A. D. PETERS

PRINTED IN GREAT BRITAIN BY
MORRISON AND GIBB LIMITED, LONDON AND EDINBURGH

Contents

Author's Note

The order " Hands to dance and skylark " was used in the Royal Navy during long voyages in sail when the Captain thought his ship's company needed some fun and games to liven them up.

PART ONE

I

"*Enter ODO and DODO, two Dukes of Mercia.*" On the margin of the script there was a note in Mr. Gurney's spidery handwriting that the names could, if it were thought preferable, be spelt ODDA and DODDA or even UDDA and DUDDA; the authorities differed. But Lance, rolling them round his tongue, thought that all three versions were equally ridiculous, and the quaintness of the sound tickled his fancy, so that he laughed aloud. To him on this May morning it seemed that the whole world was composed of such delightful curiosities, life was a ceaseless cornucopia pouring out before his eyes a many-coloured bounty of these toys of his imagination, strange, wondrous, absurd, beautiful, but all new-minted and bright-shining as the first of May. For he was a poet and he was young.

From his couch among the sweet-smelling grasses at the top of the little haycock-shaped hill he looked down upon the sunlit scene into which Odo and Dodo, Odda and Dodda, Udda and Dudda, had possibly strolled, about the year 700. On the spot where they had installed (according to Mr. Gurney) a devoutly religious hermit, walling him

up to the glory of God in a cell with a six-inch grating
through which he could glimpse the sky, there rose up
now a great Norman abbey, with the assorted buildings of
the small compact town clustered about it : cottages, pubs,
shops, large private houses, and even a factory which made
balloons, all huddled together like sheep in a storm. Ringed
by roofs, the twelve chestnut-trees in the churchyard,
known as the Twelve Apostles, bubbled up like a pale
green foam; Lance was too far off to see their candles of
white and red. But beyond them in the Vicarage garden a
minute black figure moved, which was certainly his father
pottering with the rain-gauge or taking a reading from the
hygrometer, as he did about six times every day. The old
man's addiction to the study of meteorology, which he
practised with tireless devotion and remarkable muddle-
headedness, was yet another of those bright and curious
fragments which the cornucopia poured out before Lance's
wondering and delighted eyes.

It was market-day, and the silvery-grey backs of the
sheep in the market-place made a pattern of blobs, five to
a pen, while other blobs ran to and fro down the alley-ways
and gradually filled up the empty pens, as if somebody
were playing one of those games with silver balls in a box
which has to be tilted to and fro until all the balls are
distributed among the various compartments. In the streets
moved crepuscular cows, chivvied by crepuscular collie-
dogs, and down the steep hill towards the river-bridge
poured more sheep, a whole flock reddish brown from
recent dipping, so that they looked like a trickling subsidence
of soil.

Two rivers tied a knot round the town, a bowline in a bight, and joined together just below it. Thence the broadening stream ran on through emerald water-meadows towards the weir. Surely, thought Lance, these meadows had never been so green before, the patches of ladies'-smocks in the damp places had never since Shakespeare looked at them shone so quicksilver-bright in the sun, the buttercups had never made such a thick-piled carpet of gold ; and nearer at hand, the blackbirds had never sung so loud nor with so sweet a melody, and the dapple-winged orange-tip butterfly had never so exquisitely matched the lacy umbel of hedge-parsley on which it poised. At twenty-two Lance was quite certain that no bygone spring had been so beautiful as this one nor would the years bring one so beautiful again. Its transience tormented him, and he stared greedily at the green-and-gold meadow as if it might fly away like the transient cuckoo calling faint and far-off among the church-yard chestnut-trees.

It was upon this great field beside the river, known as the Bloody Meadow because of the ancient battle which had been fought there, that the town's pageant would be enacted in ten weeks' time. Mr. Gurney, the industrious local archæologist, had routed out the history and devised the episodes:

THE COMING OF ODO, DODO AND THE HOLY HERMIT
(only that queer girl in the Festival Office had typed it HOLLY HERMIT);
DAME JOANNA, POETESS AND PRIORESS, FOUNDS A NUNNERY
(Who on earth was she ? thought Lance);

ROBERT FITZHAMON DEDICATES THE ABBEY;
GREAT FIGHT DURING THE WARS OF THE ROSES;
SURRENDER AND DISSOLUTION OF THE MONASTERY;
VISIT OF THE LADY MARY, DAUGHTER OF HENRY VIII AND
    AFTERWARDS QUEEN OF ENGLAND;
VISIT OF WILLIAM SHAKESPEARE POSSIBLY APHOCRYPAL
    (the queer girl's typewriter had slipped up again);
SKIRMISH DURING THE CIVIL WAR;
FLIGHT OF CHARLES II FOLLOWING THE BATTLE OF
    WORCESTER.

After that, it seemed, history had ceased, or Mr. Gurney's
interest in it had petered out ; for there the script ended,
save for the non-committal words GRAND FINALE. It was
Lance's task to " link the episodes together by means of
Choruses in verse," and when eight choruses, one prologue,
and one epilogue had been duly delivered and approved,
he would receive the modest reward of ten pounds, which
worked out at approximately one shilling a line.

Lance did not—as many a high-minded young poet
might have done—look askance at this meagre fee ; for
he reflected sensibly that it was as much as Dr. Johnson
had been paid for his first poem, and more *pro rata* than
Shelley got for *Adonais* or Keats for *Endymion*. Nor
indeed could he afford to despise it, for he had just been
sent down from Oxford in considerable disgrace and was
reduced to living on the charity of his father, who was
fortunately well acquainted with the parable of the
Prodigal Son.

He therefore applied himself earnestly to the unpromising

task of writing a Chorus on the subject of Odo and Dodo, and for a few minutes his pencil scratched some tentative fragments of blank verse on the back of Mr. Gurney's Draft Synopsis. Soon, however, the essential absurdity of the names got the better of him and he found himself laughing at his own lines, which is a very healthy and excellent thing for a young poet to do. But it is not the way to write deathless poetry, and Odo and Dodo began to take on in his mind some attributes of musical comedy:

Odiododiododiododiodo

Humming this air to himself, he stuffed the sheet of paper into his pocket and ran down the hill, taking huge strides over the springy turf for the sheer joy of being alive. He became caught up again in wonder at the whole world's absurdity; and in particular at the beautiful absurdity of the microcosm which lay below him, his beloved, his native town—its Mayor portentously announcing "our not unworthy contribution to the Dollar Drive and to the entertainment of the foreign visitors," Mr. Gurney the antique-furniture-dealer taking lucky dips out of history, Stephen Tasker, the indigent little bookseller, accepting the job of producer on the strength of having once organised a Boy Scouts' entertainment, that pale wisp of a girl who couldn't spell apocryphal wrestling with an old typewriter in the back room of the bookshop now converted into the Festival Office, Councillor Noakes pompously booming, "I don't know much about Modern Poetry, young man, but make it *clean* and make it *wholesome*."

At the bottom of the hill he turned left along the tow-path which ran beside the river towards the town. Some moorhens delighted him with their antics as they swam downstream like clockwork toys, heads wagging stiffly, little white scuts rhythmically rising and falling in perfect time with their heads, as if the same unwinding spring controlled the whole anatomy ; and he found himself repeating a poem in which Gerard Manley Hopkins praised God for

" All things counter, original, spare, strange."

That included Mayors and moorhens, old kindly Vicars pottering with rain-gauges, small-town pageants, pompous Councillors, Odo and Dodo, everything; it surely included the tubby, the almost globular figure of Mr. Handiman who now approached him along the towpath, Mr. Handi-man the ironmonger who was also Treasurer of the Festival, and who was apt to shut up his shop on any bright day in order that he might indulge his passion for angling. Lance was particularly fond of Mr. Handiman because he had bought fishing-tackle from him ever since he was so-high, hooks for a penny, bright-painted tiger-striped floats for twopence, twenty yards of stout watercord line for sevenpence-ha'penny, even a varnished bamboo rod beautifully dappled with brown and yellow blotches for four-and-sixpence. Moreover, Mr. Handiman had given long credit to generations of small boys, who forgot to pay as often as he forgot to remind them; which was one of the reasons why he was so poor.

" Any luck? " Lance asked him; and Mr. Handiman shook his head.

" It's close season, Mr. Lance, for everything except eels; and they're not biting this bright morning. But somehow, just to be beside the river on a day like this, it takes you out of yourself, don't it? "

" 'Too lovely to be looked on, save only on holy-days,' " said Lance half to himself, thinking of the green-and-gold field with the quicksilver patches of ladies'-smocks.

" Ah, that's Izaak Walton, that is. My Bible," smiled Mr. Handiman. " Every time I comes along here in the spring-time I calls it to mind."

" In a week or two, I suppose, they'll be putting up the stands," said Lance, " and then we shan't see the buttercups. How are the bookings going? "

" Bad; but it's early yet. And there's a lot of apathy in the town. They seem more interested in the Beauty Queens than in the Pageant. I sometimes wonder," added Mr. Handiman, " whether we was altogether *wise* to mix up Beauty Queens with our History. It don't seem proper somehow. What does your father think about it, Mr. Lance? "

" Oh, *he* says we must cater for all tastes. But he's more concerned about the weather than about Beauty Queens."

" A very clever gentleman, your father. Last year, a whole month before the event, he said it would be fine for the Bellringers' Outing; and fine it was. But about this Beauty Competition: what I says is that it makes for bad feeling in the town. There was booing in the cinema when they chose the finalists—booing and catcalls. The young men take sides, you see. I shouldn't like to be the man who has to judge the final, and that's a fact!"

"Nor should I," said Lance, as Mr. Handiman climbed down the steep bank and began to bait his hook with a gross and flaccid worm. "Nor should I; because I think they're both so beautiful that there's not a pin to choose between them!"

And indeed that was true; for as Lance continued on his way along the towpath he racked his memory to discover one minute particular in which the charms of Virginia exceeded those of Edna and *vice versa*; and he could find none. Virginia was a shade the taller, certainly, and she walked with such an airy grace that a man would have to be a Herrick or a Lovelace to do it justice; and she had calm grey eyes and the slender delicacy of a flower, you could compare her with a sprig of the lilac ladies'-smock misty with the dew! Yes; but Edna with the yellow hair and the high frank breasts and the glowing skin, so that there was a sort of incandescence about her—you had to liken her to those buxom marshmallows which offered themselves so artlessly to the sun. Between ladies'-smocks and kingcups, who could make a judgment? Between Pallas and Aphrodite, who could choose?

It was true that the name "Virginia" was greatly to be preferred to "Edna," and this might seem to give her a trifling advantage in the eyes of a poet, until one recollected that her surname was Smith, whereas Edna bore the more romantic one of Shirley. Once more the balance was even; by not a minim nor a single hair did the loveliness of the one outweigh the beauty of the other; and when he asked himself which of them he would have beside him now, if Edna could be miraculously translated from the balloon factory where she worked or Virginia from the office of the *Weekly Intelligencer*, he had no doubt whatever about the answer. He would have them both.

So Lance, as he walked along the towpath with his hands in his pockets and his head in the air, made the discovery that he was in love; not with one girl or even with two, but with the whole blessed lot. For when his thoughts dwelt for a moment upon the tawny-haired barmaid who had been the immediate cause of his removal from Oxford University (for the proctors had been waiting for him beneath when he lowered himself from her bedroom window like Romeo upon a rope) he could scarcely deny that he was in love with her too. And when he allowed his fancy to play about the girl in the Festival Office, he had to admit that although she couldn't spell and appeared to be witless there was nevertheless something fey and secret about her which could easily win a man's heart. Astonished by this revelation, and as if to test further the huge catholicity of his taste, he even permitted himself to consider the claims of Miss Foulkes, a waspish redhead who was said to be a member of the Communist Party and whose lively opposition to the Festival was causing considerable embarrassment to the Mayor. Lance had once danced with Miss Foulkes at the annual beanfeast of the Tennis Club; upon that occasion their conversation had been confined to the subject of Dialectical Materialism. And yet he could not be absolutely sure, upon this bright May morning, that the multitudinous freckles upon her nose had actually displeased him nor that there had not passed through his mind a momentary speculation whether her rather pretty mouth could be put to better purpose than repeating the dogmas of Karl Marx.

The fact of the matter was that Lance was in love with Life. Being a poet, he was naturally a kind of Pantheist; and being young he was a Pan-amorist as well. As he strode through the buttercups which gilded his shoes, and sang to himself some improvised and exceedingly improper verses about Odo and Dodo, his heart felt as if it would burst with an overflowing and comprehensive love of Virginia and ladies'-smocks and Edna and marshmallows and barmaids and buttercups and of the kingfisher which suddenly shot like an azure arrow out of a hollow tree and with its beautiful darting swiftness took his breath away.

Tirra-lirra by the river sang Sir Lancelot.

II

POISED ON top of the step-ladder, Stephen looked down upon his box-shaped front shop, the black cat rippling and purring in the window, the Rowlandson prints above the fireplace, the table littered with the unsorted and probably unsaleable books which he'd bought yesterday at an auction, the glass-fronted bookcase which contained his few first editions. Because he had never considered the shop from this angle before he felt curiously aloof; the ladder was a point of vantage from which he surveyed not merely his private world but the past five years he had spent in it. It didn't seem so long since he'd put up that rather foolish motto above the shelves, a tag out of his little Latin which steadily became less: QUOD PETIS HIC EST. It was foolish because hardly any of his customers understood it and in any case it wasn't true. What they sought was only occasionally and by fortunate chance to be found in those short inadequate shelves. "Have you got an up-to-date book on metallurgy, please?" "I want something on spiders, suitable for a boy." "Anything about embroidery." "Do you happen to have the *Poetical Works of Ossian*?" Or Councillor Noakes whispering furtively: "*I want you to get me a little book on Flagellation.*" If Stephen had learned anything during his five years as a bookseller, it was that the frontiers of the human mind were immeasurable, and that people were like ants questing hopelessly within that vast wilderness. But what diverse and diverting ants they were! It was an odd paradox, thought Stephen, that the experience of keeping a bookshop had taught him less about Letters than it had taught him about Life.

The glass-fronted door of the shop was suddenly darkened and from his high perch he looked down upon a bald and shining pate. The old gentleman who owned it clutched to the bosom of his black cassock a bundle of books in shabby green bindings, and Stephen laid a bet with himself that the books were by Dickens, that they were believed to be first editions, that half the plates were missing and that the other half were foxed.

B

The old gentleman looked up.

"Ah, there you are! I've brought you a few old books. They're not Theology this time, you'll be glad to hear."

Stephen came down the ladder. "I was cleaning out some cupboards," the Vicar went on, "and really, nowadays, one simply hasn't got room——"

Stephen had known, too, that the explanation would run like that: there was always so little room, there was never so little money. As he glanced at the damp-stained title-pages, the Vicar said:

"They're first editions, at least I've always understood so."

"Yes, they're the first bound editions," Stephen explained patiently; "but I'm afraid they're not very rare. You see, most of these books first came out in parts, and collectors like to have them in the original state, with the paper-wrappers and the advertisements all complete. I'm afraid——"

"You can't make an offer for them?" The Vicar was rubbing his old rheumaticky fingers where the thin string had cut them.

"Well . . ." Stephen began to tie up the bundle, and as he did so he felt his absurd weakness getting the better of him, his uncontrollable impulse of compassion. "Well, of course, they *might* sell." Angry with himself, he added almost roughly: "Perhaps I could give you a pound for the lot."

"You and I never argue," said the Vicar brightly. "A willing buyer and a willing seller can always do a deal. I should hardly have troubled you, but expenses have been rather heavy lately. That boy of mine—you heard he was —er—sent down? Some foolish escapade; I didn't inquire into it. Boys will be boys. Have you managed to sell many copies of his book? "

" Poetry is a bit difficult." And indeed, out of the fifty copies of that slim volume which Stephen had bought in another of his moments of compassionate folly, there were still forty-seven left. It was called *La Vie est Vaine*, and needless to say the Vicar had paid for its private publication. His printer had certainly cheated him, for the arty pink wrappers were fading to dirty orange and the bindings were springing, so that each of the little books had begun to open like a flower in the sun.

" You wait till the Festival visitors begin to arrive," beamed the Vicar. " Then they'll sell like hot cakes. Ah, thank you "—as Stephen took a pound out of the tobacco-tin which served as a till—" I can't deny that it will come in handy, just at the moment. Boys like mine are very expensive. Besides, I'm saving up for an anemometer."

" I beg your pardon—a what? "

" An instrument for measuring the velocity of the wind."

" Oh, I see."

" And by the way, I've got some good news for you," added the Vicar, pulling up the skirt of his cassock in order to pocket the pound note, " some very good news indeed. I've been looking at my long-range weather-charts, and there's an extremely promising fine-weather area building up in the Atlantic. It's going to be fine for the Festival! " He patted Stephen on the shoulder and went out, calling

back from the doorway: " I'll see you at the Committee
Meeting this afternoon." The wind billowed out his shabby
cassock and, as he hurried across the street on his short legs,
he looked rather like a plump blackbird. But it was an
illusory plumpness, Stephen knew, like that of a bird's
puffed-out feathers on a cold day, for the old man half-
starved himself on a stipend of three hundred and fifty a year
out of which he had to maintain his large and dilapidated
Vicarage. He had been selling his library piecemeal ever
since Stephen had taken over the bookshop. Most of it,
alas, still occupied Stephen's shelves.

Climbing up the step-ladder again, painfully because his
shrapnel-shattered knee was contradicting the Vicar's
weather forecast, Stephen resumed his self-imposed task of
taking stock. He hated this annual formality, which
assumed the shape of a prolonged inquest upon all his
follies—why on earth had he paid fifteen shillings for that
deplorable set of Gibbon's *Decline and Fall*, why had he
failed to notice that the Byron first edition lacked a fly-leaf,
why had he allowed a tearful widow to persuade him to
buy no less than five copies of her late husband's uninspired
work on Liverworts and Mosses? Like shabby and faintly
disreputable acquaintances whom one avoids if one can,
the same books turned up at every stocktaking, the old
bound *Punches*, the inevitable Longfellows, the Complete
Works of Sir Walter Scott. They would be with him, he
thought, until the end of his days.

For the rest, stocktaking only served to prove on paper
what he already knew: that he was losing money. Immediately after the war, when there were still a few

American soldiers about, he had made a substantial profit; for the G.I.s having bought up everything in the town from beer to bicycles could find nothing else to spend their money on save books. But the profits of those fat years had been eaten up by the subsequent lean ones. His war gratuity had gone too, and all he had left was the small capital sum left him by his father. He had seriously thought of giving up the bookshop, and trying to get a job in a library, when Councillor Noakes had suggested that he should organise the town's Festival and produce the Pageant, for which service the Committee had voted him a hundred and fifty pounds. "Perfect arrangement all round," said Councillor Noakes. "We use your back shop as an office, find you a Secretary, and pay you a fee. Visitors flock to the town, good for trade, fill your shop with customers, everything hunky-dory." But already Stephen was beginning to doubt whether it was going to work out like that. For one thing he knew little about producing; the sum of his experience was *A Midsummer Night's Dream* at school, some musical shows in the Army, and a Boy Scouts' Pageant at the very thought of which he blushed still, for the script had been written by a local Lady Bountiful who fancied herself as a versifier and must on no account be displeased. Her inspiration had reached its climax in a scene on a desert island, when the principal character standing beside an unfurled Union Jack suddenly exclaimed:

> "*What is that voice which I have heard before?*
> *It is my mother, washed up on the shore.*"

The repetition of this couplet, at ten rehearsals and three performances, had caused Stephen the most acute embarrassment; and he was by no means certain that something of the kind might not occur again, for the names of Odo and Dodo were ominous indeed.

Moreover, he had discovered that he was not merely expected to produce the Pageant, but to cast it, advertise it, oversee the dressmakers, hire the horses, engage the programme sellers, arrange the box-office, sell the tickets, and do everything else which was necessary; and to help him in this tremendous task the Mayor had wished upon him the extraordinary girl whose typewriter in the back room now tittuped in a series of short bursts with long pauses in between: like a Lewis gun, he thought, operated by some gallant but incompetent defender of an outflanked salient, continually jamming itself, repeatedly cleared so that it could fire another few rounds, but doomed irrevocably to silence in the end.

She was a farmer's daughter, to whose father no doubt the Mayor had been under some heavy obligation; and her shorthand and typing were self-taught. She had sat in the back room for five days now, placid, self-possessed, apparently incompetent, and quite unresponsive to Stephen's kindly attempts at conversation about such subjects as saddle-back pigs and shorthorn cows. " Yes, Mr. Tasker," she said demurely; and sat so still in the straight-backed chair that Stephen became most foolishly embarrassed and made an excuse to go into the front shop. Only her wide blue eyes were continually in motion, making examination, as if they were amusing curiosities, of her shorthand, the typewriter, the book-lined room, and himself. She was beginning to get on Stephen's nerves.

TitumtitumtitumtitumtitUM, went the typewriter, like a line of bad blank verse, and suddenly stopped. No doubt the letter " t " had become tangled up with the letter " y " and Miss Pargetter was staring wide-eyed at the interesting phenomenon. At that moment the shop window was darkened again and there fell on to the sunlit floor of the shop a shambling, flapping, curiously corvine shadow. Corvine too was Mr. Gurney's exclamation when he opened the door and saw Stephen on top of the steps.

" *Quark!* " he said, like a suddenly-alarmed bird. " What you doing? "

As usual he carried an umbrella, although it was a cloudless day, and as usual he carried it like a rifleman, at the trail. His shadow lay across the floor like that of a hunch-backed giant with a spear.

" I'm stocktaking," said Stephen.

" *Quark!* " Mr. Gurney was horrified. " What you want to do that for? "

" I do it every year."

" Make any money? " grinned Mr. Gurney.

" That's what I'm trying to find out."

" Foolish, foolish," said Mr. Gurney, clicking his tongue. " Let sleeping dogs lie. If you find you've made a loss you'll start worrying, and if you show a profit the Income Tax will have it sure as nuts. Beware the Jabberwock, my boy; beware the Income Tax. I never take stock."

Stephen wasn't surprised. Mr. Gurney, who kept the antique furniture shop next door, observed none of the conventions of retail trade. He opened when he felt like it and shut when he became bored. If the conversation, manners or faces of his customers displeased him, he compensated himself for having to put up with their company by doubling his prices. On the other hand, if he liked the look of a person he was apt to knock off twenty-five per cent. Since almost every article in his shop was skilfully faked he could afford to do this. From time to time he would " dodge out," as he put it, for a drink, sticking up in his window a peculiarly discouraging notice which said *Back in half an hour*; and often, like Mr. Handiman the ironmonger, he would take himself off for the whole day, leaving no apology at all.

" What's all this about an extra episode? " he said, while Stephen sat on the top of the ladder, fascinated by a bird's-eye view of Mr. Gurney's enormous jowl bulging out over a butterfly collar.

" Well, the Committee feels that we can't just stop at Charles the Second. *Something* must have happened, even in this place, since then."

" A great many things have happened," said Mr. Gurney. " People have been born, have loved, married, had children, hated, dreamed, cheated, thieved, prospered, and starved; and in due course have died wondering what it was all about. But that, Noakes tells me, is not History." Mr. Gurney bore an ancient grudge against Councillor Noakes, of which the origin was lost in obscurity. " History, according to him, consists of Battles, Kings and Queens."

" And Odo and Dodo," said Stephen, " and Dame Joanna. By the way, I shall have to know a bit more about

that lady. Apparently she was our only local poet, but
what did she write? "

"Reams," said Mr. Gurney, "and all in practically
undecipherable manuscript at the Bodleian. Most of it is
extremely coarse."

"But she was a Prioress! "

"There are suggestions that her nunnery was not
everything that it should be."

"Look here," said Stephen, "how am I expected to
produce an episode in which somebody founds a nunnery
which is not everything that it should be? "

"That's your headache," said Mr. Gurney cheerfully.
"My job is simply to give you the facts." And with that
he was gone. His grotesque shadow lifted itself like a
cumbrous bird off the worn carpet on the floor and flapped
away. "Remember what I said about the Income Tax! "
he squawked from the door. "Beware the Jabberwock,
my boy! " He waved his umbrella in valediction, and then
the sunshine flooded back into the small square room.

Stephen once more turned his attention to the top shelf,
where all his worst bargains stood in a row, skied there like
second-rate pictures in an Art Gallery because it was incon-
ceivable that anybody should buy them. He heaved down
Jacob's *Law Dictionary* in two volumes, price one guinea,
and noticed that the ghostly mouse, which nobody ever
heard or saw, had been nibbling the edge of the leather
binding. The beast was untrappable, since it unnaturally
preferred old calf to cheese.

The damaged books certainly weren't worth a guinea
now, so Stephen marked them down to ten-and-six, more

as a gesture than in any hope that they would sell. Next to them stood Macaulay's *History of England* in eight scrubby volumes, all with broken spines, and then came *The Art of the Farrier Improv'd in All its Parts with some Original Observations concerning The Thrush in Horses*, and then *Annals of My Village*, by the author of *Select Female Biographies* and *The Conchologist's Companion*: a versatile writer, thought Stephen, if a dull one. From each of the books, as he pulled them out of the shelf and opened them one by one, a year's accumulation of dust rose up, drifted away on the draught, and formed eddying nebulæ which were caught in a slanting shaft of light from the window. He became aware that Miss Pargetter, who always walked as softly as a cat, had emerged from the back shop and was standing beneath him gazing up at the swirling dust-particles with large inquisitive eyes.

" It reminds me," she observed quietly, " of the Universe according to Sir James Jeans."

Stephen was so astonished that he nearly dropped *The Art of the Farrier* upon her head; for until this moment he had entertained some doubts whether she could even read.

" I bet there are millions of germs there," she added. " You can get awful diseases from second-hand books. When I was at school I caught measles from *David Copperfield*. A girl had accidentally brought it out of the san."

" You can get more dangerous things than diseases from books," said Stephen. " You can get ideas."

" Yes, Mr. Tasker." She relapsed into her formal manner, and stood at the foot of the ladder, gauche, disinterested and immobile, with her shorthand notebook open in her hand.

"I couldn't read my notes," she said. (She never apologised for anything.) "The Earl of Somerset laid, and then there's a squiggle."

"The Earl of Somerset laid?"

"Yes, laid a what?" said Miss Pargetter patiently.

"Does it look like 'egg'?"

She studied her book without smiling, and at last said: "No."

"Then try 'ambush.'"

"Yes, Mr. Tasker." Softly as a cat, she went towards the back room. Stephen called out to her:

"I've got to go to a Committee Meeting this afternoon. You'll look after the shop?"

"Yes, Mr. Tasker."

"The prices are all marked plainly inside the front covers."

"Yes, Mr. Tasker."

"I don't suppose anybody will come in, though," said Stephen. He put the *Annals of My Village* back on the shelf and jotted down its price in his notebook. Titum-titumtitUM went the typewriter, like a brief despairing fusillade. Then silence returned. The Earl of Somerset had laid an ambush; and Miss Pargetter was stuck again.

III

"MEANWHILE OUR maidens," wrote Mr. Runcorn, "emulous in pulchritude," and looked across his office, as if for inspiration, at the impeccable profile of Miss Smith who sat at her little desk in the far corner of the room. But he was old and desiccated, and the broad smooth brow, the grave eyes, the slightly-parted lips and the faultless permanent wave (free to finalists) held no inspiration for him. Indeed it struck him as more than a little unseemly that the *Weekly Intelligencer* should number a potential Beauty Queen among its staff; and he recollected the words which he had spoken, only ten years ago, to a cub reporter who came to the office in ankle-length plus-fours: "In our profession, we do not unduly draw attention to ourselves, Mr. Cole." The plus-fours had been bad enough; but a Beauty Queen was unheard of. Nothing of the kind had ever happened in the office before, and the files of the paper, which was one of the oldest in the United Kingdom, went back to 1772. Nor had the style of its leading articles changed much since then; for Mr. Runcorn was a practised exponent of the art of circum-locution, which he had learned from his ancient predecessor nearly fifty years ago. His mentor, in turn, had picked it up from *his* predecessor; and thus the laboured, elaborate and somewhat facetious prose which distinguished the

Intelligencer from any other newspaper had been handed down through an apostolic succession of editors from the original founder: a turgid stream flowing direct from its muddy source. That first editor, when he wished to imply that the champion beast at Christmas market had been slaughtered by the town's leading butcher, used to write that it had " made the acquaintance of the pole-axe at the hands of our chief practitioner of the executioner's trade." Mr. Runcorn still used the same phrase in his Christmas number, merely substituting " humane killer " for " pole-axe " out of deference to the R.S.P.C.A.

It would be a serious breach of the rules to write of a Beauty Competition as a Beauty Competition, it would be almost as bad as describing the scarlet-coated followers of the chase as mere huntsmen, and Mr. Runcorn had already employed " pulchritude " twice; so his old eyes in search of a synonym fixed themselves upon the trim head of Miss Smith, the plucked eyebrows, the darkened lashes and the well-powdered nose.

Miss Smith, however, deep in a brown study, was unconscious of his stare. She, too, was in search of a word, but she didn't mind what it meant so long as it was sufficiently mellifluous and began with a V. For a long time she had been troubled about the ordinariness of her surname, which whenever she shut her eyes she was apt to see in large shining letters upon a cinema screen: " Starring Virginia Smith." But " Smith " was clearly impossible, and since she firmly believed that her success in the semi-final had brought her one step nearer to Hollywood, the problem of a substitute now became urgent. The prize for the winner of the Beauty Competition was a film-test; thence it was but a short step to becoming a Starlet, and thence to a Star. Most of her favourite film-stars bore alliterative names, but her vocabulary was somewhat limited and she knew very few words beginning with V. " Virginia Vale " had tempted her, but she thought it sounded rather like a suburb or a telephone exchange, and now she was weighing up the respective merits of Virtue and Verity. For this purpose she shut her eyes until she could feel the long lashes tickling and watched in her imagination the familiar flickering screen with the incandescent captions: " Starring James Mason and Virginia Verity," " Starring Virginia Virtue and Stewart Granger." She was thus occupied when a banshee scream, rather like a railway engine's whistle only hoarser and more throaty, awakened her out of her daydream with a start.

It was the voice-pipe by which the office downstairs communicated with Mr. Runcorn and *vice-versa*. This horrible instrument, which she felt sure was full of spit, had been a daring innovation when it was first installed about 1850; and Mr. Runcorn, who now had a telephone on his desk, nevertheless obstinately insisted that the voice-pipe should still be used for speaking between the offices. In order to work it you took a deep breath, put your lips to the mouthpiece, and blew. This produced the whistle. Thereafter you shouted your message in such a loud voice that the person below would hear you even without the aid of the instrument. Its use, in fact, was simply a convention, quite unrelated to any utilitarian end.

With revulsion, Miss Smith put her shell-pink ear to the

repellent mouthpiece and felt a scorching sirocco blowing into it, which was the spotty office boy's breath. When it had blown itself out she wiped the mouthpiece with a tiny blue handkerchief and cautiously spoke into it, removing her lips from it very quickly lest they should be contaminated by the office boy's reply. A wheezing noise came out of the pipe, and she shouted " Speak louder " at the top of her voice. He did so, and she was able to hear him through the worm-eaten floorboards: " The Mayor to see the Boss." Mr. Runcorn, who had also heard although he was several yards from the voice-pipe, looked up from his writing and inclined his head. She shouted back " Send him up, please," and the office boy's shrill unbroken tenor came up through the floor: " Okay."

The Mayor was a small sandy man called John Wilkes, who invariably signed his Christian name as Jno. He was without presence, dignity or ambition, and he was always in a hurry because he was always " doing things for people." He had been chosen as Mayor for no other reason than this: that he was kind. And because he was also humble, so that none of the Councillors had cause to be jealous of him, he looked like remaining in office until he died; for there was no great competition for the Mayoralty of the small decaying town. The little man was literally killing himself with kindness, for he could never bring himself to say no to anybody who asked him to do anything for them. He lived in a state of perpetual breathlessness.

He now burst into the room, greeted Mr. Runcorn, and rushed across to shake Miss Smith's hand and congratulate her upon her success. Her mouth was full of antiseptic

lozenges, so she said nothing, but fluttered her eyelids at
him and gave him what she believed to be an enigmatic
smile. " Really, Runcorn," he said, " you're a lucky dog,
you know: sitting in here all day with nothing to do but
stare at a Beauty Queen! Poor me, I've just come from the
Council and now I'm off to a Festival Committee."

He threw himself into the visitor's chair opposite Mr.
Runcorn's desk.

" Frankly, I'm worried about the Festival. There seems
no interest, no real enthusiasm at all. I say to them, ' Let's
relive our glorious 'istory,' and they only shrug their
shoulders. I tell 'em it'll help to earn dollars for the country,
and they just don't care. What they don't realise is that
the foreign visitors will put money into *their* pockets——"

" I suppose," said Mr. Runcorn sepulchrally, " that there
will be some foreign visitors? "

" Swarms of 'em, don't you worry. With money to
burn. That's the line for you to take, if you don't mind
me making the suggestion. Visitors from all over the
world! "

Mr. Runcorn nodded without enthusiasm and made a
note on his blotting-pad: " *Viators and peripatetics from
other climes.*"

" I'm relying on you," added the Mayor, " to lift them
out of their apathy. Rouse 'em, Runcorn, rouse 'em! "

" It isn't apathy alone," said Mr. Runcorn, picking up a
typewritten letter off his desk. " It's active opposition.
Read this."

The letter began:

" *We the undersigned workers wish to protest against the*

diversion of valuable man-hours and material, at this critical moment in our history . . ." It went on for nearly three pages and bore twelve signatures, the first of which was " Enid Foulkes."

" That's bad," said the Mayor, shaking his head. " That's a blow beneath the belt, that is."

" They're all employed at the balloon factory," said Mr. Runcorn.

" I wish nobody any harm," sighed the Mayor, " but do you know, if I owned the balloon factory, I'd be almost tempted to *purge* that Enid Foulkes." He was about to hand back the letter to Mr. Runcorn when he hesitated.

" I suppose it wouldn't be possible——"

" Yes? "

" Just this once——"

" Yes? "

He became aware of the eyes of Mr. Runcorn, like those of an immensely old lizard, unblinking and cold.

" To tuck it away," he stammered.

" Yes? "

" On an inside page."

There was a long silence during which it seemed as if the shades of five sea-green incorruptibles, Mr. Runcorn's predecessors in the editorial chair, were gathered behind him where he sat hunched at his desk, as still as a lizard on a rock. The Mayor dropped the letter on the desk.

" This," said Mr. Runcorn, tapping it, " is a matter of public interest. I think I need say no more."

An atmosphere of bleak and wintry indignation filled the room. The Mayor got up to go.

C

"I'm sorry, Runcorn," he said, "I oughtn't to have suggested that."

"No," said Mr. Runcorn.

"I could bite my tongue off," said the Mayor. "Please forget it."

He went out, and even Miss Smith, who had seen Councillors and Town Clerks and on one memorable occasion the Vicar himself dismissed in the same way, felt sorry for him. Mr. Runcorn looked across the room at her and, forgetting for a moment that she was a Beauty Queen, saw her only as a member of the staff who must therefore participate in his sense of outrage.

"The *Weekly Intelligencer*," he observed, "may not be the *Manchester Guardian*; but we share certain principles."

Miss Smith said nothing; for a number of painful experiences had convinced her that people liked her much better when she didn't talk, and she had developed a kind of defensive mechanism of silence. So she fell to daydreaming again, and, closing her eyes, saw herself in the dress which the Beauty Queen would wear for the Grand Procession. This dress was to be specially designed by a young man called Robin who had been engaged to design all the dresses for the Pageant; and he, protesting that he couldn't possibly contrive clothes for somebody he didn't know, had invited her to tea in his studio. Miss Smith had politely declined, while consenting to go a walk with him instead on one of her afternoons off; for the young man, though attractive, had a reputation for unconventional behaviour and she was well aware of the special dangers inherent in artists' studios. A Beauty Queen could not be too careful; for that matter—a film-star could not be too careful! Fluttering her eyelids slightly, Miss Smith faded out the long taffeta dress with puff sleeves and replaced it with a dark oblong upon which convolutions of light hurled themselves towards her, formed fantastic patterns, and at last resolved themselves into her own name. Starring Virginia Verity? Virtue? Vane?—Oh no, that was liable to misinterpretation—Valley? Vance? Virginia Vance, she decided, was almost perfect; in quaint gothic letters for a Period Picture, in square modern ones for a Tense Drama, in blue, in old gold, in rose, in emerald green for a piece in technicolor, the beautiful name pirouetted before her eyes.

The girl, thought Mr. Runcorn, must surely have fallen asleep; and although he could but disapprove, some ancient courtesy forbade him to wake her. Instead he stared hard at the almost Grecian profile, stared and stared until suddenly inspiration came. He picked up his pen and began to write, firmly crossing out " pulchritude " and putting " callisthenics " instead.

IV

THE FACTORY down by the river was making beach-balls for Australia, which in six months' time would be bouncing over the firm sands of Sydney. Children tawny as the sand would play with them, strong swimmers would push them far out to sea, small Bradmans with improvised bats would smite them to tideline boundaries, swift brown girls chased by swift brown youths would toss them like Atalanta's apple to the eager pursuers. Meanwhile it was Edna's task to see that there was no flaw in them, and with deft fingers she drew them one by one over the nozzle of the compressor, turned on the air, and watched them swell till they were as big as ripe melons. It was a sight for the Garden-god, who surely has an eye for such things, when Edna lifted the many-coloured ball off the air nozzle and stood for a moment holding it before her. For in a splendid way they matched. There were no angles, no straight lines such as nature abhors; but tumescence in the happiest conjunction, a symphony of curves.

In a light haze of french chalk a dozen women and girls worked on the bench with Edna, putting in the valves and rubber patches and blowing up the balls to test them. Close at hand Jim and Joe, who six years after the war still wore their green Commando berets, stood as it were at the head of the production line. Jim operated by hand a somewhat primitive-looking machine which lowered the formas into liquid latex, and after an appropriate interval transferred them to a homely little oven where they were dried by means of naked gas-jets in exactly the same way that one cooks a Sunday joint. When they were done Joe took charge of them and dipped them into a tank of water on top of which floated a scum of mixed rubber paint, iridescent like petrol in a pool. When they emerged from this bath they were rainbow-tinted with streaks and whorls of red, yellow, blue and green. After a second drying they were peeled off the formas and passed to Edna and her women for testing.

Upstairs in the packing-room eight more women were employed; and at busy seasons there would be at least another dozen at the long testing-bench. But to-day the work went leisurely in an atmosphere like that of a family party. The compressor kept up a low whine, and the air released from the beach-balls made an intermittent soft sigh, but since there was no noisy machinery everybody could talk to everybody else. When Jim in his harsh corncrake's voice said: " Carrots is right. What we wants is 'ouses," the conversation at once became general.

" 'Ouses and a bit more rations," agreed Joe, " instead of these faldadiddles and goings on."

" Mind you," said Jim, " I ain't against fun, don't anybody think that, us all needs a bit o' fun these days. But who's going to pay for it, that's what I wants to know? "

" Us," said Mrs. Greening, the blowsy woman next to Edna. Her name was pronounced Grinnin.

" Us? How? " said another woman.

" Bit on the fags, bit on the booze, bit on the pools, bit on the PAYE. We allus does pay for everything."

" 'Course," added Jim, with a glance at Edna, " I'm not saying aught against Beauty Competitions. Apart from putting ideas into folk's heads, I dare say they don't do no 'arm."

" You'll be too snooty to know us, ducks," said Mrs. Greening, prodding Edna in the ribs, " when you're on the fillums and we pays sixpence to go and see you."

" Not me "—Edna laughed—" I only went in for a lark.
I haven't won it yet, anyhow."

" But you will, ducks. You got more personality than
her. The stuck-up bitch," said Mrs. Greening.

" Oh, I dunno. She's all right. We shan't quarrel,
whoever wins."

" You're too easy-going, ducks."

" Well, it's only a lark."

The whole of life was a lark to Edna: the cheerful
companionship of the long bench, the chi-acking over cups
of tea, the naughty stories Mrs. Greening whispered in her
ear, the Saturday-night dances at the Town Hall, walking
out on Sunday afternoons, holding sticky hands with boys
in the pictures. It was " just for a lark " that she had
accepted Robin's invitation to tea in his studio, after he had
explained with engaging frankness why he couldn't possibly
design the same dress for both the finalists and must
therefore have a design in readiness for whichever of them
turned out to be the chosen Queen. " Your personalities,
your colouring, and if I may say so your figures, my dear,
are absolute opposites." Edna had giggled; and she had a
charming giggle, which came from very deep down and
was like the gurgle of a mountain stream bubbling up
between the ferny rocks. It wasn't long before she and
Robin were holding hands, and being of a yielding and
generous nature she didn't leave his studio until long after
nightfall. But that, too, was " only for a lark." She wasn't
going to fall in love with Robin, oh dear no, not after
seeing all those sketches of women without any clothes on
decorating the studio walls. She had found it difficult to

believe his protestations that he had painted them out of his head.

Joe said: " Here's the last batch of mucking old beach-balls, and then we've finished."

" Finished? " said Edna. " What's the next job? "

" Kaput. Finished," croaked Jim. " No more orders for nothing, that's what the Boss said."

" No more export? "

" The Yanks," said Joe, " 'ave got tired of poppin' balloons at Christmas parties. Likewise the Aussies and the Argentinos. But we're going to make a few fancy lines on spec, like, teddy-bears and jumbos, and then it's curtains unless something turns up."

" One thing," said Mrs. Greening, " he won't put us off, not until he got to."

" Not him," said Joe. " When he was wounded at Walcheren, wounded and very near drownded he was, the first thing he wanted to know was about us chaps. Was Jim and Joe all right, he said. *And* shot through the stummick! "

Just then the big creaking double-doors opened—the tumbledown place had been a warehouse, and long ago a tannery, before John Handiman the ironmonger's son converted it into a balloon factory in 1946—and there entered a very small messenger-boy carrying a very large bunch of flowers. " For the office," he said, and marched through the shop towards the door marked " Private," at the far end. All the women at the bench turned round to peer at the dewy pink petals just showing above the tissue paper.

"Roses this week," sniffed Mrs. Greening. "Must 'ave cost a packet."

"It was tulips last time," said Joe.

Mrs. Greening gave Edna another friendly dig in the ribs. "Ain't you jealous, ducks?"

"Good luck to her," laughed Edna. "But I do wonder who her boy is."

Jim's voice like a saw cutting a rough piece of wood grated through the whole shop:

"Must be rich, must be crackers, must 'ave plenty of guts."

He peeled off the last batch of beach-balls and tossed them to Edna. Adroitly she stuck the valves in and slipped them over the air-nozzles, plugging each ball in turn as it was blown up. The sunlight coming through the open double-door fell on her as she held a whole bunch together, like giant grapes, and for a moment she ceased to belong to the dingy factory with its leprous coating of french chalk, she was a Bacchante strayed there, a vision of the vineyards glowing and shining, a beaker full of the warm South.

It was a fault inseparable from Miss Foulkes' colouring that when she blushed she went salmon-pink, arms, neck and face, and when the flush subsided it left her unnaturally white, with the freckles standing out against her pallor like specks of sand. She always blushed when the flowers arrived, and there was always an uncomfortable silence in the office afterwards.

John Handiman busied himself ostentatiously with his letters. Miss Foulkes said to the messenger-boy: "Put them down there," and he laid the roses on the filing-cabinet next to the bowl of fading tulips which he had delivered last week. The week before it had been anemones, and the week before that hyacinths. Whoever the sender might be, he was a most faithful and persistent fellow, and John was profoundly puzzled, because however hard he tried he could not for the life of him imagine Enid Foulkes with a young man.

But why not? he asked himself. She was only twenty-nine, her flaming hair was a challenge, she was not at all bad-looking, she was clever—and yet there was something which seemed to obviate the very possibility of courtship. It was a sort of angularity, he decided; her bare elbows lying on the desk were little sharp nobbles, and her shoulder-blades showed like knife-edges through her thin dress. Perhaps that was because she lived chiefly on nuts. But hers was not simply an angularity of physique, but of disposition. Her character was all sharp corners; there was no smooth side to it, no place for compromise, it would cut a man to pieces, thought John oddly, to match his mind to hers. Perhaps the unknown suitor had learned this lesson, and was trying out the softening effect of roses.

"The debit balance at the Bank," said Miss Foulkes, white-faced now that her blush had faded, "is two hundred and seventy-three pounds eight and a penny; leaving two hundred and twenty-six pounds eleven and eleven pence to carry on with before we reach the limit of five hundred." She ruled a neat red ink line at the bottom of the sheet of paper. Miss Foulkes' accounts, even when they were only memoranda, were always decorated with red lines, single ones and double ones and in certain complex cases treble ones, and these lines were never smudged or crooked, but were as thin as hairs and as straight as ramrods. Somehow they seemed to express her personality; for Miss Foulkes was meticulous. She was so meticulous that when she found a halfpenny one day upon the office floor she put it into the Petty Cash and now, three years later, that tiresome halfpenny still appeared in the monthly totals, in the annual balance, and even in the audited accounts. John Handiman loathed the sight of it.

" You haven't allowed for this week's wages? " he said.

" No."

" Then unless some money comes in soon we're going to be in a jam. And we can't hope for anything much before the beginning of July."

Miss Foulkes promptly handed him two typewritten sheets headed respectively " Creditors " and " Debtors," each heading being underlined in red. There was not much comfort to be found in them; and it ran through John's mind that the adventure which he had embarked upon so eagerly after the war, which had seemed almost like another Commando operation because Jim and Joe were in it with him, was likely to end, as adventures so often did, not with a bang but a whimper. There would be no sudden and startling bankruptcy; but the orders would dwindle away, the profits would gradually contract, the chatter and the laughter at the long bench would die down, and one morning Miss Foulkes would rule a treble red line, just a shade thicker than usual, at the bottom of the last page in the ledger. When that happened she and Jim and Joe, Mrs. Greening,

Edna, and the rest would have to look for new jobs; and
he would be back in his father's little shop selling fish-
hooks to urchins.

He said:

"Look here, Miss Foulkes. You juggle with figures
eight hours a day. Tell me frankly, what's going wrong
with this show?"

She answered without hesitation: "Too small a profit-
margin on a small output."

"Exactly. But we had to accept that in order to export
at all."

"Then why export?"

"To earn dollars. It seemed a good thing to do." And
indeed he had done so for the same unformulated reason
that in 1939 he had joined the Army.

But Miss Foulkes clicked her tongue. She disapproved
of dollars.

"And look where it's got us," she said. "We missed the
home market when the home market was good, and now
the Americans don't want our stuff any more. So we've
made the worst of both worlds."

"Yes, I've been a mug, I dare say." He grinned wryly.
"I'll have to tackle the dear old Bank again."

"The Bank!" That was another thing she disapproved
of. Every Monday she had to go to the Bank to pay in:
every Friday she went there to draw the money for the
wages: and on these occasions she entered the place with
the air of a teetotaller who is compelled to visit a pub or a
very Low Churchman whose painful duty of sightseeing
takes him into Saint Peter's at Rome. As such a one would

sniff the incense, so sniffed Miss Foulkes at the odour of high finance. Disdainfully she stood at the counter with her sharp nose in the air, disdainfully and without a word of thanks she received the packets of notes and the paper bags of coins, deliberately counting them three times as if to demonstrate her mistrust of the whole capitalist system.

"The Bank!" she repeated, in that superior and dismissive tone which she reserved for the objects of her ideological disapprobation. John had once amused himself by mentally making a catalogue of them: Banks and Yanks, foxhunting, debutantes, *Punch*, Boy Scouts, beefsteaks, Saint George. . . . He suspected that she secretly disapproved of balloons also, since it was frequently their destiny to be popped by drunken revellers at night-clubs, and of beach-balls, since the Idle Rich were apt to play with such idle toys when they disported themselves on the Riviera.

And yet, oddly enough, he liked her. The complexities and nuances of character, which he didn't understand, always puzzled and disquieted him; so he would pick out from a person's make-up some simple virtue and cling to his belief in it for dear life. In Miss Foulkes' case the virtue was loyalty. It was a loyalty, he knew, which he shared with the Communist Party; and this amused him, since he didn't take politics very seriously. If at some time in the fantastic future the Communist Party should take it into its crackpot head to order Miss Foulkes to blow up the factory, then poor Miss Foulkes, he imagined, torn asunder, schizophrenic, would probably go mad. Meanwhile he found a strange comfort in her loyalty, and now that things were going badly he relied upon it more and more.

"Bank or no Bank," he said, "we'll carry on, shall we, until we're down to that last halfpenny in the Petty Cash?"

She nodded, unsmiling, for she didn't think there was anything funny about the halfpenny.

"We'll make a few thousand elephants on spec," he said. "Elephants always do go well at Christmas. Or shall it be pigs?"

"Pigs were more in demand last year."

"Shall we put a squeak in them?"

"It adds to the cost, but they go better with a squeak."

"Our last dying squeak." Still she did not smile. "Now I'll go and tell Jim to change the formas. You'd better put those roses in water," he said.

The salmon-pink blush rose like a tide up her neck and arms and he hurried to the door, aware once again of her vulnerability, puzzled and embarrassed by it because it didn't fit in with the rest of her, it was one of those complexities which he didn't understand.

V

THE COMMITTEE MEETING, that typically and terribly English thing, had been going on for nearly two hours, and Stephen's wounded knee, cramped under the table, was nagging him like a toothache. The end was not yet in sight.

Originally the Committee had consisted of eight; but
its membership had been doubled by the co-option of
people who were said to have " felt hurt." To-day there
were several new members whom Stephen did not even
know. The deliberations of this multitude, as it seemed to
him, followed a course as tortuous as that of the town's
own river. They meandered, they ran in circles, they tied
themselves in knots; unpredictable cat's-paws of wind rippled
them and uncharted currents stirred their depths. A
proposal to insure against rain had just given the Vicar an
excuse to deliver a considerable sermon on the subject of
anticyclones. Stephen, who had heard it several times
before, let his mind wander away while the voice of the
Vicar bumbled on and a distant cuckoo mocked the whole
proceedings through the open window.

His thoughts went back through time and space to a
spring morning in 1944, that had been full of unseen
cuckoos too, and to an olive-grove in Thessaly. The
occasion was the only one in his life when he had been
really important; and his importance was due to the fact
that a crumpled parachute lay in folds at his feet and he
held a tommy-gun in his hands. Until that moment he had
been a very ordinary person: in peace-time a history master
at second-rate prep schools eking out his miserable pay by
conducting archæological tours to Greece every summer
holidays, in war-time a clerkly intelligence officer, one more
dogsbody among all the dogsbodies on the swollen staff at
Cairo. Then, quite suddenly, he had been translated—there
was no other word for it—into a sort of Prometheus; for
he brought fire from heaven, in the shape of grenades and

mortar shells, to the men who had fought for years with old rifles and their bare hands. For thirteen months he had lived like an Olympian; until on VE-day a bone-shaking lorry had carried him back to Athens with a shattered knee, back to the ordinariness of hospital, demobilisation, unsuccessful bookselling, and small-town Committee Meetings at which the subject under discussion at the moment was, of all things, horse-manure.

" A dollop of muck," Mr. Handiman was saying, " from the Council's stables would do 'em a world of good."

Nearly two years ago, when the Festival was first mooted, Mr. Handiman the ironmonger had received a poetic inspiration, although at the time he was fishing with maggots for eels. Born of the sunshine and the buttercups, it had concerned flowers: let every cottage garden at Festival-time put on a special display, let every street corner blossom its welcome to the visitors from afar! When he began to elaborate this pretty notion, his thoughts naturally turned to roses, red roses and white, the favours of Lancaster and York. The ancient borough should be embowered in roses! The Council, in a mood of midsummer madness, had approved the idea and passed a resolution asking every gardener to plant roses where they could be seen from the streets. More daring still, it had even voted a halfpenny rate as a contribution towards the cost. The imaginative gesture had earned the town a good deal of free publicity, including a neatly-turned fourth leader in *The Times*; and the only protests had come from Miss Foulkes, who wrote to Mr. Runcorn pointing out that the workers couldn't eat roses, and from Mr. Gurney, who unkindly drew attention to the fact that Councillor Noakes was in business as a nurseryman and florist.

But now Mr. Handiman's innocent suggestion about a free dollop of muck for the roses seemed to cause some embarrassment to the Mayor, who at last had to admit that Councillor Noakes regularly took away the horse-manure " under a long-standing arrangement." Stephen was aware of deep currents stirring as Mr. Gurney demanded " What does he pay for it? " and Councillor Noakes shouted " I protest! " The argument went on for quite a long time, with the Mayor patiently explaining that there were only two old horses which pulled the dust-carts " so the amount involved is really very small," and Mr. Gurney muttering something about " wheels within wheels."

" The next item on the agenda," said the Mayor swiftly, " is headed ' Sideshows.' " And at once there rose up a large lady in furs and feathers who observed—and Stephen could hardly believe his ears—that she was the President of the Fur and Feather League, and what about an exhibition of chinchilla rabbits? During the subsequent silence Stephen took pleasure in watching the expression on Lance's face; for the young poet, whose bright new world was brimming over with fascinating absurdities, was delighting in the discovery of a new one, and had plainly taken the furry lady to his heart. He stared at her in an ecstasy of wonder, oblivious of Robin, who had a simpler sense of fun and was poking him in the ribs with a pencil.

" I'm not absolutely certain," murmured the Mayor, " although of course we want to encourage all local activities, whether *rabbits* . . . But perhaps you'll have a word with Mr. Tasker about it afterwards? " And with a kindly glance at Stephen he passed on to the next item, which concerned the unveiling of a statue of Dame Joanna, poetess and prioress, in the Pleasure Gardens.

Stephen, who had been growing steadily more apprehensive about the Festival for several weeks, felt that the prospect of a rabbit show justified his worst fears. Already it had been decided that the Women's Institute would be allowed to tell fortunes, that the Rowing Club should bring Bloody Mary ashore in a decorated barge, and that the Master of Foxhounds should gallop with his pack past the grandstand tally-hoing an imaginary fox. " What am I but a hack? " Stephen asked himself miserably. " The Town Hack, and a poor, ineffectual, useless one at that? " He was sick and tired of the whole business already; it could end only in ridicule, of which he would be the principal butt. There would be four more of these dreadful Committee Meetings before the Festival achieved its consummation in farce or shame or a ghastly mixture of the two; and this one was by no means over. His knee was hurting so badly that he was quite unable to concentrate on the proceedings; but fortunately he had no responsibility for the statue of Dame Joanna (it was practically the only thing he wasn't responsible for) so he allowed his wayward mind to stray again, and like a homing bird it flew straight to the olive-groves.

Lately he had often caught himself looking back upon his year in Greece as if it were an experience in a frame, a sort of illuminated picture, or a theatrical interlude played within the arch of a proscenium. It glowed in his memory

D

with an unnatural brightness; the sky was a painted cyclorama, extravagantly blue, the snow was whiter than white,
the glaucous olives seemed carved in relief on tawny hillsides,
the anemones were projected in technicolor on to emerald
alpine meadows. Against this incandescent background
moved figures larger than life, and in particular one figure,
gigantic among giants, that of his friend and companion
Polycarpos. Huge and heroic, laughing at the sky, a bottle
of wine in one hand, a grenade in the other, Polly stood
outside their headquarters on VE-day. "Let's have a good
bang," he said, "to celebrate. . . ."

Suddenly the Mayor's voice ("Our 'ome-made Pageant,
our 'ome-made 'istory") brought Stephen back to the
present with a jerk. There was an argument going on
about the vexed question of an extra episode, and Mr.
Gurney had just remarked that in his humble opinion the
town had been going from bad to worse for three centuries,
and that the trivial doings of its wretched population during
this period were of no conceivable interest to anybody. The
Mayor ignored this and proceeded to make a suggestion
of his own. He was not, he said, like Councillor Noakes a
literary man; he was not like Mr. Gurney a scholard. But
Pageants were meant for ordinary chaps, and what could
appeal more to ordinary chaps than the paragraph he had
chanced upon in the *Intelligencer* only last week under the
heading "Seventy-Five Years Ago"? He fumbled in
his pocket for the cutting, put on his spectacles, and
solemnly declaimed the following passage from Mr.
Runcorn's predecessor's extraordinary prose:

"Last Saturday upon our hallowed greensward the

wielders of the willow included among their number one
whose fame resounds far beyond the confines of this his
native county, nay, throughout the whole civilised world.
In the course of scoring 172 Dr. W. G. Grace kept the
leather-chasers on the run for nearly two hours ere his
seemingly impregnable citadel fell; and towards the close
of his innings he smote the spheroid three times in succession
into the willow-girt river. . . ."

The Mayor looked up.

" I don't know," he said modestly, " whether you'd call
that 'istory? "

There was a murmur of applause. Everybody seemed
delighted with the idea except Lance, who was appalled at
the prospect of having to write a Chorus about cricket, and
Stephen, whose already enormous cast would be increased
by twenty-two. " Mr. Tasker will see to it, then," said the
Mayor, flushed with triumph. " No doubt the Cricket Club
will co-operate. And now it only remains for me to thank
you for your attendance and to say how safe we feel our
arrangements all are in Mr. Tasker's capable hands. . . ."
He got up to go.

Stephen had scarcely taken three steps to ease his throbbing
knee before the furry lady was on to him, babbling of
chinchillas. Why did it seem so much worse, he wondered,
to wear your own rabbits than to eat them? She terrified
him, and mumbling some excuse, he made his escape from
her, hurrying down the stairs although all the nerves in his
left leg seemed to be dancing an infernal jig together. At
the bottom of the stairs something like panic overtook him
as there flooded into his mind the full realisation of what

lay ahead: W. G. Grace and chinchillas superadded to Odo and Dodo and the Beauty Queens. He had an impulse to turn back, intercept the Mayor, and hand in his resignation on the spot; but he lacked the courage to do so, and he limped on down the slumberous street, past the offices of the *Weekly Intelligencer* outside which Virginia, on her way home, favoured him with an Enigmatic Smile, past the Mayor's shop, JNO. WILKES, LADIES' OUTFITTER, displaying grey bloomers, dreadful pink corsets, and peculiar garments called spencers, past the poor little dusty window of Mr. Handiman's ironmongery with its fishing-floats, its mouse-traps, its rusty garden trowels, and its bundle of skates which had hung there ever since the great frost of 1946—Mr. Handiman having routed them out from his store-room just in time for the thaw. Festival Committee Meetings always had a curious effect on Stephen: they implanted in his mind a rebellious disbelief in history; and now as he paused outside Mr. Handiman's to rest his knee, he found it quite incredible that great events had ever happened here —that the knights had clattered down the street on their heavy chargers, striking sparks from the cobbles, pennons bravely flying, a red rose or a white one worn for a challenge in their shining helmets—that a Prince had been slain but half a mile away, and a King hunted like a fox had given the slip to his foes—that Shakespeare himself, if Mr. Gurney was right, had set foot here, had trodden where Stephen now trod! Yet these were the ancient glories he must somehow bring to life: with Councillor Noakes the literary man dressed up as Shakespeare, with a foxhunting squire in armour as Prince Edward of Wales.

He knew that he could not do it. In a moment of self-revelation he saw himself as he was, well-meaning and timid and ineffectual, a faint-hearted dabbler alike in books and living. He had only been brave and competent once, and that was when he had Polly beside him—Polly laughing at the sizzle of bullets from the hidden ambush even as he cried " Get your head down! " and then suddenly toppling forward with a grunt. Stephen had lobbed three grenades one after another into the blackness of the wood, dragged Polly into the truck, and driven away. It had not occurred to him even that he had done well until Polly, returned from hospital, had thanked him for saving his life; and they had got rather drunk together on some wine that tasted like resin.

Three days later the news of Germany's capitulation came through on the wireless, and they got drunk again. It was a particularly exhilarating experience to drink with Polly, who when he was at the top of the world somehow managed to carry his companions there with him. He and Stephen danced down the village street with the whole population of sixty at their heels, and Polly kissed all the women, including an old crone who was said to be a hundred and hadn't been kissed, she croaked, for seventy years. Then Polly climbed a chimney, the tallest in the place, and unfurled a Stars and Stripes at the top of it; for although his father had been a carpet dealer from Salonika he was an American citizen, whose home was in New Orleans. He made a long speech in Greek, and another in English, and sang some scandalous songs in both languages, and danced a hornpipe on the top of the chimney before he could be persuaded to come down. Then they went back to the Headquarters and drank some more wine; and Polly, swaying in the doorway, took a grenade out of his pocket and very slowly, almost thoughtfully, pulled out the pin. " Must have a bang, Stevie. . . ." In a world of bangs he always wanted another. But the baseball player's pitch for once in a way failed to come off; the grenade hit the telephone wire in front of the Headquarters, and fell to earth within ten yards of Stephen. He was lucky indeed to lose no more than his knee-cap and half his shin.

Yet oddly enough he bore Polly no ill-will; indeed it was impossible to feel resentment against such a man. Somehow it cheered him up, now, simply to remember Polly, to remember his hip-swinging walk, his slow wide grin, his laughing dark eyes which spoke of the Mediterranean even while his mouth drawled of New Orleans. And the extraordinary hats he wore, a match for Mr. Churchill's—once he had gone out on patrol in a ridiculous little baseball cap, perched with the peak pointing skyward on top of the big prognathous head which had caused Stephen to nickname him the Piltdown Man; and the five Bulgarian prisoners he brought back in the morning had seemed more alarmed by his cap than by his tommy-gun.

Indeed there was nobody in the world like Polly! Nobody, surely, who could do so many things so well—from driving a truck at fifty along the side of a precipice to handling a boat in a rough sea; from climbing a mountain to riding a half-wild horse; from singing songs to making love! And in this latter respect he was indeed unique, for he had not only made love to all the eligible young women in a valley forty miles long (the population, though small, was widely scattered), but he had done so in spite of an embarrassing idiosyncrasy at the memory of which Stephen nearly laughed aloud. Whenever Polly experienced the least premonitory stirrings of passion he sneezed; sometimes indeed the sneeze came first, and gave him early warning that yet another affair of the heart was on the way. " I bin to a psychiatrist about it, Stevie," he confessed gravely; " but the guy said there was nothing to be done. I reckon it's something like hay-fever; but you can't get inoculated against dames." And after all, it didn't really matter, he added with a grin; for when the dames got wise to it they'd naturally take a violent fit of sneezing as an exceptional compliment.

Nevertheless, this singularity of Polly's had once nearly cost him his life. During the time of the troubles with Elas he happened to be courting a Communist schoolmistress who lived in a village held by bandits. At considerable risk he visited her under cover of darkness, entering her parents' house by means of an open window. At a tender moment he was assailed by such a paroxysm of sneezing that, according to him, the whole house was shaken by it, her father woke up, the guards were aroused, and he found himself in the same awkward predicament as Samson at Gaza. He went one better than Samson, however, for instead of carrying away the doors of the gate he fought his way out with the protesting girl slung over his shoulder; and taking her to a place of safety he was able as he put it to unconvert her from Communism in no time.

Stephen was still chuckling to himself at Polly's adventures when he arrived at his shop; and the boisterous memories had dispelled most of his gloom. But when he thought again of Odo and Dodo and W. G. and the chinchillas, he wished, oh, he wished, that he had Polly's company in this desperate affair, for then surely all would be well. On the spur of the moment he pulled out his notecase and hunted through it for Polly's address; and when he found it he went into the back shop where Miss Pargetter was sitting very prim and still at her typewriter and told her:

" Put one of those Festival folders in an envelope, please, and send it by airmail to this address. I'll write a letter to go with it." Then he spelt out the address to her very slowly: *Mr. Polycarpos Gabrielides, 1256 Esplanade Street, New Orleans, Louisiana, U.S.A.*

He went back into the front shop to write his letter. He had got as far as " My knee is still a better weather-forecaster than the Met used to be" (and was wondering whether it was quite fair to Polly to mention his knee at all) when he was aware of Miss Pargetter standing at his side with her notebook held out in that helpless and appealing attitude which she adopted when she was Stuck.

" Polly-something," said Miss Pargetter abruptly. " I can't remember whether it ends with us or os."

" Polycarpos," said Stephen, spelling it again.

" Yes, Mr. Tasker."

" It means ' many-seeded,' " added Stephen.

" What a funny name."

" Yes; but apt. By the way," said Stephen, " I don't suppose you sold any books? "

"I'm afraid there was only one customer all the afternoon."

"That's above the average," said Stephen.

"He wanted something to read in a bus. I sold him these." Miss Pargetter stared for a long time at her notebook. "I put down the titles in shorthand for practice," she said. " *The Feeling for Nature in Scottish Poetry*—and, oh, yes, I've got it, *Meditations on Death and Eternity*."

"If you sold those books," said Stephen, "you could sell anything."

"Yes, but—I'm afraid I knocked sixpence off *Death and Eternity*." Miss Pargetter still looked as solemn as an owl. "I felt sure you wouldn't mind. He was a Scottish Minister," she said, "and rather poor."

PART TWO

I

THERE WAS a long sultry spell, as May melted into June ;
the close sticky nights were shot with sheet-lightning,
and black thunderstorms punctuated the scorching days.
The Vicar announced that his promised fine-weather system
was building up slowly. Nevertheless, some of the storms
were heavy, and in one twenty-four-hour period he had
the satisfaction of registering no less than .62 inches of rain
on his gauge. The Vicar always did record more rain than
any other observer within a hundred miles; and on the
charts at the Air Ministry the neighbourhood was shown as
a pocket of exceptional rainfall and pointed out to students
as a remarkable phenomenon, due perhaps to the effect of
the nearby hills. But it is possible that the true cause was
to be sought in the mischief of the choir boys who under
cover of darkness would play an exceedingly naughty trick
as they went home through the Vicar's garden after a late
practice.

The thundery and electric atmosphere got on everybody's
nerves, and as the days went by Stephen had a sense of
mounting tension. Disaster was in the air, and its pre-

monitory rumblings were as plain to him as those of the
circumambient storms. The first rehearsal had been a
ludicrous failure, for owing to a typing mistake in Miss
Pargetter's circular to the performers—she had put " Thursday " instead of " Tuesday "—half the company failed to
turn up. The rehearsal therefore became a sort of Tactical
Exercise Without Troops; but even so tenuous an affair
resulted in five separate and distinct quarrels among the
leading actors. In addition, Odo and Dodo, complaining
perhaps with reason that their parts were not sufficiently
spectacular, had resigned from the company; they would
be knights or nothing, and there were not enough horses to
go round. A savage rainstorm had finally drenched everybody before they went home.

Stephen had other troubles too. Lance's choruses had
turned out to be incomprehensible to anybody but their
author, and in order to persuade him to rewrite them it
had been necessary to apply the ultimate sanction to which,
alas, young poets are singularly vulnerable: the Committee
had withheld his fee. The Wardrobe Mistress threatened to
throw her hand in because she couldn't understand Robin's
designs. The men who were building the grandstand went
on strike. Mr. Gurney and Councillor Noakes were like
two old tomcats snarling at each other in dreadful under-
tones every time they met. And the Beauty Queens, it
was rumoured, had had a row in public at a local dance.

On the first of June, according to plan, a pink nettlerash
of posters had broken out all over the town. Designed by
Robin, they were somewhat impressionistic, and seemed to
represent a crowd of knights and ladies in a blurry snow-

storm of red and white roses—pretty enough when you looked at them closely, but on the hoardings they might have been advertisements for strawberry ice-cream. During the night following their appearance somebody plastered a second lot of posters side by side with them. These declared in bold scarlet lettering:

WE DON'T WANT FESTIVALS
WE WANT HOUSES, WORK AND WAGES

and were generally attributed to the machinations of Miss Foulkes.

All that morning Stephen's inadequate office in the back shop was overcrowded with Councillors and members of the Committee who had looked in to discuss this atrocity. He now had two telephones, which went continually as well-meaning people rang up to tell him about the posters or to ask him what he was going to do about them. Councillor Noakes, fleshy and perspiring, fussed around as usual, got in everybody's way, and frequently and unnecessarily patted Miss Pargetter on the shoulder, who in her summer dress was the only cool and placid person in the room. At last Stephen could stand it no longer, and making the excuse that he must personally inspect the outrage he escaped from the shop and followed in the footsteps of Mr. Gurney, who had just " dodged out " (*Back in half an hour*) to have his mid-morning drink at the Red Lion.

Even in the sleepy High Street one could not help being aware of conflict, frayed tempers, and a population at odds

among themselves. Wherever two passers-by had paused
to have a word together, or a small group stood gossiping
outside a shop, it was ten to one they were disputing either
about the Festival or about the Beauty Queens. No longer
had the Mayor any reason to complain of apathy. " Rouse
'em, Runcorn, rouse 'em," he had said; and Mr. Runcorn
had responded with a colourful leader about " the verdant
meadow, known as Sanguinary, encompassed by um-
brageous trees." It had finished neatly with a quotation
from Shakespeare: " This green plot shall be our stage."
Probably hardly anybody had bothered to read it, but the
unpredictable citizens had roused themselves with a
vengeance. Unfortunately theirs was not exactly the
enthusiastic awakening the Mayor had looked forward
to; it was more like the resentful agitation of ants in a
suddenly disturbed anthill.

Half-way up the street Stephen found the Inspector of
Police, with two of his men, scraping the offending posters
off the walls. This pompous and lugubrious individual,
whose unsuitable name was Heyhoe, hinted to Stephen that
although he was doing his duty he didn't hold with the
Festival either. " I looks around me," he said, " and what
do I see but trouble, trouble everywhere? " He was,
however, already on the track of the culprits, for he had
searched the balloon factory " from floor to ceiling " and
at last had discovered a paste-pot. The paste, he said, in
the tone of one speaking of bloodstains, was *still wet*. He
had impounded the pot in case it should be required as an
exhibit in court.

Next Stephen called at Mr. Handiman's shop, which had recently been opened as the Festival Booking Office with Virginia in charge. She had been lent to the Committee by Mr. Runcorn, an act of self-sacrifice more apparent than real; and now she dreamed her day-dreams over an immaculate seating-plan, as virginal as herself, that had not so far a single X in any of its multitudinous squares. It was Councillor Noakes who had urged that a Beauty Queen would be the very person to sell tickets; but Stephen had his doubts when he entered the shop and Virginia did not even look up from the sheet of paper on which, in round schoolgirlish characters, she was copying something from a magazine.

He coughed, and she came to earth from the dizzy heights of stardom, fluttering her eyelids at him.

" Not very busy yet," he said.

" Ay'm not expecting a rush till nearer the tame."

He glanced over her shoulder at the sheet of paper and read: K2 tog, P1, K2 . . .

" It's a pettern," she explained, " for a twin-set."

" Oh, I see." Glancing out of the window, from which Mr. Handiman had at last removed the unseasonable skates, Stephen became aware of a square poster stuck on the outside of the pane, next to Robin's oblong one.

" Good Lord, look at that ! " he said.

It was quite easy to read the big letters backwards: WE DON'T WANT FESTIVALS. . . .

" Well, Ay never ! " was all Virginia said.

Stephen went out and scratched off the poster with a penknife. There was something of the Nelson Touch, he thought, about Miss Foulkes' campaign; and he smiled as there came into his mind's eye a picture of that angular little figure padding about the town in the small hours, probably wearing gym-shoes and the kind of dirty old mackintosh which revolutionaries all over the world seemed to favour; dabbling away with the paste-brush, scurrying round corners, lurking breathless in the dark shadows, and imagining herself to be at last of true fellowship with Sacco and Vanzetti and Dimitrov and all the other martyrs in the Leftists' hagiology. (But Dimitrov, Stephen remembered, had deviated; he had been liquidated and expunged from proletarian memory.) Poor little Miss Foulkes! he thought, and hoped sincerely that Inspector Heyhoe wouldn't catch her and drag her to court on some such silly charge as Unauthorised Billposting—if indeed there was such an offence in the catalogue. The way to deal with Miss Foulkes was not to take her seriously; and to laugh off the posters as if they were a boy's prank.

Stephen threw the bits of paper into the gutter and continued on his way to the Red Lion.

II

LOUNGING ON the bar, in a canary-yellow polo jumper and a segmented tweed cap with a little button on the crown of it such as English milords are supposed by the French to wear, Sir Almeric Jukes, Baronet and Master of

Foxhounds, was holding forth on the subject of the Beauty Queens.

"A good-lookin' pair of fillies," he said. "High-spirited. A fine pair of fillies."

The Festival Committee had appointed him Master of the Horse. He had also been cast originally for Edward Prince of Wales; but he had seemed to think that his horsemanship would show to better advantage if he were on the winning side, so he was going to lead the victorious charge of the Yorkists on his own grey steeplechaser. He was an arrogant and supercilious young man, who had made it clear at the first rehearsal that he did not intend to take orders from anybody—least of all from a second-hand bookseller. Stephen disliked him intensely.

"I dunno which of 'em to put my money on," he drawled. "'Pon my word I don't."

He was addressing Mr. Gurney, who sat in his customary corner with his umbrella between his knees. At the other end of the bar, Florrie, the old barmaid, had just hung up one of Robin's posters, and her two most faithful customers, Mr. Oxford and his friend Timms, were admiring it and talking about History.

"What I always says," declared Mr. Oxford, whose real surname was possibly Huxford, but he had persuaded the world to accept his own version of it, "is that 'istory is tradition and tradition is 'istory, if you see what I mean."

"Plain as a pikestaff, old man," agreed Timms the piano-tuner—at least that had been his profession long ago, but the owners of pianos nowadays mostly regarded them as pieces of furniture, which had to be dusted but need not be tuned, so Timms had drifted into a more profitable job, that of bookie's runner to Mr. Oxford. Fortunately, for he was as scrimp and meagre as Francis Feeble, he didn't have to do any running; his morning round of half a dozen pubs was accomplished at a leisurely pace, for Inspector Heyhoe was the last man to look for trouble, though he found it everywhere ; and besides he liked a little flutter himself. Regularly at twelve o'clock Timms brought the betting-slips to the Red Lion, where he met his employer, and they drank together till closing time, doing a bit of business now and then. At night they went round the pubs wearing broad and benevolent smiles as they distributed largesse in furtive little envelopes to those of their clients who happened to have won. It was a pleasant, profitable and not a very arduous existence if you had no particular desire to look upon the world with a clear and sober eye; and neither of them had any such ambition.

" Now take those knights," Mr. Oxford went on, prodding a fat finger into the poster, which was still sticky with printing ink. " Just like the good old 'Ome Guard, I bet they was, comin' in 'ere arter the battle for their pints of mead or sack or whatever they drank in those days. There's tradition for you! "

" Quite right, old man."

" What's more," said Mr. Oxford, " I've heard that battles were nice comfortable affairs then, nothing like Arras and the Somme where *we* got our feet wet, and I dare say the 'habitants of this town were standing on the touch-line 'avin' a bet on the result: just like you and me at a game of football. An Englishman will bet on anything."

E

" Just like you said; tradition," echoed Timms dutifully.

" I knew a Rechabite once," mused Mr. Oxford, " who had two children called Peter and Josephine; and although he disapproved of 'orse-racing, he had a standing order with me for five bob each way every time an 'orse ran with Peter or Josephine in its name. He put his winnings into Savings Certificates for his kids. But Josephine didn't get much, did she, Timms? "

Timms shook his head.

" The name was too uncommon," said Mr. Oxford. " But it just shows you: an Englishman, be he Rechabite or racing-man, will bet on anything. For example, there's Sir Halmeric wantin' to 'ave a pony with me on the Beauty Comp. Two to one bar one, Sir Halmeric, two to one bar! "

" Which d'you bar? " asked Sir Almeric swiftly.

" We'll discuss it together later," said Mr. Oxford with fine sensibility. " It wouldn't be right to bandy the names of ladies about over the counter, like. But, as I say "—he jabbed the poster again—" that's tradition, that's England. And these Communists or whoever they are that are kicking up such a row, they ain't got no tradition, they ain't what I call English."

" I'd put the rats up against a wall," said Sir Almeric.

" That's right. Shoot 'em," said Timms into his whisky glass. " Jolly good tradition."

Just then John Handiman came into the bar and Florrie made haste to serve him.

" You look tired, dearie," she said. " Need a nice glass of stout to buck you up."

An empress in black lace with jet buttons and a pink artificial rose, she had ruled over the Red Lion Bar for nearly thirty years. Like a constitutional monarch, although she took no part in the conduct of affairs, she had a clearer view than the more active participants of everything that went on. She knew all about the balloon factory and John Handiman's financial troubles, and because it was unusual for him to drink in the morning she guessed that he was on his way to or from an uncomfortable interview at the Bank. She knew all about the ups-and-downs of the Festival too, about the midnight doings of Miss Foulkes, about the Beauty Queens' quarrel and about the tentative and tangled courtship of the Beauty Queens by Robin and Lance. She knew that Sir Almeric hadn't as much money as he pretended to have and that Mr. Oxford had a great deal more; that Mr. Gurney made a good thing out of selling " antique " furniture with artificial worm-holes in it, and that Stephen's bookshop was tottering to its ruin. And she locked up all this knowledge in her large and compassionate heart, regarding the whole distressing scene with the tolerance and calm of one who had married three husbands and buried them all.

They had been no ordinary husbands either. Her first was said to have been a lion-tamer from a circus. Her second had endeavoured to predict the winners of horse races by studying the stars, and had lost all her savings, as as well as his own, through a trifling miscalculation about the date when Jupiter entered the aqueous sign of Pisces. Her third had possessed the absorbing hobby of collecting the labels off whisky-bottles and sticking them in a scrapbook; he had drunk himself to death during the war and left the labels of ninety-nine different brands as his strange memorial. From these and other experiences Florrie had acquired her comfortable conviction that it took all sorts to make a world.

But the manager, Old Screwnose as she called him, who now came creeping into the bar through the door at the back, nevertheless tried her patience sorely. He was carrying by their necks, as if they were snakes which might bite him, two bottles of whisky. "This is all you get," he said defensively, dumping them on the counter. "It's our Allocation." That was one of the words which he always spoke reverently and as it were with a capital letter, as if they were some sort of abracadabra or mumbo-jumbo of which he stood in awe: Allocation, Triplicate, Quota, Directive; for in the war he had been a Temporary Civil Servant. To Florrie, who had worked for nearly a dozen innkeepers in her time, good and bad ones, drunken and sober ones, gamblers, spendthrifts, wife-beaters, likers of bits of skirt, and even one who had cut his throat in the cellar all among the beer barrels, Mr. Hawker was a source of perpetual astonishment and dismay. Not that there was anything remarkable about him, except his crooked nose; he was just an ordinary petty puritan, with a thin peaky face, sandy moustache, and rimless glasses, habited in the shiny black pin-stripe which had been his bureaucratic uniform. Among Licensed Victuallers, however, puritans and teetotallers are rare birds; and Florrie often caught herself staring at him as if he were a hoopoe hopping about on the lawn. All her previous employers, even the worst of

them, had been like large or lesser suns, giving out light and
warmth to customer and crony. They shone, they glowed
in her memory, each the centre of a miniature solar system
which revolved merrily about him. But Mr. Hawker
generated no warmth; he was as cold as a dead star; he
possessed no planetary cronies. His only interest in the
customers took the form of a niggling apprehension lest
they should misbehave themselves; and his only concern
about the bar was how many glasses had been broken last
week. He disapproved strongly of the Festival because he
thought it would bring undesirable charabanc people to the
town.

"It's our Allocation," he repeated. "Two for the
Saloon, two for the Public; and lucky to get it." The
poster which Florrie had hung up over the Price List of
drinks caught his eye, and he said:

"You oughtn't to clutter up your bar with advertisements. I've told you before, you want to keep it dignified.
And that one hides the prices."

He shut the door behind him with a petulant slam just
as Florrie was beginning to fluff herself up like an angry
old hen.

"Well——" she said, taking a deep breath; and with
her bosom heaving expressively she drew pints of beer for
Lance and Robin, who had just come in together. Mr.
Oxford resumed his historical discourse—"Take Lords and
Ladies now——" and suddenly broke off, looking at Lance.
Stephen was staring at Lance too, and Mr. Gurney had put
down his drink and turned round in his chair in order to
get a better view; for Lance had a really remarkable black

eye. Robin's swollen lips and bruised chin were only slightly less obvious.

"Well, here's to you, my dear chap," said Robin, with a painful grin.

"Bless your old heart," said Lance, raising his glass.

Florrie winked at Stephen, as if to say: "I know all about it"—which undoubtedly she did; and Robin and Lance clinked their glasses together as if they were drinking a loving-cup. In his lazy and offensive drawl Sir Almeric addressed them both:

"A little difference of opinion over a lady, perhaps?"

Lance swung round angrily, and Stephen had the pleasant fancy that his sword-hand moved towards his hip. Once again Stephen was aware of the feeling of conflict he had had in the street, which had reminded him of Verona: "And now, these hot days, is the mad blood stirring." Lance and Robin might indeed have been two tall young Elizabethans, lean, eager, quick on the draw, their days and nights gloriously compounded of poetry and brawls and Juliets and Rosalines; nor did it take much imagination to turn the arrogant Sir Almeric into Tybalt. The thought occurred to Stephen suddenly that the real Pageant was here, in this bar, in the streets, in the shops and houses, in the balloon factory; and that whatever happened six weeks hence in front of the grandstand on the Bloody Meadow would be by comparison but a rattling of dry bones.

Robin touched Lance on the arm and they drew apart, taking their beer into the farthest corner of the room, where they soon began to chuckle together over some private

joke. The Mayor had just come in, with Councillor Noakes
as usual at his heels; and now Mr. Runcorn joined them,
and the three Elder Statesmen, sipping their drinks, began
to shake grizzled heads over the Outrage of the posters.
Mr. Gurney put in some sharp comment which Stephen
couldn't hear, and Councillor Noakes snapped back at him;
you could almost see the sparks fly. The Mayor, turning to
John Handiman, said genially: " Well, John, I suppose your
factory's full of flat-footed policemen this morning, eh? "
and John, looking straight at him, replied:

" That's nothing. We're expecting the bailiffs at any
moment."

There was an awkward silence during which Stephen in
embarrassment glanced about the bar, and then forgot his
embarrassment as he became fascinated by the assortment
of faces. His glance travelled from John's fine-drawn face
to the Mayor's kindly and puzzled one; from Florrie rising
majestic behind the counter to Sir Almeric lounging upon
it, and Mr. Gurney contemplating his umbrella-handle and
thinking his thoughts; from Councillor Noakes who
collected " little books printed in Paris " to those ardent
young men, Robin elegant in a flowered waistcoat, Lance
wearing his black eye with an air of You-be-damned; and
as Stephen looked about him he was struck not for the
first time by the infinite permutations and combinations of
character which even a small town could afford. " What a
rich hotch-potch," he said to himself, " is there within these
four walls now, and how it sizzles and steams and boils up
like a witch's cauldron! " He felt life swirling about him;
man's proud and angry dust was bestirring itself, the air was

charged with emotions as it was charged with thunder; and in a flash he thought of his Festival as a sort of Frankenstein's monster which perhaps would take command of those who were trying to create it.

The long silence was broken at last by the voice of Mr. Oxford as he resumed his history lesson. It was at this time of day—and Florrie could predict it almost to the minute—that Mr. Oxford became more and more pontifical, his voice boomed louder, and somehow he seemed to grow bigger, to swell like a great bullfrog. But conversely Timms dwindled away; his interjections became the merest echo; one felt that if the bar had remained open for another hour he would disappear altogether.

" Take"—said Mr. Oxford, as if he was reciting a recipe for some extravagant dish—" take Kings and Queens. Take Henry the Eighth——"

" Lots of wives," said Timms almost in a whisper. " Chopped their heads off."

" And *that* ain't a bad tradition either," said Mr. Oxford, laughing hugely as he slapped his fat thigh. And " 'Dition " repeated Timms with a sort of midget's giggle.

As he listened to them, Stephen suddenly had a mischievous impulse. For some inexplicable reason the ridiculous names of Odo and Dodo came into his head; and the longer he looked at Mr. Oxford and Timms the better those names seemed to fit them. But light-hearted mischief was a thing foreign to him, and even as he edged his way across the bar towards them he was appalled by what he did.

" Look, I've got a job for you two."

"Want to have a little flutter?" said Mr. Oxford heartily.

"Not at the moment. You've been talking so much about history that I think you ought to take part in the Pageant."

"What, us?"

"All you have to do is to walk on with a Holy Hermit. 'Enter Odo and Dodo.' And then you found the Abbey."

"Ah, the Abbey." Mr. Oxford's finger sought the tower which loomed in the background of Robin's poster. "Now that's old, real old. Reeking of 'istory. 'Ow often, on my way down the street to do a little business at the Black Bear, 'ave I looked up at it and said to myself, 'That's a bit of old England, that is.'"

"'Dition," said Timms automatically.

"Odo and Dodo, then?" said Stephen, glancing from one to the other, awe-stricken by his own folly.

Mr. Oxford heaved a long sententious sigh.

"Well, I will undertake it," he said at last; in the very words, as it happened, of Bottom the weaver.

III

"WOULD YOU say it was cinegenic?" asked Virginia, trying to keep her head still while Robin with his quick pencil made a series of jabs at the sketching-block on his knees.

"Would I say it was what?"

"Cinegenic. That means it takes well," she added helpfully. "The photographer said it was ever so."

"I wouldn't know," grinned Robin. "Photographers and painters aren't interested in the same thing. Anyhow, I'm not drawing your face."

"Then what are you doing?" asked Virginia reasonably; for she had been sitting for half an hour in a most uncomfortable attitude on a sort of nursery-rhyme tuffet at the top of the hill. Short sharp grasses prickled her behind, and all manner of poisonous insects, she was sure, were crawling up her legs.

"I'm taking notes," Robin said. "I'm getting Inspiration. I can't design you a dress without Inspiration. At the moment I'm seeing you in white draped chiffon; or maize taffeta, just off the shoulder, I'm not quite sure which. Sit still and look at that sunset."

It was as if the gods had lit a bonfire behind the black hills away to the westward. Out of the crimson heart of the blaze shot orange streamers, teased-out witches' brooms, curly unfolding fronds of flame, pink tendrils climbing into the duck-egg blue. High above the whole conflagration hung a huge dove-grey cloud like a mushroom of smoke.

This cloud cast a long shadow over the Bloody Meadow with its skeleton grandstand, but the town beyond lay in a pool of the softest pink light, the roofs of the houses and the tall Abbey tower were rosy-flushed above a shimmering river-mist, so that the place did not seem to belong to the English countryside at all, but to the fabulous East; it was Bokhara, Tashkent, Samarkand.

"Turner's sunsets," said Robin, "were wishy-washy to this one."

But Virginia was not looking at the sunset; the stupendous bonfire burned for her in vain. She was thinking that perhaps she had been unwise to trust herself on the hill with Robin, and that even the scandalous studio might have been safer, and would certainly have been more comfortable, than this anthill or whatever it was with its population of creepy-crawlies. She was not sure that she liked Robin's manner, which was brusque and domineering, nor his preoccupation with birds, which bored her; she had not the slightest ambition to listen to a nightingale. On the other hand, she had to admit that his merry brown face was attractive—it was rather like a nice monkey's when he grinned, and she liked his clear blue eyes which had little crinkles at the edges of them, and the touch of his strong hands when he helped her over stiles. And although she didn't approve of fighting with fists, which she thought was not very refined, she could hardly be indifferent to the fact that Robin and Lance had come to blows on her behalf. She had read in the paper about a French film-star whose admirers had fought a duel with pistols or rapiers, she couldn't remember which; and that was romantic indeed. Robin's swollen lip was less so, but it was not so bad as Lance's black eye. Presumably Robin had won, otherwise she supposed Lance would have invited her to walk on the hill and listen to the nightingales. The only thing which puzzled her was the continued friendship of the two young men. She had seen them coming out of the pub together only this morning, arm-in-arm. It was quite true what her best girl-friend often said to her, the one she went to the pictures with twice a week: You never knew where you were with Boys.

"And now," said Robin, putting away his pencil, "those nightingales will be just about piping up at the edge of the birch-brake. Come along."

"Can't I see your drawing?" she temporised.

"No, it's only a lot of squiggles. You wouldn't make head or tail of it." He slipped the sketching-block into his big pocket and got up.

"The long grass will be all wet with dew," she said.

"Do your feet good. Milkmaids used to bathe their faces in it, for the sake of their complexions. Come along, Virgie."

"Ay wish you wouldn't call me Virgie," she said in the mincing tones she always used to repel advances, "it doesn't sound nace somehow."

She got up and brushed a lot of imaginary insects from her skirt. Robin set off at a great pace up the hill, and she nearly had to run to keep up with him. The little bracken-fronds, rough as a coarse blanket, tickled and scratched her bare legs. Tiny green caterpillars, suspended from the birch branches on invisible threads, waylaid her just at eye-level, and when she put her hand to her face she found one of them wriggling upon her nose.

Robin stopped suddenly.

"Listen!" he said.

She could hear a very faint trilling sound, uttered, it seemed, by something as breathless as herself.

"Is that the nightingale?"

" Of course not; grasshopper warbler. The first I've ever heard here. Rather exciting! "

Virginia didn't think the indistinct chirrup was in the least exciting; but Robin stood stock-still, with his head on one side, obviously fascinated by it.

" You're blowing like a grampus," he said. " It's all that sitting in the pictures. Bad for your wind. Now come into the wood and we'll listen for nightingales."

The brake, which had a ride running through it, looked black and forbidding. A network of green caterpillars swaying in the breeze defended the entrance to the ride.

" It's getting awfully dark," Virginia said. " Oh, Robin, let's go home."

But Robin had already climbed the gate and was waiting for her impatiently among the dangling caterpillars. Once more he had cocked his head on one side, and he was listening, not for the nightingale's song, but for the squeal of a rabbit. Last night he had set half a dozen traps along the edge of the wood, and he had forgotten to inspect them in the morning. This was a shameful thing, and contrary to his nature; for he was not thoughtlessly cruel, despite his preoccupation with killing beasts and birds. Robin poached indefatigably, partly for profit but mainly for pleasure, and although he would poach anything from a brace of pheasants to a salmon, or even a fallow-deer from the Park, he had no interest in lawful game, and always refused the kindly invitations of local landlords to join their shooting-parties. Such orderly sport bored him; but in the woods at night " at the season of the year," holding his breath, straining his ears for the sound of a twig cracking beneath the keeper's boot, every nerve deliciously a-tingle —there he found true happiness. It was better even than sunsets or girls.

He had remembered his traps remorsefully just before he called for Virginia; and he had brought her up to the birch-wood for no other reason than that he wanted to put the rabbits out of their misery. Virginia, however, hesitating at the gate, seemed to think she would be outraged if she ventured over it. At last she took the plunge—literally, for her high heel caught in the top bar and she went head first into the bracken. Robin picked her up and, taking her hand firmly in his, led her unprotesting down the sepia path which was like a tunnel between the trees.

After about a hundred yards the path became green again, and with deep thankfulness Virginia perceived at the farther end of the tunnel a shining patch of sky. They had come to the other side of the wood, where Robin had set his traps; and as they emerged into the twilight three deep bubbling notes suddenly rang out over their heads, *jug, jug, jug,* so close that Virginia started. There was a pause, while Robin whispered " Be quiet " and drew her to his side. Then the bubbling started again—it was as if a number of stones were being dropped one after another down a very deep well and the successive *plops* were echoing musically upwards—but this time it didn't die away, the melodious bubbles grew bigger and came quicker until the notes seemed to shower down in a silver spray, a fountain of notes, a cascading waterfall of sound. And the nightingale was answered or challenged by another along the edge of the wood, and two more began to sing out of the blackness of the ride, and just within earshot a fifth joined in the chorus. It was as if the very trees were singing.

Robin stood entranced. Bird-song at dawn and dusk always moved him, and dawn and dusk were his favourite times of day. He was, indeed, a creature of the half-light, never so contented as when with his gun under his arm he lurked by a willowy pool or in the rushes by the river, waiting for the swift teal and widgeon or the wild duck with their panting wings. At such times the pastel shades of sky and water, the light on the land intensifying or fading, gave him the keenest joy; and he never discovered any inconsistency in his appreciation of beauty and his purpose to slay something beautiful.

But though he had listened to the birds so often in the exquisite moment of the longest shadow, he had never experienced anything quite so dramatic as this, nor heard the nightingales in a lovelier setting, with the delicate birch branches fretting the argent sky, meadowsweet and campion at his feet, and the silver-white trunks rising ghostly all about him. Because he was moved he imagined Virginia must be moved too, and thought himself for a moment to be in love with her as he let his hand rest lightly on her arm just above the elbow and then brought it slowly upwards underneath her sleeve.

"Little tiny throats," he whispered, "pulsing and swelling. Windpipes no thicker than the inside of a grass stem. Lungs as big as the end of my thumb. A heart not much larger than a pea, but beating oh so quickly. How do they do it, Virginia, how do they *do* it?"

She was silent, and he thought she must be caught up

in the wonder of it too; she gave a little shudder and he thought it was acquiescence. He increased the pressure of his hand.

"Robin——" she said, in a queer tone.

"Yes."

"There's something horrible—one of those caterpillars —crawling on the back of my neck."

Love is a strong plant, but how tender a seedling. Let it but once take hold and it will withstand the cruel frosts and the perfidious winds: not even the long drought of a heart unresponding will wither it. Yes, but before it has rooted it is as frail as a tropic orchid in a wintry clime. The soil may be fertile, the tilth well prepared, the season favourable and all the stars propitious; yet if there blow then the merest ghost of an intempestive zephyr, the seedling will droop, the bud will canker, the young stem collapse, and in the morning there will be nothing left but a vanishing smudge on the earth which failed to quicken it.

So now Robin's seedling withered.

His hand fell away from her elbow.

"Please take it off," she said. She bent her head forward and he plucked the little green looper from the very spot where a soft imperceptible down ran between her shoulder-blades. But that touch which a moment ago would have set his pulses dancing affected him not at all.

He squashed the caterpillar, and as if at a signal the nightingales suddenly stopped singing. In the profound silence something stirred, a scuffling, a thump, a brief flurry among the herbage at the wood's edge.

"What's that?"

" Perhaps a rabbit——" he said, remembering his traps.

Again the scuffling; and Robin's sharp eyes picked out a small circular depression in the bracken, where the fronds had been laid flat. But Virginia, astonishingly, was quicker than he was. She had run forward and was bending over the hollow place.

" Oh, Robin, Robin ! It's a cat ! "

" Take care, then," he cried. " Don't touch it! "

Virginia couldn't, at first, see the trap; for the big tabby was crouching over it, pressing itself into the earth, with only its head raised to snarl at her dark figure against the sky. The soil was kicked up all round it, and there was a hot sweet smell of bruised bracken.

" Leave it to me! " said Robin sharply, as Virginia stretched out her hand towards it and the cat rose up, a spitting, snarling fury, tugging at its torn leg held between the trap's steel jaws.

Robin said uncomfortably:

" Do go away, Virginia. I'll deal with it. I'll get a stick."

" No," she said quite calmly. " No. Take off your coat."

The extraordinary thing was that her tone had a sort of authority; and Robin took off his coat.

" Now," she said; and as he threw it over the cat and drew it tight about the struggling body, the astonishing girl knelt down and tried to open the trap with her fingers. It was too strong for her, but Robin with his free hand pulled the jaws apart, and Virginia lifted out the mangled leg and ran her thumb and forefinger gently along it.

" No fracture," she said, confident and authoritative;

F

and then Robin noticed that a whole tuft of bracken had
caught in the trap as it closed, so that the jaws had not
quite met. But the skin was ragged from the cat's elbow
to its paw, and there were the two ends of a severed tendon
sticking out from the wound.

" Tear up a handkerchief," Virginia commanded. Robin
did so, holding the wriggling coat between his knees, and
watched Virginia as she deftly bound up the cat's leg,
dividing the end of the bandage to make a small neat knot
where it ended.

Her utterly unexpected competence bewildered him; it
didn't fit in with anything he knew about her. She was
ineffably silly, her head was full of film-stars, she was
frightened of harmless little caterpillars, and yet in this
business she was more capable than he was; for Robin
could kill but he couldn't succour, he could maim but he
couldn't mend.

" Where did you learn to do that? " he asked her; and
tucking in the loose ends of the knot, she said : " V.A.D.
Just at the end of the war. I rather liked it." And indeed
there were times still when the film-dream for a moment
faded and she looked back upon that year in hospital as
the happiest of her life. She'd never go back to it, of
course; to dictatorial matrons and emptying slops and
turning heavy mattresses, not she. But it was something
she was glad to have done, though if anyone had asked her
why she couldn't have told them; she didn't understand
that she had liked it because when she was doing things for
other people she forgot about herself.

" Now lift the coat off it and let it go," she said. " With

luck it'll run home on three legs and its owner will look after it."

Robin wasn't so sure; for the tabby, he suspected, was a poacher like himself, a rabbiter, a hedgerow-hunter, perhaps a chicken-stealer. Good luck to it, he thought, as it streaked away.

He was sorry he had caught it, of course, but he didn't trouble himself for long with uncomfortable reflections about its fear and its pain. What teased his mind at the moment was the puzzle of Virginia. Her metamorphosis had been so sudden and complete that it almost startled him.

She gave the trap a little kick with her high-heeled shoe.

"Horrid thing! Chuck it away, Robin, so that the beast who put it there can't find it."

Robin pulled up the peg and heaved the trap into a clump of bushes; taking good care to mark where it fell.

"And now let's go home, please."

They left the twilight behind them and walked back through the ride. Between the trees the night was black velvet, the still air seemed heavier somehow, Virginia had a strange fancy that she had to *push* her way through it. The silence was heavy too, now that the nightingales had stopped singing. The dew on the bracken soaked through Virginia's shoes and there were queer damp smells everywhere, some sweet, some sharp. Virginia walked close to Robin, for she didn't like woods even in daylight and dreaded them in the dark, erroneously imagining them to be populated by adders.

Nevertheless, she felt pleased with herself. It had been

nice to be able to save the cat (although as a matter of fact, she wasn't very fond of cats) and she was glad that she had tied up its leg so swiftly and neatly. She was rather good at that sort of thing; and she remembered with pleasure the grudging praise of a horse-faced old matron when she had completed a difficult dressing: " You may be a fool, Smith, but you've got quick fingers." Nurse Smith! It sounded funny now. It might come in useful for publicity, she thought; the kind of publicity they gave to starlets when they were building them up into stars. " At the age of seventeen Virginia Vance, undreaming of her bright future, was making beds in a military hospital. . . ."

They walked arm-in-arm, and Robin, feeling her so close to him, wondered whether he'd been wrong about her after all. She'd been so sensible about that cat, so competent and yet quite unsentimental, she hadn't cried about it and made a fuss as some girls would—perhaps, then, she wasn't such a silly floosie as he'd thought? And if so, perhaps he'd been wrong about other things too. Perhaps she wasn't, as he'd imagined, one of those Take-your-hand-away-or-I'll-scream girls.

He put his arm about her tentatively, and she made no protest. Indeed for a moment a little flicker of warmth was engendered between them. Virginia saw the last of the sunset breaking through the tracery of branches at the end of the ride, and felt quite safe at last. She even dared to lean her head on Robin's shoulder as lovers sometimes did on the pictures: a position, she discovered, of acute discomfort when one is walking.

Perhaps at that moment Robin's little seedling of

affection might have taken root; perhaps the fading plant did quicken—but not for long. She said suddenly:

" Do you like Virginia Vance? "

" I don't know her," said Robin, genuinely surprised.

" I mean the name, silly."

" Well, who is she? "

" Me. I thought of Virginia Valley," she explained patiently, with her head at an angle of forty-five degrees, " and Verity and Virtue and Vane. If I get that film-test, you see, I can't be just Smith. Virginia what? "

" Stock," said Robin automatically; " or creeper." But she didn't see the joke. " Stock? Creeper? " she repeated, puzzled. " I think those are very ugly names. Honestly, Robin, don't you think ' Virginia Vance ' sounds pretty? "

So it had only been a flash in the pan after all, he said to himself; she really was as dumb as she seemed, as dumb as he had dismally anticipated, after that silly fight with Lance when they had got drunk and quarrelled so absurdly over the Beauty Queens. . . .

Robin vaulted the gate and Virginia climbed over it clumsily, getting her shoe as usual caught in the bar. The dying sunset lay before them, a long streak of orange low in the dark sky. The lights of the town were beginning to stipple the pewter-coloured river.

" Thenk you for the natingales," said Virginia primly, coming up to his side. " And Robin——"

" Yes? "

" It was awfully naughty of you and Lance but it was nace of you to—to fate for me."

Robin didn't say anything. She couldn't guess, the silly

little floosie, that they had fought about Edna; and that when they had made it up afterwards, solemnly shaking hands in a ridiculous welter of English sportsmanship, they had decided to toss up for the Beauty Queens; and that Lance, alas, had won.

Less than two hundred yards away, as it happened, Lance and Edna had made for themselves a couch among the bracken, which had begun as a very small one, a mere dimple on the hillside just big enough for two, but had unaccountably extended itself to cover an area of many square yards. They had been much too preoccupied with each other to notice the nightingales; but within their private battlefield, hidden from the world, they now lay at peace.

" You know when Joe dips the balloons in the paint? " said Edna; and indeed Lance did know, for he had called for her just before seven at the factory and had been not a little embarrassed to find himself in the company of nearly a dozen young men who were also waiting for their girls: a lengthening queue. It had occurred to him that it would be extremely awkward if his father came along, on his way perhaps from visiting the sick; so he had made the excuse to John Handiman that he would like to see over the factory and had taken refuge there until the day-shift came off duty. Thus he had watched Edna putting the squeals into a score of pigs and inflating them until they swelled like uberous sows, deep-bellied, huge-hammed, luxuriantly fecund. Ripeness is all.

" And you know how the balloons come out all the

colours of the rainbow?" she went on. "Red and yellow
and green all mixed up together?" She giggled delight-
fully. "Your eye's rather like that."

Lance watched the stars coming out, and heard a little
breeze sigh through the ferns, and smelt the queer bruised-
bracken smell, thinking that he would remember it for the
rest of his life. His head was full of tenuous rhymes, and
words came from nowhere like the wind in the bracken and
whispered through it. *Violet-weaving, shimmering-throned
Aphrodite*, he said to himself. (He had been reading
Sappho.) He felt so happy that he was sure, if only he had
a pencil and paper, he could have written the saddest poem
in the world.

Edna stretched herself like a contented kitten, and let the
tip of her finger rest lightly on Lance's swollen temple.

"Poor eye," she said. "And I'm sorry for Robin too.
But I'm *glad* you beat him, Lance."

IV

FAITH PARGETTER, the farmer's daughter, had been
properly brought up in one of those big, gracious
farmhouses "where all's accustomed, ceremonious." In
the spotless kitchen with its stone-flagged floor there were
never less than two sides of bacon slung high above the
chimney-piece, and two treacle-cured hams, spiced with
juniper berries, in pickle for Christmas. The shining pots

and pans and the dull-gleaming coppers which hung upon
the walls were of a size which spoke of generous hospitality.
The scrubbed table was laid as a matter of course for twelve
people because the household consisted of ten and " You
never knew who'd drop in for a bite." To this table in
their appointed seasons came Aylesbury ducklings, turkeys,
geese, fat capons, rook-pie, pigs'-fry and faggots, lambs'-
tails, and such time-honoured delicacies as frumenty, biffins,
lardy-cakes, sparrib-pie, love-in-disguise, fairings and
gingerbread-husbands. There was always a bowl of cream
big enough to drown a cat in, and a Double Gloucester
cheese the size and shape of a grindstone, and without fail
on Michaelmas Day Mrs. Pargetter made three dozen
Christmas puddings just as her mother and her grandmother
had done before her: never one more nor one less.

Miss Pargetter was therefore very shocked indeed when
she discovered that it was Stephen's habit to nibble a couple
of small sandwiches for his lunch. She had an agricultural
contempt for sandwiches; they were all right for the gentry
who went picnicking for fun, but you wouldn't think of
sending your own men out with sandwiches for their mid-
morning bait. You would cut them inch-thick slices of
bread, well daubed with butter and accompanied by slabs
of cold meat or fat bacon plastered with mustard; and if
you forgot to add a quarter of a pound of Double Gloucester
the men would come home grumbling at dinner-time.
Sandwiches were therefore anathema to Miss Pargetter.

She dealt with the situation in her own way. Without a
word to Stephen she brought in four brown eggs and four
slices of ham. At lunch-time, which she called dinner-time,

she locked the front door of the shop and went up uninvited into Stephen's little flat, where she spent rather a long time scrubbing the frying-pan with wire-wool, having fore-sightedly provided herself with this necessity. She then cooked the ham and eggs and called " Dinner's ready."

Stephen, in his office, was on the telephone. The voice of Sir Almeric Jukes was drawling contemptuously into his ear:

" And if you think I'm goin' to risk my valuable cattle in the company of diseased ridin'-school hosses you're wrong, Mr. Stephen Tasker, you're wrong."

" I'm sorry," said Stephen patiently. " I didn't quite gather what you thought the horse was suffering from? "

" Strangles," shouted Sir Almeric. " D'ye hear, strangles? I felt the brute's neck and there were lumps on it. So unless you get the vet and he gives it a clean bill of health you'll have none of my horses for your Pageant. And that's flat, Mr. Stephen Tasker," he added offensively.

Stephen wearily put down the telephone. It had been his worst morning so far. Everybody was in a muddle, from the Wardrobe Mistress to the lighting man, and they had all brought their muddles in succession to the small back room. The knitters of chainmail had run out of wool; the painters of chainmail had run out of silver paint. The carpenters, admittedly, had settled their strike, but the electricians were just starting one. The printers had lost the block which was to go on the cover of the programme. Robin had declared he could design no more dresses unless he was provided with an expensive and unobtainable book on heraldry. The Cricket Club had failed to agree about who should represent W. G. Grace: a part which required not simply a beard from Clarkson's but the ability to hit sixes which Clarkson's couldn't provide. The Rowing Club, with nobody's authority, had spent twenty pounds on decorating a barge for Bloody Mary more elaborate than Cleopatra's. The Bank Manager was concerned about the increasing overdraft and had rung up to ask who was going to guarantee it. Finally, just before one, the Vicar had arrived with a bundle of nineteenth-century *Punches* for which he had practically demanded twenty-five shillings. Outside it was mizzling with cold rain, water poured in runnels off the Vicar's bald head and the silvery drops furred his old cassock, which he shook all over the shop like a dog which has been in the river. "The pride of the morning, my boy," beamed the Vicar, pocketing a pound note and two half-crowns. "Just the pride of the morning. The glass is going up; there's an anticyclone on the way. You mark my words, it'll be fine this afternoon."

Although the telephone was ringing (with Sir Almeric raging at the other end) the Vicar showed no inclination to leave.

"You'll sell those *Punches*," he said, "when the American visitors arrive. Bit of old England: just the sort of thing the Americans love." (Shades of the *New Yorker*! thought Stephen.) "But it's always pleasant to do a deal with you, my boy. No haggling, no hums and hahs; and both of us go away happy. You'll be particularly pleased, I think, if I tell you something."

"What?" said Stephen.

The Vicar patted his pocket.

" This is *just* sufficient, with what I've saved up, to pay for that anemometer I told you about; and, bless your heart, I'm going to send off for it this afternoon! "

Beaming, the Vicar went out.

" Dinner's ready," called Faith again.

Stephen went up. Faith looked homely in an apron (she must have brought it with her) and the ham smelled very good.

" Faith," he said. " What the devil's strangles in horses? "

" Abscesses in the neck," she replied promptly. " Difficult to distinguish from glanders."

It seemed there were certain advantages, apart from ham and eggs, in having a farmer's daughter for your secretary !

" Is it catching? " he said.

" Very."

" Sir Almeric thinks one of the riding-school horses has got it."

" Most unlikely," said Faith. " It attacks young horses generally; all the riding-school hacks look about a hundred and one. But we'd better ring up the riding school and ask them to get the vet."

It was strange, thought Stephen, that he should have once thought her half-witted, for although her typing and short-hand were as bad as ever, and she had a slap-dash way of doing things which resulted in some terrible muddles, she possessed a kind of rough-and-ready country common sense which made up for everything. More and more he found himself asking, and taking, her advice. It was she who had settled the row about the programme sellers' uniforms, which had been specially designed by Robin and rejected by the lady in charge of the programme sellers, who had threatened mass resignations on account of them. "What you don't understand," Faith had explained patiently to Stephen, "is that Robin designs dresses for pretty girls with good figures. Since half the programme sellers either bulge in the wrong places or are as scraggy as old ewes they know they'd look silly in them."

"But that wasn't the reason they gave at all."

Faith had looked at him with amused pity.

"Do you really imagine they admit it even to themselves?"

He began to rely on her in all sorts of ways. (Relying on Faith! he thought—it wasn't a bad motto for his Festival.) Unusual properties were always being asked for by the stage manager. He wanted a set of hames and traces, and Faith, who knew all about harness, obtained them next day. He wanted a Very Light pistol and Faith rang up a Group Captain at the nearest aerodrome whom she charmed so completely that he risked court-martial and lent her two. But she wasn't always charming, by any means; in her abrupt countrified way she could be devastatingly rude, and since Stephen was by nature unqualified to assert himself, Faith's rough manners sometimes came in very useful. She had been so rude to Councillor Noakes, whose perpetual pawing she resented, that he no longer hung about the office all day; and that, at any rate, was a blessing.

Eating his ham and eggs, Stephen tried to sort out the

events of the morning. " Knitting wool and silver paint,"
he said, " and we must have a new block made for the
printers."

" Have done," said Faith with her mouth full.

" And the Cricket Club wants to hire a pro for W. G.
Grace. The Captain thinks *he* ought to have the honour but
the team say he's not good enough."

" Quite right. Had an average of eight last season."

" And we want a donkey. Mr. Gurney says the Holy
Hermit's got to be led on to the field by Odo and Dodo,
riding on a donkey."

" What, Odo and Dodo? "

" No, the Hermit."

" Well, that's lucky," said Faith. " If they were as drunk
as they were at the rehearsal last night they'd fall off."

" But can you get a donkey? "

" Of course. Old Mother Perks at the bottom of our
lane has one in her orchard. It's older than I am so it ought
to be quiet."

" Good girl. What a life it is ! "

She put down her fork and examined him for a moment
with her pitying and curious stare.

" Does it ever occur to you," she said, " that if we're
going to play to empty stands all this hurly-burly hasn't got
much point? "

And indeed it had occurred to him. He was only too
well aware that the turmoil in his office was, in a sense, a
sort of bombinating in a vacuum. You had only to look
at the seating-plans in Virginia's booking office to discover
that the public at large regarded the Festival with supreme

indifference. There was a thin speckling of crosses in the half-crown section, mostly representing charabanc parties, and here and there a few of the more expensive seats had been sold; but Stephen suspected that the purchasers of these were devoted or dutiful friends and relations of the performers. Virginia, knitting away uninterrupted, had finished her twin-set in record time and started on another one; her total takings amounted to less than a hundred and fifty pounds.

Encouraged by this, the anti-Festival faction had become more vociferous. The opposition was by no means confined to Miss Foulkes' supporters and the workers in the balloon factory; letters began to appear in the *Intelligencer* signed "Ratepayer" and "Pro Bono Publico" asking who was going to foot the bill if the Festival lost two or three thousand pounds. Mr. Runcorn, meeting Stephen one morning in the street, declared in his most sepulchral tone: "I have my finger on the pulse of the town, Mr. Tasker; I do not like the feel of it at all." Councillor Noakes haunted the booking office anxiously, peering short-sightedly at the seating-plans over Virginia's shoulder and sighing deeply while he gave her small consoling pats upon various parts of her anatomy. In fact the only remaining optimists were the Mayor, who held fast to his belief that there would be a last-minute influx of Foreign Visitors, and the Vicar, who insisted that when the anticyclone arrived the bookings would be immediately trebled.

"Buzz-buzz-buzz," said Faith, "like blowflies in a bottle. We make ourselves so busy we forget that nobody's taking any notice of us."

"We've spent more than we ought to on advertising already."

"Just ordinary advertising. Posters and things. That's no good. We must do something *different*. Have some cheese?"

"No, thanks, I'm full."

Faith helped herself to a lump of Double Gloucester.

"Something different," she munched.

"Yes, but what?"

"Bloons."

"What?"

Faith finished her cheese in her own time and said:

"Balloons. Kill two birds with one stone. Win over the opposition by supporting a local industry and advertise the Festival all over the place."

"I don't quite get it," said Stephen.

"You print on the balloons a neat little caption about the Pageant. You fill them with hydrogen. You ask for volunteers to let them go. (That's more publicity because people love letting off balloons.) And they sail away wherever the wind listeth. I thought of it in the bath," said Faith.

"Wouldn't most of them come down in open country where they'd never be seen?"

"Yes. You'd want a lot of balloons."

"How many?"

"Twenty thousand," said Faith coolly. "At least. And perhaps you'd have to offer rewards and prizes to start people looking for them. But I worked it out in the bath and I thought that if five per cent were picked up, we'd have set a thousand people talking. There's a lot of publicity in that."

It sounded to Stephen a crazy idea. In any case, he protested, the factory couldn't make them in time. There were only three weeks to go before the Festival; and to do any good the balloons would have to be dispatched within ten days.

" They can make them in ten days," said Faith.

" What? You've talked to John Handiman already? "

" Have fixed," said Faith. " One hundred and fifty gross at twelve-and-six a gross. Delivery to-morrow week. That just gives us time to persuade old Runcorn to write a leader about it, asking for volunteers to let them go from the top of the hill."

Faith helped herself to another piece of cheese.

" I do hope it blows like hell," she said.

V

A DEFLATED pig lay upon John Handiman's desk; it was a sample of the latest batch, which Miss Foulkes had put there. Beneath it were two letters which had arrived by the morning post. John removed the pig and read them for the third time.

The first was from the Bank. It ran:

" Dear Mr. Handiman: I am disappointed to find that the promised payment into your company's account has not materialised. You will realise of course that it is impossible for me to allow any further increase in the overdraft, which stands at £571 3s. 6d. and that provision must therefore be made for your Wages Cheque on Friday. I can only suggest that you take the necessary steps to ensure that the cheque due to you from your Agent is received by that date. . . ."

The second was from the company's Agent in London. Certain currency difficulties, it said, had cropped up in connection with the Argentine payment. No doubt all would be well in the end, but the money had not yet arrived and no settlement could be expected for at least a week. " Meanwhile," the Agent added, " we enclose a translation of the explanation we have received from the Argentine importer."

The " explanation," if it was one, was wrapped up in Latin courtesies. It spoke of pesos and Exchange controls as if they were the language of love; and the very literal translation finished with a flourish: " Your servants who kiss your hand."

So this, thought John, was the end: not with a bang but a whimper. On an impulse he blew up the pig and stood it on his desk. Its long falsetto squeal was dying away when Miss Foulkes came in, and she regarded it with disapproval as the wrinkles began to appear on its back and with a final faint squeak it toppled over as if it had been pole-axed. She didn't think that balloons in the shape of pigs were very funny. Then she noticed the bowl of scarlet peonies on the filing-cabinet and began to blush.

" The messenger-boy brought them and I put them in

G

water," said John, trying not to look at her. "There was no message."

"Thank you. By the way," she said briefly, "the shop stewards have called a meeting. It's just starting now."

The "shop stewards" were Jim and Joe. They were in fact the only Trade Unionists in the factory, and their title was an honorary one, bestowed upon them by Miss Foulkes.

"A meeting? Oh, yes. I suppose I ought to go and give them a sort of farewell talk or something. On the lines of 'It was a good show while it lasted'?"

"This is a private meeting," said Miss Foulkes, "for the workers."

"Oh! All right. Enid," he said, "I'm sorry about it all."

"So am I."

"I should have liked to do that job for the Festival. I wonder if we could carry on just long enough——"

"Wait and see," snapped Miss Foulkes.

In the small yard at the back of the factory, a desolate place full of empty latex-containers, some of which had rolled down into the mud at the river's edge and stuck there, with bits of old bicycles, motor tyres and a half-submerged punt, Jim was making a speech. It was a long, confused and rambling speech, which would surely have puzzled any student of industrial relations, and it was delivered in the voice of a raven with tonsillitis. The B. capitalists, Jim said, had made another B. muck-up. A proper military muck-up it was, like Dunkirk. The Argentinos were partly to blame for it too. Run away without paying. He never did hold with that Peron.

Anyhow, the long and the short of it was there was no money in the B. kitty. Pretty kettle of fish. Just the sort of thing that happened under B. capitalism. Always would happen until the whole shooting-match was in the hands of the workers. Then they'd show 'em.

Not that he had anything against Mr. Handiman. They ought to have seen him at Walcheren. Shot through the stomach and half drownded, and asking about Jim and Joe.

No money in the kitty. And along came this contract for a hundred and fifty gross of balloons for the Festival. What the hell the Festival wanted balloons for Jim couldn't say. He didn't hold with the B. Festival. Since there was no B. copper listening he didn't mind admitting he'd had a hand in sticking up them posters. Him and some others he wouldn't name.

That Inspector Heyhoe was a Fascist Beast, he was, proper.

Now the B. puzzle was, what happened next? Did they go on the dole or did they work out that contract on half-pay, overtime chucked in, and have the other half when and if there was something in the kitty again? Union Rules? To hell with Union Rules. Who was talking about Union Rules anyway? He and Joe were the only loyal Trade Unionists there, and if they couldn't say to hell with the Union who could?

" We wants to do fings proper and we wants to do fings Democratic," croaked Jim, " so we'll put it in the form of a resolution and settle it by a show of hands. The proposition is—but I'll ask our secretary to read it out. Go on, Joe."

It was a very complicated resolution, and it took the

shape, for some obscure ideological reason, of an ultimatum to the Management. Because Joe had forgotten the last part of the sentence, it ended " or else——"

" Or else what? " put in Mrs. Greening.

" Or else it's a lock-out, see," said Jim. "Not a strike, but a B. lock-out. Some of you scabs that ain't in the Union don't know the difference. If he don't accept it, then it's simply another B. lock-out. Now put it to the meeting, Joe."

A woman at the back of the crowd said:

" What about the Festival? We don't want it to go out as we holds with it, do we? "

" Amendment accepted," said Jim with alacrity. "Put in somefing to that effect, Joe—while not in favour of the Festival at a time when man-hours and materials—you remember that piece Carrots had in the letter to the paper? "

" It makes it sound a bit round-the-'ouses," protested Joe.

" Never mind. We wants to say what we means. Put it to the meeting."

Joe did so.

" Now we wants a proposer."

Mrs. Greening put up her hand; Edna seconded, because she liked Mrs. Greening and was sorry for John Handiman; and twenty-nine men, women and girls, who lived in leaky tumbledown cottages in the back alleys of a rural slum, the rag-tag-and-bobtail of the town, raised their hands in favour.

" Carried unanimously," said Jim; and a corncrake mocked him from the long grass of the Bloody Meadow.

It was Joe's duty, as Secretary, to lay the resolution upon

John's desk. He did this without undue ceremony, because he could never quite make up his mind, when he entered the office, whether he was the accredited spokesman of the workers or Private 256389 Collins, J. He stumped in with his beret on, gave a sort of compromise-salute which could be interpreted either as a token of respect or a comradely acknowledgment of John's greeting, observed that it was a proper muck-up, regarded Miss Foulkes' peonies with interest, and stumped out.

John read the resolution four times before he understood it. At last he looked up.

" Enid. You knew about this? "

" I dare say."

" You know what it means? "

" No beer or cigarettes for anybody for a fortnight— won't hurt them, anyhow—and then if the Argentine pays, and we get some more contracts, we might just scrape through."

" If I can raise a hundred and fifty pounds. That's half the wages, for two weeks."

" Can you? "

" Somehow. The Lord knows. I've got to."

" Then we'd better get started," she said, " on those Festival balloons."

John looked at her for a little while in silence; and then suddenly he grinned.

" Enid."

" Yes? "

" Are you quite sure that this is in strict accordance with the Party Line? "

" If you're thinking of the Festival," she said, pursing her prim little mouth, " we are still opposed to it. Our solidarity—you needn't laugh."

" Go on. Your solidarity——"

" It isn't funny."

" By God, it isn't!" he said gravely, looking down at the resolution on his desk.

" Well, what I mean to say is, we're doing this for the factory, not for the Festival." She had a watertight-compartment mind. In her woodcut-world there were no half-tones, the black never merged into the white. " As for the Festival," she said, bloody, bold and resolute, " we shall continue to fight. Joe, Jim and I propose to picket the entrance with banners."

VI

M R. HANDIMAN senior never went fishing on Sunday, because he was strict Methody, but it was his custom to take an afternoon stroll by the riverside instead. There could be no harm in watching other fishermen who had been brought up more easy-going, nor in marking down a likely eddy or a deep quiet bream-hole where the fish might be biting later in the week. Besides, the slow-flowing, peaceful river acted as a sort of salve upon his spirit; it soothed all his worries away. Merely to walk beside it, to listen to the song of the larks upspringing or spiralling down, to watch the silly ducks dabbling, to see the loosestrife and the willowherb and those yellow waterlilies that boys called brandy-bottles (because they smelled like brandy, he supposed, though never a drop of it had passed his lips)— all this afforded him a deep contentment. He described it to himself as "communing with Nature," and every Sunday afternoon between the time when he finished his nap and the time when the Abbey bells called the High Church folk to evensong he communed with nature in his chapel-going bowler hat.

But he had never needed this communion so much as he needed it now, nor ever had less hope of comfort from it. When he thought of the terrible thing he had done, the deceitful, wicked, almost criminal thing, his heart nearly stopped beating and he asked himself why God did not strike him dead then and there. This morning in Chapel, while the Minister was praying, he had hung his head and staring at the bare stone floor had fancifully contemplated the possibility that it might suddenly open and swallow him up; for he worshipped, without knowing he did so, a devil called Jehovah, who was certainly capable of such acts of vengeance.

His dreadful deed, at the time, had seemed comparatively innocent; though he had performed it with trembling fingers and a quickening breath. But now he could see there had been no excuse for it at all; except the folly of a doting old man.

John had come to his shop late on Thursday evening and had asked for the loan of a hundred and fifty pounds. He had explained all about the troubles of the factory, and about the Festival balloons and the people working on half-pay. He had promised that the money should be paid back within a fortnight; and he had ended: "I wouldn't have troubled you, Dad, not for worlds, save that you told me to if ever I was in a jam."

And that was perfectly true. When John had come back from the war to discover that the ironmonger's shop had shrunk while he was away and become too small to contain him, like his civilian clothes; when he had planned to strike out on his own and set up the balloon factory, Mr. Handiman, full of pride, had suggested that if he ever wanted a temporary loan he knew where to look for it. "You come to me," he had said. "You come along to your old dad and he won't let you down." It was, as he saw now, a vain and foolish thing to say; why, then, had he uttered it? Because John had looked so fine in his uniform, because he had fought so many fights and killed so many Germans, because he had been wounded, because he was surely the most upstanding son that a silly old widower had ever doted on. But now those unconsidered words had come back to roost with a vengeance. Mr. Handiman hadn't got a hundred and fifty pounds. He had less than fifty; and out of that small sum he owed a quarter's rent. Yet with John sitting there before him, anxious and apologetic, he couldn't bring himself to say so. It was as if Satan had entered into him and spoken the words:

"Just a minute, my boy, while I think it out. Just let me reckon up my resources."

And all the time he wasn't thinking of his resources at all. That was the monstrous lie. He was thinking of that paying-in book with the thick wad of notes in it, and the slip made out ready for the Bank, which he had put away in the shop safe and forgotten about for nearly a week. He was thinking, with appalling casuistry, that since the balloons had been ordered by the Festival, and would have to be paid for by the Festival, it wouldn't be stealing or anything like stealing, it would merely be " putting down a deposit " or " making a payment on account." But he didn't say so to John; he dared not; for John would have seen through that flimsy argument at once. And thus he had made John an unknowing party to his crime; for he had said, or Satan had said, so calmly and smoothly:

" Now you sit yourself comfortable here while I go and see what I've got."

What *I've* got!

He had still kept up the pretence that he wasn't stealing —or embezzling, did they call it? That sounded even shabbier. He had written plainly on a blank paying-in slip " Paid to J. Handiman junior on a/c for balloons. One hundred and fifty pounds: J. Handiman senior, Treasurer." Yes, but that didn't excuse him morally or legally as he knew very well. For one thing he hadn't asked John the price of the balloons. It might be much less than a hundred and fifty. For another, all Festival payments had to be made by cheque; and the cheques had to be countersigned by Councillor Noakes. That prudent rule had been passed at the first meeting and it was in the minutes; indeed he had proposed it himself.

When he returned with the notes John had said seriously: " You may have saved the factory, Dad," and then had laughed:

"You old *miser*! You oughtn't to keep so much money in the shop, with all these spivs and cosh-boys about. You ought to pay it into the Bank regularly."

These words had mocked him for three days. *You ought to pay it into the Bank regularly*. For it was only a matter of time before somebody else said that—Mr. Tasker, or Noakes, or even the Mayor; and what then?

At one moment, yesterday, he had actually resolved to go to the Mayor and confess; and the resolution had lifted a cloud off his mind, until he realised that he could not do so without incriminating John. For who would believe that John had not known where the money came from? To confess would be to bring John's precarious house-of-cards tumbling about him; and about his wife and two kids as well. It was unthinkable that he should ruin John.

So there was nothing for it; he must carry his shame about with him for a fortnight and hope, like all the wretched and foolish little men who ran away with the funds of slate clubs, that "something would turn up" before he was found out. For now he was of their fellow-ship. He thought and felt as they did. He made the same feeble excuses to himself: I wasn't really dishonest, I meant to pay it back. He was blood-brother now to that poor weak creature Watkins who had spent the Christmas share-out money belonging to the Black Bear Goose Club and got six months in gaol. Watkins had meant to pay it back too, and perhaps he would have done so if the right dog had won on his last, desperate evening.

The Bloody Meadow formed an island in the loop of the

two rivers and was joined to the town by an old stone bridge. It was a huge field, nearly a mile across, and it generally took Mr. Handiman two hours to walk all the way round it. But he walked more quickly to-day, because he spent less time talking to his friends on the bank, those easy-going fellows whom he secretly envied. He asked them the usual question: " Any luck? " but he hardly listened to their usual excuses, that the sun was too bright, the water too clear, the wind too strong, or the fish off the feed. In his own favourite fishing place, a cow-drink between two willows, he found Robin baiting his hook with something out of a jar which Mr. Handiman could have sworn was illicit salmon-roe; for Robin rarely indulged in any lawful form of angling. However, he hadn't caught anything (or if he had he wouldn't admit it) and was obviously disinclined to say what he was fishing for. Instead he asked: " How are the Festival bookings going? Is the money beginning to roll in? " at which Mr. Handiman's heart gave a terrible bound, though he was able after a moment's pause to answer quite calmly:

" Very slow, Mr. Robin, very slow indeed."

He hurried away. This was another nightmare which he shared with the slate-club secretaries: the suspicion of being suspected. Even the most casual pleasantry—*Is the money beginning to roll in?*—took on a frightening significance.

Yesterday when Virginia had handed him her day's takings—only five pounds seventeen and sixpence—she had said jokingly: " Don't spend it all at once, Mr. Handiman," and for a second he had imagined that she knew and was trying to tell him so. When he realised that she couldn't

know—for he had the only key to the safe—he had felt the
damp cold sweat on his forehead, and heard the surging in
his ears, just the same as that time after a bout of 'flu when
he had fainted in chapel and was coming to afterwards.

Such experiences, thought Mr. Handiman wretchedly,
were part of his punishment. And it was part of his punishment too that even his beloved river gave him no joy this
afternoon. The beauty was tarnished, the magic gone, he
took no pleasure in the gobbling ducks and the tight, bright
buds of the brandy-bottles. All along the bank, spaced out
at intervals of about ten yards, were new wooden pegs,
consecutively numbered; and these displeased him, for
they were a reminder that on Saturday week, for ten miles
upstream and five miles down, the river would be lined
with thousands of anglers from Birmingham and the Black
Country, taking part in the first big angling competition of
the year. Mr. Handiman, because he had fished there since
boyhood, felt that he had a proprietary right to the banks
of the Bloody Meadow, and he disapproved of these
spectacular fishing matches to which the contestants came
in noisy charabancs, bringing with them their wives and
girls. There were umpires every mile or so along the pitch,
who started the match with pistol shots as if it were a race,
and bookies, even, ran along the banks taking bets on the
result. The women sometimes put on paper hats, which
they seemed to think were necessary to the enjoyment of a
day in the country, and when they had gone they left
behind them a distasteful debris of stout and pop bottles,
cigarette packets, newspapers and partly-nibbled sandwiches.
The whole thing shocked Mr. Handiman profoundly, and

he looked upon it as an almost blasphemous parody of his cherished sport; it pained him as it would pain a member of the M.C.C. to see the cricketers at Lord's going out to field in comic hats and false noses. For " Study to be quiet," Izaak Walton had said; and he had recommended his innocent recreation especially to contemplative men. What would he have thought of the screeching wenches in paper hats and the drinking that went on in the pubs afterwards— he who had declared, " I had rather be a civil, well-governed, well-grounded temperate poor angler than a drunken lord; but I hope there is none such" ? What would he have thought of the bookies, and the betting, and the elaborate precautions against cheating, who hardly ever failed to speak in the same breath of " anglers, honest men" ?

Oh, dear, there I go again, thought poor Mr. Handiman, wishing that *The Compleat Angler* hadn't laid such emphasis upon honesty. Stephen Tasker had once shown him a copy with Walton's own handwriting on the fly-leaf (it was one of the very few rare books Stephen had ever had in his shop) and the inscription so plainly written in faded brown ink was simply, " *For my friend Honest Will Iles, Iz. WA.*" How right and proper, he had thought at the time; for surely all Izaak's good friends must have been as honest as the day. He had felt absurdly proud, as he handled the book reverently, that the man who wrote it had been an iron-monger like himself.

Then there was the famous recipe for cooking pike: " This dish of meat is too good for any but anglers, or very honest men; and I trust you will prove both." Alas, he had forfeited his claim for ever. He was no more of that honourable brotherhood. He was—with shame and horror he forced himself to formulate the word—an *embezzler*. No better than that.

In his distress, Mr. Handiman no longer paid much attention to where he was going; and straying off the tow-path he found himself among long mowing-grass full of moondaisies in which there lay—right at his feet, for he had nearly tripped over them—a couple hotly embracing. The spectacle filled Mr. Handiman with embarrassment and dismay; for though he turned away at once with a mumbled apology he couldn't fail to be aware that the young man was Mr. Lance the Vicar's son and the girl was that Edna Shirley from the balloon factory. Moreover, although his glance before he averted it had fallen only for a second upon the girl's bright head and Lance's dark one, upon a confusion of limbs, a preposterous heap which he refrained from anatomising in his mind, he had seen something else which had embarrassed him much more than the embracing couple. For as in common decency he had looked the other way, his attention had become fixed upon a bright patch in the grass, and he realised now that this had been a dress —in fact, he could even remember the pattern, which was one of yellow flowers. Worse still, the dress had been neatly folded, and this fact deeply troubled his unwilling imagination. For it was clear that the girl had taken it off, you might say, with malice aforethought. Such an action was altogether outside Mr. Handiman's experience, and it seemed to him to be very wicked indeed.

He had known Mr. Lance since he was a schoolboy in shorts, coming to the shop for fish-hooks on tick.

" What's the right size to catch a roach, Mr. Handiman? "

" You'll want a Number Twelve for him, Mr. Lance; very small mouth a roach has got "—and somehow that seemed to make it worse that he should have taken a factory girl, even though she was a Beauty Queen, for his lie-beside. That was a bad word which they used in the alleys; but it could hardly be too bad for a young woman who would take off her dress in an open field, even though the mowing-grass *was* very long, and tidily, providently, *fold* it. . . . What in the world would the old Vicar say if he knew?

Down what dangerous paths, thought Mr. Handiman, is this Festival leading us, with its play-acting and Beauty Queens, its jealousies and its quarrels? But even as he shook his head in disapproval, the recollection of his own wickedness came flooding back. Who was he to cast stones, while that empty paying-in book lay in his shop safe? Who indeed?

He put his hand in his pocket and felt for the key. Then he remembered that he had left it in the drawer where he kept his private papers, and he had a moment's unreasoning panic, for it suddenly seemed important that he should have the key in his own possession always. Unconsciously he began to hurry; and he didn't notice the fishermen any more nor ask them if they had had any luck, he had no eyes for the loosestrife which stained the banks like dark arterial blood, no ears for the larks which poured down their sweet trickles of song all about him. He went so fast, on his short legs, that he was almost running; and his guilt ran beside him, beneath the accusing sky.

VII

IT WAS Noakes, the old fool, who had insisted on folk-songs. "Consider the visit to our town of Mary Tudor," he had said. "The King's daughter. What more natural than that the simple country people of those days should seek to entertain her with their simple folk-songs?"

Lance thought it highly improbable; but Noakes was determined.

"Have a hunt round for something suitable, there's a good chap. Go over to the Public Library and ask the Librarian to help you. There are sure to be plenty of the right period—I can so well imagine the scene, the King's daughter sitting entranced in her barge while the yokels chant their pretty songs in her honour, clear and sweet as the blackbird, pure as the morning! Much better, if I may say so," added Noakes nastily, "than some of this meaningless modern stuff."

Very well, you shall have your folk-songs, thought Lance mischievously. But he had no desire whatever to spend a fine summer day in a frowsty old library, and he therefore proposed to write them himself. This he was now doing, with considerable enjoyment, as he leaned back in the garden-chair which he had placed in a spot well suited to inspire pastoral poetry, being half-way between a bower of honeysuckle and a bed of white tobacco plants which were just beginning to shed their sweetness on the waning air.

He wrote swiftly:

> *When I was a youngster on Midsummer Day*
> *I tumbled the wenches about in the hay,*
> *With a heigh-ho frolicsome——*

"Lance!" he heard his father calling. The old man had just come out of evensong and was ambitious, Lance knew, to fix up his newly-arrived anemometer before it was too dark. There was no point in doing this, for the air was quite still, but the Vicar was like a child with an exciting toy and he wanted to play with it immediately.

"Lance!"

"Coming."

But I must get this chorus finished first, he thought; it's going to be rather authentic.

> *With a heigh-ho frolicsome,*
> *Goosegogs and sillabubs,*
> *Puffballs and pillikins,*
> *Kecksies and crazies and*
> *Codlins and cream!*

That would teach Master Noakes a lesson. ("Meaningless modern poetry!" thought Lance.)

He had as little difficulty with verse two.

> *The birds they were singing in Merry-come-sorrow,*
> *"Come Michaelmastide you pay back what you borrow,"*
> *With a heigh-ho frolicsome,*

H

Goosegogs and sillabubs,
Puffballs and pillikins,
Kecksies and crazies and
Codlins and cream!

Just the thing to sing to Bloody Mary in the Bloody
Meadow!

"Lance!" His father sounded very petulant indeed.
"I'm stuck on the ladder. Do come."

Lance put away the notebook in his pocket. His father,
he found, with reckless enthusiasm had put up a rickety
ladder against the old dovecote which he had long ago
selected as the ideal site for his anemometer; his weight had
broken two rungs of the ladder and he now hung on by
his arms alone while his feet clove the air where the rungs
should have been. Lance went up the ladder, seized his
legs, and guided him down. The Vicar's wife, meanwhile,
hearing his cries, put her head out of a bedroom window,
and called:

"You'll break your old neck if you aren't careful. I said
you'd be punished for doing it on Sunday."

"God is very tolerant of an old man's foibles," said the
Vicar mildly. "Be a kind chap, Lance, and fetch another
ladder from the coach-house—the big fruit-picking one if
you can manage it."

Lance did so, while couplets of delightful nonsense
rhymed themselves in his head.

The cobwebs were hanging upon the bright thorn,
(Come tiddly, come toddly, come Michaelmas morn!)
With a heigh-ho frolicsome——

By the time he returned with the big ladder the Vicar had the instrument out of its wooden packing-case and was assembling it.

"This is the recording device, and these are the connecting tubes. And this, of course, is the vane which keeps the tube facing the wind. What a miracle of ingenuity! And yet, on what a simple principle it works! We've certainly advanced a long way since Dr. Thomas Rory Robinson invented the first of these machines at Armagh Observatory in, let me see, 1846. Now all we need to do, Lance, is to secure the anemometer to the platform I built on top of the dovecote and plug in the connection. Then I can read off the velocity and pressure of the wind on this dial which I propose to place at eye-level upon one of the supports of the dovecote. If you like to carry the instrument up the ladder, you'll find that I've put the screws and screwdriver on the platform all ready."

The instrument was not very heavy, and Lance soon had it firmly screwed in place. It was the work of a few minutes only to connect up the tubes which registered the pressure on the recorder, and to secure the recorder to one of the legs of the dovecote. The Vicar gazed at it lovingly.

"Not a zephyr," he said.

And indeed it was the stillest, softest evening Lance could remember.

"The anticyclone has come to stay," pronounced the Vicar, with a glance at the sky, which was empty save for a small cloud the size of a man's hand just appearing over the horizon. Yet Lance fancied there was a thundery tendency in the air; for the utter stillness was almost unnatural, it was as if the whole world held its breath.

" My boy, we must celebrate this," said the Vicar suddenly. " At long last, my anemometer! Let us go in and drink a glass of the Vicarage port."

Nothing loath, Lance followed him into the house. The Vicarage port derived from the grocer's, and was described as rich ruby, but Lance was not the fellow to look a gift horse in the mouth and he was glad to accept a second glass, and then a third. His mother came in to draw the curtains and switch on the light, and remarked that it had got dark very quickly; the sultry weather had given her a headache and after a few minutes she went up to bed. The Vicar settled himself comfortably in his armchair and lit his pipe. There was a long silence, during which a cockchafer or moth banged against the window-pane several times. Lance correctly conjectured that his father was about to reopen the vexed question of his own future.

" Er—how are those choruses coming along? " said the Vicar at last; and Lance recognised the gambit.

" Finished, Father. Ten days ago." It was less than a fortnight till the Festival, and he was unable to temporise any longer.

" Ah! Then we shall have to begin—er—*thinking* again, shan't we, my boy? "

" Yes, Father."

Bang, bang went the cockchafer on the window-pane.

" Have you ever, for example, considered taking Holy Orders? "

" No, Father, I can't say I have."

" You may feel, of course, that you haven't a call. Many young men experience such a natural diffidence. But often the sense of vocation comes later; and I can assure you that from the worldly point of view it's a very pleasant life—not much money, of course, but a measure of security in an uncertain world and a modicum of leisure to pursue some pleasant pastime, such as my own hobby of the weather, to one's heart's content."

Lance was thinking that his own pleasant pastime would perhaps be considered less suitable for a clergyman than meteorology, when the tap-tapping at the window started again.

" Upon my soul," said the Vicar, " what a plague of those chafers there must be this summer! " He went to the window and drew apart the curtains. " Yet I can't see any. I believe—well, what an extraordinary thing! Yes, I'm *sure* it's the wistaria blowing against the glass. Quick, Lance, go and find a torch. We must go out and read the anemometer! The Lord has brought the wind out of his treasuries! It's really *blowing*! "

The Vicar gathered up his cassock about him and ran out through the front door. Following him with the torch, Lance was aware that the sky, which had been so blue half an hour ago, had assumed a lowering and atrabilious look. And the air, that had been so still, had set up a multitudinous sighing.

" Fifteen miles an hour," called the Vicar. " A little more in the gusts. It works, Lance! The anemometer's working! "

Some drops of rain were beginning to fall, sparse but enormous. The Vicar, however, did not heed them.

"Anemometer." He breathed the word as a lover might utter it. "Derived as you well know from the Greek ἄνεμος wind: the same root from which we get the beautiful word 'Anemone,' the wind-flower."

The rain began to patter like galloping horses. The voices in the sky became more shrill and there was a long *whoosh!* among the churchyard chestnuts. Lance fancied that he could feel all about him a quickening elemental pulse.

"Has it ever occurred to you," his father went on, "that the Latin *Animus*, meaning 'soul'—how odd that the soul-less animals are so called!—comes from this identical Greek original—'ἄνεμος' again? Wind is indeed an awe-inspiring thing; and it is no wonder that man has always associated it with the idea of the spirit. 'The spirit moved upon the waters.' 'The spirit bloweth and is still.' You remember at the Pentecost——"

But Lance never heard the rest of the sentence. It was literally and most appropriately blown away; for there came at that moment out of the ochreous-black sky a mighty rushing wind. Thus, surely, while Odysseus slept had the contents of Aeolus' rifled sack leapt forth with a howl and a hurroosh. The first wild gust twanged as if it were a violin-string the solitary telephone wire which ran from the street to the Vicarage, and at that signal the whole orchestra started. The trees screamed like fiddles played by maniacs, the thunder rolled, the rain beat a tattoo on the roof-tops. Lance and his father found themselves in the small open shed behind the dovecote; and neither of them was sure whether he had run there for shelter or been blown there by the wind. A lightning flash illuminated them and Lance saw the Vicar struggling with his cassock, which had wrapped itself round the upper part of him like an inside-out umbrella; he looked like a headless man. A second flash showed the big fir-tree on the lawn slowly toppling over, torn up by the roots; it uttered a mandrake's shriek as it fell and for what seemed to be many minutes afterwards made a noise like a brushwood fire crackling as its branches broke up on the gravel drive. A third flash, which was followed immediately by a tremendous clap of thunder, revealed nothing but the rain, which looked to Lance like a vast army of spearmen advancing remorselessly with their spears at the slope.

The Vicar, free of his enveloping cassock at last, from time to time shouted " Stupendous! Wonderful! Incomparable! " in Lance's ear.

Lance lit a cigarette and prepared for a long stay.

" I'm not sorry about that fir-tree," yelled the Vicar. " I was always afraid that it might act as a wind-break so that I wouldn't get a true reading on the anemometer."

A number of tiles from the old roof now began to clatter down on the front porch.

" I hope Mother's all right," Lance said. " She doesn't like thunder."

" Yes. We'd better make a dash for it," said the Vicar.

So they charged out among the silver spearmen, and the wind seemed to pluck them up like the blown leaves of autumn and deposit them outside the front door. Lance

ran upstairs and found his mother on the landing playing
what looked like a game of chess with six slop-pails and a
chamber-pot; however skilfully she deployed these pieces
there was always an eighth leak, worse than all the others,
which demanded that the knights or the castles should be
moved to intercept it. Lance went downstairs and found
three buckets; and with these reinforcements the *status quo*
was restored.

"It's your father's fault," said his mother unreasonably.
"That wind-thing! One can't help feeling he's brought
this upon us. I told him he shouldn't do it on Sunday.
Where is he, anyhow, and why doesn't he come and help
us? For all he cares I might have been drowned in my
bed."

"He came in with me," said Lance; "but I rather
suspect he's gone out again."

"In this? He'll catch his death."

Just then they heard the Vicar's heavy tread upon the
stairs.

"Lance! Emily!" he called. "I've been out to make
sure the anemometer hadn't been blown down. It's still
working. Guess what the recording is for the strongest
gust so far."

He arrived, dripping and breathless, upon the landing.

"You'll never guess. Eighty-one miles per hour—Force
Twelve on the Beaufort Scale. In fact a hurricane!"

Beaming with joy, he stood and watched the dribbles of
water falling plop-plop into the assorted receptacles. A
new leak had started and his wife moved her Queen, which
was the biggest bucket, into position close to the window.

The big drops seeping through the ceiling rattled it like a kettledrum.

"And it's still pouring," said the Vicar with satisfaction. "I shan't be at all surprised if I measure an inch of rain in my gauge to-morrow. An inch, Emily! Think of that. A whole inch! One hundred tons to the acre! One hundred and one point three eight to be precise!" Suddenly his face fell.

"Upon my soul, what a selfish old fool I am! I'd forgotten about the Festival." He shook his head gravely. "I hope very much that we aren't going to get a flood."

PART THREE

I

SLOPPING ABOUT in his sea-boots and croaking from time to time in protest or complaint, Jim was more than ever reminiscent of a frog. Thus, grumbling and muttering oaths, he had waded out to the little motor-boat beneath the smoky skies at Dunkirk; thus, still grumbling, he had splashed ashore under a spatter of bullets through the cold grey sea at Walcheren. He was therefore truly in his element.

The water had been into the factory before—in March, 1947, when the big snows melted on the hills—and Jim had spent half an hour of his working time marking the highest level on the wall with his carved initials and the date. But some anonymous tanner in 1875 had recorded a still greater flood; and the water now stood exactly half-way between the two marks. Jim, who had a passion for records and could have told you offhand the fastest time for the Derby, the heaviest pike ever caught, and the greatest number of goals ever scored in a soccer match, was naturally ambitious to inscribe a new set of initials above those of his unknown predecessor.

" Four inches to go," he croaked. " Still rising."

" So what? " said Mrs. Greening.

" If it comes up another four inches it's an all-time high."

" If it comes up another four inches," said Mrs. Greening, " it'll be over the top of my gumboots and I'm off home."

Edna giggled.

" Isn't it a lark? "

But Joe, who was temporarily in charge of the oven since the present batch of self-coloured balloons needed no dipping into the paint, said gloomily:

" It only wants about two inches to get into the gas-mains; and then we're done."

" Kaput," said Jim. " And no balloons for the B. Festival; though unless they're going to turn it into a B. Regatta I can't see as they'll want 'em."

Although the gas continued to function, the electric light had failed, so they had opened wide the double-doors on to the yard. This gave a view across the turbulent brown river to the Bloody Meadow, now a lake dimpled all over with raindrops, in which the grandstand rose gauntly, stripped of most of its wooden seats. Some men in punts were paddling round retrieving these planks, which they secured with ropes and tethered to the main structure. It certainly didn't look as if a Pageant could be held there in less than a fortnight's time.

" It makes you almost cry to see it," said Mrs. Greening, unexpectedly. The catastrophe had brought about a curious change in everybody's attitude to the Festival. Now that the whole project lay in ruins, many of those who had opposed it decided perversely that it had been *their* project after all, and became its enthusiastic supporters. When the Mayor put up a notice outside the Town Hall: " Whatever happens we're going to CARRY ON," the gesture pleased the townspeople, who went about talking of the Dunkirk spirit and felt themselves for the first time to be participants in a great venture. Only Miss Foulkes remained implacable, because she was a believer in Logic and realised therefore that the trifling accident of a flood couldn't make any difference to the Party Line.

There was something rather Russian, John Handiman was thinking, even about her get-up to-day. She was wearing a pair of very shiny black gumboots with pointed toes and they fitted, like jackboots, tight round the calf. Her red hair was tucked up under a coloured handkerchief knotted at the nape of her neck. She had the air of one who goes sternly forward to meet a crisis, and under her arm she carried a broom.

John seemed to remember photographs of women snipers in 1942 who wore the same cossack boots and had the same aspect of bleak determination. They kept the tally of their victims nicked upon their rifle-butts, and with faces devoid alike of triumph and humour posed for their pictures as they added the fiftieth notch to their score. In similar circumstances, he thought, Miss Foulkes would have done the same. She now took the broom purposefully in both hands, opened the office door, and began vigorously to sweep out the water which was just beginning to trickle in over the doorstep and threatened to leave a muddy stain on the carpet.

Regarding her narrow and angular back as she did so, John had a sense of profound and hopeless pity. For this morning he saw her with new eyes and for the first time he realised her complete defencelessness. It so happened that he had got up at six to help Jim and Joe shift the heavy barrels of latex out of flood's way; and when the job was finished he had decided that it wasn't worth while going home to breakfast and had gone straight into the office instead. The morning's letters, which Miss Foulkes generally sorted, were still in the letter-box, and having nothing else to do he opened them himself. He half hoped to find his Agent's cheque among them; but there was nothing but circulars and bills. He stared at one of these bills for a long time before he understood it.

In account with Noakes and Sons, Florists

May 2	To Anemones	6	0
9	To Tulips	7	6
16	To Roses	7	6
23	To Ditto	7	6
30	To Peonies	5	0
		£1 13	6

At last he looked on the outside of the envelope and saw that it was addressed to " Miss E. Foulkes."

So there wasn't a young man after all. There never had been a young man. She had sent herself the flowers.

John was not a very imaginative person, but as he crumpled the bill and put a match to it—for the torn envelope was past repair and she must never suspect that he had seen it—he caught a brief glimpse of the tragedy of the unloved. He had no clear understanding of Miss Foulkes' motive: was it himself or the girls in the factory whom she wished to impress with this fiction of an attentive lover, or did she, in some vague incomprehensible way, even seek to deceive herself? In any case it seemed to John to be rather silly, and a great waste of money into the bargain. He was contentedly and unadventurously married, to a girl to whom Miss Foulkes' behaviour would have seemed even sillier than it did to him; two boisterous children fulfilled their marriage. But what do we know, he asked himself, about the unfulfilled, and by what standard can we judge them? He brushed the white ash off his desk—old Noakes would have to send her an Account Rendered—and put the disquieting puzzle out of his mind. But now at the sight of her defiant back as she brushed out the water it came back to trouble him, and it occurred to him that the soul or spirit of Miss Foulkes, wherever that might reside, must be as tender and red and raw as her pale skin became on those first week-ends of summer when she unwisely indulged in sun-bathing because she thought it was healthy.

"Well tried, Canute," he said.

Still sweeping, she glanced over her shoulder.

"It'll ruin the carpet and the furniture."

"So much the worse for the bum-baillie," he laughed.

"I wish you wouldn't talk like that. We're going to pull through."

He stepped past her, into the flooded factory, and she

went on sweeping—sweeping with the inadequate little broom which was more fitted for the destruction of cobwebs than the stemming of a flood. Thus, when facts rose up and challenged her orthodoxy, she would strive gallantly to brush them away. Did the papers say that the Soviet was a police state? That there were concentration camps in Siberia? That North Korea had been the aggressor? And what about those Russian wives?

Lies, lies, lies, because *Pravda* said so. Brush them away!

But such a cobweb-brush was a frail armament against the world; and to John Handiman this morning she seemed infinitely pitiable and forlorn.

Splashing through eight inches of water, he made his way into the busy shop with its queer mixed smell of ammonia and hot methylated spirits which had formed for the last five years a background to his life. He would miss that sharp tang if, next week or the week after, he sniffed it for the last time; and he would never forget it, he thought, for as long as he lived.

Jim squelched towards him, hunch-shouldered, widemouthed, Batrachian, grumbling as he came.

" Busting up the B. floor again," he said. The flood had done the same thing last time, and it had cost twenty pounds to fill in the holes with concrete. But perhaps that would be somebody else's headache now.

" And if it gets into the gas we're finished, and if it gets into the dynamo we're finished likewise, 'cause there won't be no B. air for testing."

" Is it still rising? " John asked.

"I wouldn't say it was rising and I wouldn't say it was
falling." Jim was still hankering after his all-time high,
because records gave him some obscure spiritual satisfaction.
"I'd say it was just B. well hanging fire." Muttering to
himself that there had been more water at Walcheren, he
went back to his job.

The factory certainly was a bit of a shambles. The surface
of the flood-water was covered with a mixture of oil and
rubber paint, an iridescent film, so that it resembled that of
some filthy pond. Cardboard boxes, tin canisters, and
innumerable cigarette-ends floated about in it, and John
noticed that the big latex barrels beside the long bench,
into which the girls were supposed to throw the faulty
balloons for salvage, had been carried away out of their
reach. Consequently the girls were dropping the rejects
into the water at their feet, and two or three score of these
objects, borne along by a sluggish current, now processed
round the shop, looking like the spat-out skins of white
grapes.

The row of girls at the bench had their backs to John
and their silhouettes made a curious frieze against the open
door; and because of the certainty in his mind that the
factory couldn't carry on much longer he stood and stared
at this familiar sight, thinking that he would remember it
with absurd affection in the years to come: a score or so
of backs, some shapeless, some shapely, bent over the long
bench like housewives over the wash-tub; handkerchiefs
tied round their bobbing heads; sleeves rolled up, french
chalk powdering the bare arms; the balloons swelling and
collapsing; the hiss of the air going into them, the faint

sigh as it went out. How often, on his way through the shop, had he paused at the bottom of the shaky stairs and listened to these women chattering like a flock of starlings! For their perpetual gossip was indeed a sort of murmuration, which from time to time broke out into shrill squeaks and cries when the flock was startled (or pretended to be) by one of Mrs. Greening's outrageous tales. They were a pretty mixed lot—" his sluts," as his wife called them. Ruth, at the end of the row, had had two illegitimates and looked as if she were going to have another; Mrs. Hawkes had been bound over to keep the peace with her next-door neighbour; Mrs. Townshend was regularly drunk on Saturday nights; the lame girl, Doris, had been convicted of shop-lifting; the two seventeen-year-olds next to Edna daubed their faces with rouge and their eyes with mascara so that they looked like tarts and set out down the main road each night in search of lorry-drivers.

But these also, like the ammonia smell and the fog of french chalk, had become part of John's background. They were his people, and he would miss them too when the final bust-up came.

He went up the stairs to the packing-room and at the top he paused again. For the sound which came from the bench now was more rhythmical than the usual bandying of gossip and dirty stories. Raggedly and untunefully the women were singing. Their feet were cold in the leaky cheap gumboots, they were on half-pay, next week they might be out of a job; so they sang. It was the latest silly catch from America, with a trivial tune and moronic words:

I

I'll do anything for you,
Anything you ask me to . . .

but somehow it moved him that they should sing at all in
such circumstances and he was reminded of his soldiers
singing, in all the wettest, dreariest, darkest moments of
the war.

II

ON THE morning of what Faith called Balloon Monday
she saw the mare's-tails in the sky and, being more
weather-wise than the Vicar, knew that her hoped-for blow
was on the way. And sure enough in the late afternoon a
dry north-easter came tearing out of the streaky blue, giving
long manes to the little white horses which pranced over the
flooded fields and kicking the spray high over the main
road; so that the crowds who were walking out from the
town along that narrow causeway said it was " just like the
seaside " and felt exhilarated by the sprinkling of spume.

By six o'clock there must have been more than two
hundred people on the haycock-shaped hill overlooking
the town; and at least another hundred were making their
way there. " Sound the trumpet, Runcorn, sound the
trumpet! " the Mayor had said; and so the *Intelligencer* on
Saturday had carried a leading article in Mr. Runcorn's
most extravagant style calling for volunteers to let off

twenty thousand balloons. The composition had presented
no difficulty to him, for he had simply looked up " Montgolfier " in the Encyclopædia and then referred to the old
files of his paper to see if its founder and first editor had had
anything to say about the ascent of the first balloon in 1783.
It was unthinkable that so significant an event should have
escaped the notice of the argus-eyed *Intelligencer*; nor,
indeed, had it done so. " We are told," wrote Mr. Runcorn,
" that a sheep, a cock and a duck were the unwilling and
far from intrepid aeronauts, launched into the empyrean in
the nacelle of the Messieurs Montgolfier's revolutionary
contraption. But the balloons which our townspeople will
cast to the winds from the birch-clad eminence on Monday
evening will bear a less ponderable cargo—nothing but our
eager hopes for the success of the venture upon which we
have set our hearts . . ." and so on to the tune of nearly two
columns.

But perhaps such a highfalutin encouragement had been
hardly necessary after all; for as Faith had said, " people love
letting off balloons," and to take part in the release of twenty
thousand of them was an experience which was unlikely to
befall anybody more than once in a lifetime. Besides, ever
since what Mr. Runcorn called the Inundation, popular
enthusiasm for the Festival had been gathering momentum;
for the difference of opinion between the pros and the antis
had been like a neighbours' quarrel, which brooks no
interference from outsiders, and the sudden intervention of
the elements had had exactly the same effect as the arrival
of the policeman. Both parties had united to meet the new
challenge. Mr. Runcorn, coming from church on Sunday

morning, had made the unusual gesture of shaking Stephen by the hand. " I have my finger on the pulse of the town. I am gratified to tell you that it is quickening, Mr. Tasker, it is quickening surprisingly."

So, with no shortage of volunteers, the strange ceremony began promptly at six and continued without a hitch for nearly four hours. Stephen had at first been doubtful whether it would be possible to release so many balloons in so short a time; but for once in a way Faith's uncertain mathematics did not let him down. John Handiman had provided eight hydrogen cylinders and fitted them up on the lee side of the birch-wood. It took just five seconds to inflate each balloon and make a knot in the rubber mouth-piece; so they went off at the rate of about a hundred a minute. They were in five different colours, blue, pink, green, yellow, and white, and each was overprinted with a caption about the Festival and the symbol of a formalised rose. Streaming away in batches on the strong wind they looked like a flurry of flower-petals blown off by a summer gale; and then as they mounted into the blue-and-white sky, spiralling, somersaulting and chasing each other while the fickle air-currents whirled them along, they reminded one of butterflies on a mating-flight, when the males pursue the females until both vanish from sight in the unattainable heaven.

It was a pretty spectacle, and worth a poem, thought Lance, as he watched a little cluster of coloured specks hardly bigger than the Pleiades melting into the luminous blue. His head was always full of words and phrases, and the lines which ran through it now came from *Adonais*: " Life, like a dome of many-coloured glass, Stains the white radiance of eternity." It hurt your eyes to look for too long into that white radiance. He blinked them, and looked at Edna instead.

Edna, obviously, had decided that sending off balloons was the jolliest game in the world; a lark indeed. Every time she released one she indulged in a little jump or skip in order to give hers a better start than its fellows. Her giggles succeeded one another like the merry cascade of a mountain stream tumbling down from waterfall to waterfall. Lance thought she looked like a dancing Maenad. How eagerly the little lustful eyes of the sileni and the satyrs would watch her from the edge of the birch-brake, on what light feet would she lead them up hill and down dale in the chase that could have only one ending:

> *The ivy falls from the Bacchanal's hair*
> *Over her eyebrows hiding her eyes;*
> *The wild vine slipping down leaves bare*
> *Her bright breast shortening into sighs. . . .*

Lance reluctantly withdrew his gaze from her as he became aware of his father standing beside him. The Vicar in his wind-fluttered cassock presented an incongruous figure, for he held a big bunch of balloons in each hand. "If I could paint that picture," thought Lance, "I should title it simply ' Church Fête ' and it would somehow stand for all the nice silly homeliness of the Church of England!" The Vicar boomed cheerfully: "I feel like Noah loosing his dove. Go, each of you, and find an Ararat!" It seemed

to please his fancy to set off his balloons in flocks of seven
or eight at a time, and to watch them for as long as possible
to see which outclimbed the others. Mr. Oxford and his
friend Timms had had the same idea, and were now making
quite a good thing out of backing their fancy against
anybody who cared to risk half a crown. "Two to one
the blue!" shouted Mr. Oxford. "Fives the pink, fives
the yellow, the green's gone down in the water! Five to
one bar one, five to one bar!" He was in excellent spirits,
for he had just won a pound off Sir Almeric, who had
come down on horseback from his manor to watch the
proceedings though apparently he did not think it com-
patible with his dignity to take part.

"Put it on the bill," drawled Sir Almeric, standing up
in his stirrups and peering into the sky, "and give me
fours in half-dollars against the yellow. It's a bad starter,
but I like its action. I reckon it'll stay."

Little Mr. Handiman was listening with disapproval.
"They'd bet on anything, Mr. Lance," he whispered. "It
isn't right, to my mind, to treat money so casual in front of
folks who haven't, some of them, got much to bless themselves with." And he shook his head sadly. He was so
globular, thought Lance, that he looked rather like a balloon
himself. Fill him with hydrogen and he'd surely fly away,
over the flooded meadows, over the roof-tops, over the
Abbey tower!

"No, it isn't right, Mr. Lance, to my way of thinking."
Then his glance fell upon Edna and in sudden embarrassment
he shuffled off.

And now Virginia, who had been kept late at the

Booking Office, came wending her way daintily up the
hill, wearing a ridiculous picture hat because she knew she
was going to have her photograph taken. Mr. Runcorn's
photographer had been waiting for her, and he made haste
before the light faded to pose the two finalists on the very
summit each with a bunch of balloons held aloft. The
Mayor and Stephen stood between them.

"Forward a bit, Miss Edna; back a bit, Miss Virginia,"
said the photographer. "That's right, I want you looking
windswept. Now, when I say Go, loose the balloons."

But when he said Go, it was Virginia's hat that took the
air. Just as the shutter clicked it sailed away, revolving
rapidly like a tea-tray spun out of the hand, and because
it presented so large a surface to the wind it almost kept
pace with the balloons and Sir Almeric had time to shout:
"Six to four the Gainsborough!" before it fell into the
muddy gateway at the bottom of the hill. Faith, who was
sorry for Virginia, ran to pick it up; but Edna, although
she was sorry too, found a simple pleasure in watching the
gyrations of the hat and was unable to suppress a giggle.
Patting into place her neat permanent wave, Virginia said
in accents of dangerous refinement:

"Ay don't know whay you think thet's funny."

"Keep your hair on, ducks," said Edna tactlessly (her
own yellow curls were blown all over her face); and the
Mayor, who privately thought that Beauty Queens were
as tiresome as Councillors though one got less weary of
their faces, saved the situation by announcing in his formal
speechifying voice:

"The last batch of balloons is just going up, ladies and

gentlemen; and it only remains for me to thank you for this very fine turn-out which exemplifies, if I may say so, the magnificent public spirit that characterises our ancient town. . . ."

Pink, yellow, blue and green, and pearly-white like huge mistletoe berries, the balloons rose up into the paling sky; and everybody cheered as they sailed away—slowly and smoothly now, for the wind had dropped with the setting of the sun. Standing next to Stephen, Faith said in her matter-of-fact voice:

" So that's that. I wonder if it'll work? "

" Goodness knows," he said. " But how pretty! "

The last lot of two or three dozen kept so close together that you could have covered them with an umbrella; it was as if a many-coloured flower-bed had taken wing. The crowd stood and watched them until they were lost to view; and then, curiously hushed, like people who had taken part in some ancient rite, some strange druidical act of sacrifice, they began to make their way down the slippery slope towards their homes.

The Vicar, luckily, had left before the end; so Lance was able, unnoticed, to take Edna's hand and draw her into the bosky clumps where they hid until the last of the balloonists were out of sight. Now they shared the birch-wood, which they had come to regard as their private playground, with none but Philomel. Lance quoted:

> " So hote he lovede that by nightertale
> He sleep namore than doth a nightingale."

And Edna said: " You do talk silly," and ruffled his hair.

" It's Chaucer talking silly, not me."

"You and your poetry!" A momentary look of trouble crossed her face, wrinkling her brow like a cat's-paw of wind passing over the surface of a sunlit pool. " Lance——" she said.

" Yes? "

" We're so different, you and me. Poetry, for instance. Half the time I just don't know what you're talking about. D'you think it matters? "

" I don't suppose the nymphs knew much about poetry," said Lance irrelevantly, " nor the yellow-skirted fays either. They certainly didn't *make* poetry; but they made poets. Like you do."

" Go on! You don't write poems about me, I bet."

" You *are* poetry. Your eyes are lyrics, your hair's an aubade, a song to wake lovers with in the morning; your nose is a roundelay, your chin is a triolet, your lips are couplets better than ever I could string together, your limbs are sonnets, each of them, your——"

" Get on with you! " She laughed, and the troubled look vanished; it had never been much more than the shadow of a passing cloud in April. " It's getting dark. I can see the stars through the branches. What does your father say about all these late nights? "

" Oh, he's a Wordsworthian, my father; he believes that a poet has to spend a great deal of his time worshipping Nature."

" That's what you tell him."

" It's true. I'm very worshipful."

" Like the Mayor ! " She laughed.

" More worshipful than the Mayor." And, indeed, thought Lance, it was so. Within his narrow field of vision, circumscribed as it was by the tall ferns, he could see a single feathery sprig of woodruff, a bracken-frond half-curled and prehensile-looking, like a hawk's claw, a brave tall foxglove, a dainty yellow pimpernel, a quaint and exquisite little beetle with burnished wing-cases crawling up a stem, and Edna's soft and rounded forearm with the french chalk still powdering it like bloom on a peach. He could smell honeysuckle and meadowsweet; he could hear the brown bright nightingale amorously pouring out its heart, and Edna's delightful chuckle as she repeated, " The worshipful Mr. Lance ! " and drew him towards her. If God manifested Himself in each and all of these various and beautiful things, in bracken-frond and beetle and in the little golden hairs on Edna's arm, " Then," thought Lance, " there is truly no man more worshipful than I ! " But perhaps his was an older god than the Vicar's; a god in whose doxology the laurel, the palms and the pæon had their proper place. The laurel, the palms and the pæon, echoed Lance's exultant heart, the breasts of the nymphs in the brake !

III

O N HIS way home Mr. Handiman paused out of habit to lean upon the parapet of the old bridge and stare at the river. The parapet was made of soft sandstone and its top was notched with smooth rounded grooves where a dozen generations of men and boys had sharpened their pocket-knives. Mr. Handiman had carved his initials there with his tenth-birthday knife in the year of Mafeking. How many hundreds of times, on summer evenings, had he leaned there since!

But never before had it passed through his mind, as it did now, that a man could cock his legs over that parapet as easily as when he crossed a stile and that with the river running so full there would be quite a short drop on the other side. After that, if the man couldn't swim, there would be a minute or less of gasping and choking, and then nothing. No empty paying-in book, no kindly, puzzled, incredulous Mayor, no pompous Inspector Heyhoe reading the charge, no Quarter Sessions, no stern Recorder. He remembered how frightened he had been of the Recorder when, as Foreman of a Jury, he had helped to send a gipsy to prison for stealing a horse. All he had had to say was " Yes, my lord " and " Guilty, my lord," yet he had trembled like a man with the palsy. Now he repeated to himself the terrible phrase, " Guilty, my lord," and his mouth went dry as he did so. He leaned a little farther over the parapet, and saw the stars drowning in the swift dark current, and thought that if he sank down among them he would never have to say those words.

Yet nothing had happened to make his plight any worse to-day than it had been yesterday or the day before. John's Agent hadn't written, it was true, but John had said he didn't really expect that letter with the cheques in it before Saturday. And still nobody suspected him, Mr. Handiman assured himself: certainly not the Bank Manager, who had rung him up—a terrible moment!—to discuss the arrangements for providing the programme sellers with change; certainly not Mr. Tasker, who had sent round a batch of Festival cheques for his signature; least of all the Mayor, who had put an arm round his shoulder and called him "Dear old George" when they stood watching the balloons go off from the hill.

Why, then, he asked himself, had he known all day such panic as he had experienced before only in dreams, pounding down lightless corridors with a nameless, shapeless, stealthy, swift Thing at his heels and a closed door, which he both longed and feared to open, at the corridor's end? Perhaps it was the waiting that had got on his nerves: the waiting for somebody to find him out. Or perhaps it was the lack of sleep, for he had only dozed wretchedly and briefly during the last four or five nights. At any rate, to-day had been a long lightless corridor indeed, down which he had fled in terror, and now at the very heels of his spirit panted the pursuer. Before him lay the door which he dreaded to open, not knowing whether he would find refuge there or not.

So Mr. Handiman slung his right leg over the parapet and paused there, looking down, with just the toecap of his left boot still touching the ground.

Immediately below him was a thin streak of bubbles trailing away from the topmost twig of a submerged withy bush which jutted out into the river. He remembered the bush well, because once with a fat grasshopper on his hook he had caught a two-pound chub there; but now the flood covered it save for this one green twig, like the olive on Mount Ararat, at which the current plucked in vain.

In one part of Mr. Handiman's mind his dreadful purpose lurked still; but in another and, it seemed, quite unrelated part, there stirred all manner of speculations about the course of the eddies and little whirlpools and the way they would carry the drowned flies and beetles into the backwater just beyond the withy. There, surely, out of the current, was the very place for a big chub; for it is only the little fishes, the foolish fry, which like busybodies dart to and fro in the swift shallows, wasting their substance in the ceaseless pursuit of trifles. The old wise ones take up their station in some place where the conflicting currents cancel each other out; and in that small still pool maintain themselves with faintly tremulous fins, watching the flotsam and jetsam which the currents, like conveyor-belts in a factory, endlessly carry past them. There are dead leaves, cigarette-ends and sodden paper bags on the conveyor-belts; but there are also hairy caterpillars and fat white grubs, beetles, caddises and flies.

If you are an angler, therefore, you must chart these currents in your mind. You must cultivate a special sort of

eyesight and a special sort of imagination; and when you
have fished off and on for fifty years or so this habit of
cartography-in-miniature becomes second nature to you,
and you find yourself practising it every time you are by
the river, whether you have a rod in your hand or not.
This was what Mr. Handiman began to do as soon as the
bending twig attracted his attention; and as he speculated
he eased himself back a little so that the heel of his left foot
rested upon the ground.

Then, suddenly, he saw a dull bronze flash below the
withy bush, an arrow-headed wave, a great swirl which set
all the stars dancing in the water. The big chub was there,
and he had just taken a fly.

The spectacular confirmation of his theory gave Mr.
Handiman great satisfaction. " I *knew* there would be one
in that hole," he said to himself, " and I *knew* he'd be a
whopper. But exactly how or why I knew I cannot say.
That's experience, that is; and experience is what makes
you catch fish when other chaps catch nothing." Meanwhile,
unconsciously, he had withdrawn his right leg altogether
from the parapet and he now leaned upon it in just the same
innocent way as he had done ever since he first carved his
initials there.

The part of his mind which was concerned with fishes
continued its cogitations. Experience and knowledge of
the river: that was better than all your fancy baits and all
your expensive tackle. He had never possessed a rod that
cost more than a pound (wholesale, of course) nor owned
one of those complicated reels which required an engineer
to take them to pieces. He used an old wooden reel with a

home-made ratchet which made a noise like a death-watch beetle when the line ran out; and how many splendid fish had he landed to the accompaniment of that click-click-clicking! After all, Izaak Walton managed quite well without a reel of any kind; he had never seen one, or he wouldn't have written in his simple ingenuous way (pretending he knew all about it but not quite liking to tell a lie): "Some use a wheel about the middle of their rod, or near their hand; which is to be observed better by seeing one of them than by a large demonstration of words." He had caught his chub with a line made fast to a ring at the rod-point; and his line was of twisted horse-hair gleaned from the nearest gate!

But the week-end anglers from Birmingham, whom Mr. Handiman so greatly despised, thought you couldn't catch fish unless you had enough tackle to set up shop with. Their split-cane rods cost eight guineas apiece, their silken lines were like gossamer, and their enormous wicker creels were filled with every sort of gadget imaginable. Ordinary baits didn't suit them either; their bread paste had to be flavoured with aniseed or honey, and their maggots stained scarlet or chrome-yellow, despite the fact that fish were probably colour-blind! From time to time they came into Mr. Handiman's shop and asked him for patent spinners which he had never heard of, and luminous floats for night fishing, and special gut-casts dyed green as water-weed, and even a so-called magic oil which, when you anointed your bait with it, was supposed to attract the fish from fifty yards away. Mr. Handiman didn't stock such rubbish. "We've no call for it in these parts," he would say. And

the Birmingham men would look pityingly at his dusty
shelves and the penny hooks for the children and the rusty
skates hanging in the window.

Yet Mr. Handiman felt quite sure that with his bamboo
rod, his water-cord line, his penny hook and a tobacco-tin
of red worms from his garden muck-heap he could teach
any of those visiting anglers a lesson. He wasn't conceited
about it, for he accepted his skill with a fishing-rod in the
same way that he accepted his rotundity; it was just the
way he was made. With that skill, plus his long experience
of the river, he reckoned he could catch ten fish, any day,
to the visitor's one. But he had never put the matter to the
test, of course, because he didn't approve of fishing competitions and the Goings-on which accompanied them:
referees to see that nobody cheated, paper-hatted harridans
drinking stout on the banks behind the fishermen, and
worst of all, the bookies and the betting. Why, only last
year the winner of the All-Midlands Cup had backed
himself with ten shillings and won a hundred and fifty
pounds! Mr. Oxford had dropped into the shop to tell
him about it. " One roach, one skimmer "—that was a
little bream—" one daddy-ruffe and five eels as thick as
bootlaces," said Mr. Oxford, " and off he goes home with
a hundred and fifty smackers. Makes you think, Mr.
Handiman, makes you think! "

One hundred and fifty pounds! At the thought of that
hateful figure Mr. Handiman's mouth became dry again,
as dry and rough to the tongue as sandpaper. Once more
he saw the Recorder in his wig, once more he heard his
own still small voice in the huge cold courtroom: " Guilty,

my lord." Guilty of embezzling one hundred and fifty pounds.

But at the back of his mind another, and a most startling, picture was forming. It was a picture of one of those numbered pegs which he had nearly tripped over on that Sunday afternoon when he saw the couple in the mowing grass with the folded yellow dress beside them. On the bank close to the peg stood Mr. Handiman. Mr. Handiman was fishing.

And why not? he asked himself. There was nothing actually *wicked* about fishing competitions; they were merely distasteful. Betting? Well, that was another thing altogether; he had been brought up strict, and he didn't hold with betting. He had never questioned the ethics which his old father, and a succession of Ministers, had drummed into him ever since he was old enough to go to chapel. Gambling was sinful, drinking was even more sinful, and one didn't fish on Sunday. There were worse sins, such as fornication, but these were beyond the bounds of possibility and were neither mentioned nor contemplated.

Mr. Handiman's father had been, even by Methodist standards, pretty narrow. He had not permitted his children to read anything on Sunday except an unillustrated Bible. Mr. Handiman himself, progressing towards liberality, had allowed John, when he was a boy, the exceptional privilege of reading a Bible with highly-coloured illustrations. The frontispiece was of Adam and Eve without any clothes on. So Freedom broadened down from precedent to precedent until Sunday papers began to appear in the house, and now Mr. Handiman regularly sat in his armchair after dinner to

K

read all about the remote incomprehensible troubles of dance-hostesses, men-about-town, night-club proprietors, girl-wives, elderly clergymen and Scoutmasters. He was hebdomadally dumbfounded by these grotesque and dreadful fairy-tales, as they seemed to him, which he could never properly understand.

But betting was a reality; one actually knew people who had been ruined by betting, and its evils provided a recurrent theme for the Minister's sermons. The Minister, indeed, held it to be wrong to subscribe sixpence to a Church Bazaar sweepstake if by doing so one became liable to win a boiling fowl, an iced cake, a box of chocolates or a bottle of ginger wine (non-alchoholic). " The High people do it," he said; " but we Low Churchmen know too well how one thing leads to another." And perhaps he was right; for Mr. Handiman, who had once won a hundred-weight of coal at a whist drive, now leaned upon the bridge, saw the incautious chub rise for a second time behind the withy bush to gobble up a fly, and, with a spiritual gesture at least as impetuous, himself swallowed hook, line and sinker his principles, his scruples and his conscience, and determined to enter for the fishing competition and back himself to win. Curiously enough, he had forgotten all about his earlier intention to commit suicide; and as he walked home, and felt his heart quicken at the thought of his own great daring, he was more cheerful than he had been for ten days.

IV

STEPHEN WALKED with Faith as far as the cross-roads at
the bottom of the hill, where she had left her bicycle.
Both of them had a sense of anticlimax now that the
balloons had been launched into the void. Stephen had
never had much confidence in the idea, and Faith, its only
begetter, began to wonder whether after all it had not been
extravagantly silly. How absurd to suppose that those airy
nothings could restore the fortunes of their doomed
Pageant! Scattered upon the capricious winds, most of
them would come to rest on barren hillsides, in tangled
thickets, in sodden marshes where only duck-shooters trod,
in the fields of farmers who cared nothing for Festivals.
Faith sighed deeply.

" Penny for your thoughts," said Stephen.

" Dandelions," said Faith, " and built-up areas."

" Don't see."

" We had twenty thousand balloons; but I wonder how
many seeds on their little parachutes Nature wastes to
produce one dandelion!"

" A sobering thought."

" Yes. And built-up areas. The proportion must be
awfully small. Then there are the roofs. And chimneys
and tree-tops and rivers and lakes. And even the sea."

" Perhaps some of them will cross it," said Stephen.

" Taking a meaningless message to French peasants. I'm sorry, Stephen: I think I've been a rather silly girl."

She picked up her bicycle out of the hedge. It amused Stephen to see that she had thrown it down there in exactly the same way as an old farmer abandons his mowing-machine or his hay-rake when he has for the time being no further use for it.

" Good night," she said.

" Good night, Faith." She bicycled away into the dusk, and as Stephen watched the zigzagging will-o'-the-wisp of her lamp growing fainter in the distance—for she rode as she typed, most erratically—he suddenly discovered in his mind a dozen things which he had wanted to tell her about, the minor comedies and mischances of the day. Moreover, it occurred to him that he had this same feeling almost every evening now, when Faith left the office and went home. He was surprised, puzzled, and faintly disturbed by this revelation.

He walked back to his shop and pottered about among his books for half an hour before he went to bed. The Vicar had persuaded him to make a special display of Lance's book of poems, but in the hot window the cheap bindings had curled back like dead leaves and faded to the same autumnal brown; so he collected up all the copies he could find and pressed them underneath an enormous Classical Atlas, which had been his first foolish purchase when he started bookselling and being too large for the shelves had lain in the corner of the room ever since he had bought it. Some common fault in the binding had caused all Lance's slim volumes to spring open at the same page, so that Stephen knew the title-poem, *La Vie est Vaine*, by heart. It was an unconscious pastiche of Swinburne:

> *We have laughed a little and wept,*
> *We have loved a little and slept . . .*

and Stephen smiled at its youthful nihilism. You have to be very young, he thought, to be on such easy terms with despair!

Next he tried to make room on his shelves for the completely unsaleable set of Bulwer Lytton's Works which the Vicar had sold him for fifteen shillings that very afternoon. " I suppose, my dear Stephen," he had boomed, as he pouched the money, " I suppose such books as these might be described as the *bread-and-butter* of your trade." That would amuse Faith; he must remember to tell her in the morning. But in the morning there never seemed to be time.

The black cat sat on the table and watched him with lazy eyes as he took down in turn a Thomas Browne, a Motley's *Dutch Republic*, a Housman, a Shakespeare, a Shelley and a Byron, opening them at certain remembered pages, reading a passage or a few lines, and adding them to the miscellaneous heap on the table. All his attempts at tidying up the shop, revising his prices, or making a catalogue, petered out like this into a sort of aimless literary dabbling. Once he had thought he would turn the desultory habit to good purpose by compiling an anthology; but that project too had died away in the pages of a half-filled notebook which he had finally lost.

He had never quite succeeded in looking upon his books as commodities; which was perhaps why he was such an unsuccessful bookseller. The most prosperous dealer he knew, who occasionally called upon him in the hope of picking up something cheap or selling something dear, confessed that he never read anything but detective stories and always spoke of the world's greatest masterpieces as " titles." " I can offer you some very good titles to-day." *The Collected Works of Sir Thomas Browne* was quite a good title; you could always sell it for ten and sixpence. But Stephen couldn't think of it in those terms. He took it down from the shelf now and opened it, and read aloud to none but the luminous-eyed cat that marvellous first sentence of *Urn-Buriall*: " When the funeral pyre is out and the last valediction over . . ." But in Motley's *Dutch Republic* it was the final sentence of all which he always turned to, the perfect epitaph on William the Silent: " He was the guiding-star of a whole brave nation; and when he died the little children cried in the streets."

Thus he dipped in turn into the Housman and the Shakespeare and the Shelley, and finally hunted through the Byron until he found a half-remembered fragment which had long been teasing him:

> *The isles of Greece, the isles of Greece,*
> *Where burning Sappho loved and sang . . .*

and straightway his thoughts went back to Thessaly, to Polly and the anemones and the grey-green olive-groves, the rosy-fingered dawn over the mountains, the islands as

he had first seen them from the air in the early morning:
Chios, Lesbos and Lemnos rising up out of the wine-dark
sea.

But although they shone so brightly in his memory, they
seemed farther away to-night than ever before. Until a
few weeks ago he had looked back on his year in Greece
as if it were the only reality he had ever known; all the
rest of his life, schoolmastering and bookselling, had seemed
in comparison like a drab dream. But now he was aware
of a slow and puzzling change. The shabby and ruinous
little bookshop nevertheless had begun to mean something
to him, for the first time he looked upon it as his home.
QUOD PETIS HIC EST, said the motto over the shelves.
Perhaps what he sought was here after all. And as he passed
through the back room on his way to bed, and glanced at
Faith's untidy desk on which the typewriter had not been
covered up (for she treated it, like her bicycle, as a farmer
treats his machines)—he knew in his heart what he sought,
although he would not yet admit to himself that he knew it.

V

AND NOW there occurred one of those quirks of
circumstance, those fortunate freaks of chance, which
were easier to believe in when people thought that sportive
gods occasionally took a hand in the affairs of men. While
Stephen pottered about in his shop, wishing that Faith

were there beside him—while Edna and Lance dallied pleasantly upon their hillock—and while Mr. Handiman on the old stone bridge contemplated chub and suicide, the balloons sailed on to the south-westward. Their vanguard, caught up in a strong steady current, had already travelled about fifty miles and was passing over a small village on the Welsh border which bore the unlovely name of Goytre.

It happened that simultaneously a Mr. Emrys Jones, a hack reporter for the local weekly, was driving home in his old car after a tedious assignment at a village fête. His boredom had been slightly mitigated by the proximity of a beer-tent, in which he had spent most of his time. Being considerably fuddled, he failed to notice the first group of yokels who stood by the roadside gazing into the sky; but the second group was much larger and aroused his curiosity, so that he stopped to ask them what they were staring at. For answer they pointed upwards at a cluster of tiny globules, transparent as soap-bubbles, which freckled the clear evening blue like spots on a bird's egg.

"Flying saucers we were wondering could they be," said an old man.

Having with some difficulty focused his eyes upon the objects, which were extremely minute and in rapid motion, Mr. Jones tried to count them. He had reckoned up to a hundred and fifty when he became dizzy and had to desist.

"Terrible times we do live in," said the old man. "Saying, peace, peace, when there is no peace. Jeremiah, six, fourteen."

Mr. Jones, admittedly, was a hack. He was elderly,

disillusioned and drunken, and he had suffered for a great many years from a surfeit of bazaars run by Capel Bethesda and Capel Moriah. Nevertheless, blunted though it was by sermons, christenings, weddings, and innumerable silver, golden and diamond jubilees (and also, of course, by alcohol), he possessed still the remains of a sense of News. This now sent him full speed down the road to a public house called the Red Dragon, where he put through a call to the Press Association, and while he was waiting for it filled three pages of his reporter's notebook with swift if indifferent shorthand. He was so weary of writing about the dresses of bridesmaids (from information supplied by the bride's mother) that he reacted powerfully to the stimulus of a less factual theme; and his pencil ran away with him to the tune of three hundred and fifty words. These he dictated very slowly and impressively to the Press Association's telephonist, having first given his name and credentials; he ended, with only a little pardonable exaggeration:

". . . And these objects, described as resembling flying saucers, have been passing over at a great height for several hours, causing not a little alarm in the neighbourhood. At times several hundred can be counted in the air at once. The extraordinary spectacle has brought out large crowds into the streets of Goytre, where they stand craning their necks to watch the stratospheric phenomenon. . . ."

Mr. Jones, well satisfied with himself, then went into the bar and ordered drinks all round. He remained there, discussing flying saucers, until well past closing time, when there arrived at the back door of the pub the old man he had encountered earlier, carrying a deflated balloon in his hand. Apparently it had sprung a leak, lost height, and descended upon a hedgerow, whence the old man with due caution had retrieved it.

"How art thou fallen from heaven," said the old man. "Isaiah, fourteen, twelve."

Mr. Jones, stretching the piece of pink rubber to read the caption on it, felt as if he had fallen from heaven also. Like the balloon, he was utterly deflated. But he had retained, through all the long years of chapel bazaars, some tattered remnant of his professional honour. This he now summoned to his aid as he ordered a stiff whisky and with the air of one who says to himself, "Nevertheless, I also have my virginity," put through a second call to the P.A. It took a long time to get through from Goytre to London at that time of night; and by the time his message had been received most of the London editors were in the process of putting their papers to bed. Those of them, therefore, who had featured the strange story from Goytre found it necessary to put the denial in their Stop Press column.

"The objects reported over the village," dictated Mr. Jones thickly, "were not, repeat not, flying saucers. No, I didn't say anything about Chaucer—not flying chaucers, but balloons. Please spell that back. Balloons—B for balderdash—released to advertise the Festival and Pageant to be held at . . ." *et cetera, et cetera.*

With the telephone still held to his ear, having done his duty according to his lights, Mr. Jones then fell asleep; and he has no further part in this story.

PART FOUR

I

"VERTIGO," said Councillor Noakes as his glance fell upon the newspapers lying on Stephen's desk. "Poor fellow, it must have been vertigo. Otherwise he wouldn't have bought a ticket before he climbed up, would he? Still, it's an ill wind; and I must say you've cashed in on it very nicely."

The gods never do things by halves; it is all or nothing with the gods. On the day after the appearance of the flying-saucer story, which was featured by five papers and corrected in the Stop Press by three, a retired commercial traveller called Micklethwaite, on holiday from Scotland, had walked into the Booking Office and paid Virginia ten shillings for a seat in the grandstand. With this evidence of his ambition to survive for at least another week in his pocket, he had climbed to the top of the Abbey tower, whence he had fallen, or cast himself, into the churchyard below. Entirely unmoved by this sad event, Faith had at once despatched excellent photographs of the tower to every London newspaper with a caption typed on the back of them describing the tragedy and mentioning, of course, the forthcoming Festival. Each of the morning papers which now littered Stephen's desk displayed one of these pictures in a prominent position, giving to the town's little Festival a better advertisement than could have been bought for thousands of pounds. Heartlessly, Faith hoped for still more publicity from the inquest.

Already the bookings had taken a dramatic turn for the better; Virginia, indeed, had been hard put to it to deal with the telephone calls. Moreover, the flood had subsided, the ground was drying quickly under a hot sun, and the workmen were busily repairing the damaged stands. " Everything hunky-dory ! " beamed Councillor Noakes to Stephen. " And since that young spitfire of yours isn't here —she fairly snapped my head off the other day—I'll take the opportunity of asking you to get me a little book I've been told of "—he whispered hoarsely though there was nobody within hearing—" called *Fanny Hill*. On the strict q.t., you know; after all, a man has a Public Life and a Private Life, and in my position one can't be too careful; although of course there's not a bad word in it."

Faith had temporarily taken charge of the Booking Office while Virginia, unsuitably dressed in transparent purple chiffon with a mauve slip, and a big black cartwheel hat, went off to give evidence at the inquest. She was required to testify that the unfortunate Micklethwaite had told her he was looking forward to the Pageant very much. This was regarded—unreasonably, Stephen thought—as evidence of his sanity. Faith had urged her to make the most of it.

" Not a bad word in it," repeated Councillor Noakes, " and yet my friend assures me that it made him *wriggle*."

"Its author," said Stephen, "a chap called Cleland, is probably the only man who's ever been paid for *not* writing books. *Fanny* was regarded as so scandalous that he was given a pension on condition that he didn't write any more."

Councillor Noakes was delighted. "That's the way to make money!" he said. "I might even consider going in for it myself! And now you've told me that, I'm set on having the book whatever it costs me. Real hot, it must be. Talking of hot, have you ever read any of the poems of Dame Joanna?"

Stephen shook his head. "I thought they only existed in manuscript in the Bodleian?"

"Well, yes; but Gurney's going to bring out a little edition, expurgated of course, and have it printed by the man who does our Guides. He says it'll help to put the town on the map; because sooner or later there's bound to be a great vogue for Joanna. And I must say I agree with him. He showed me some bits he'd copied out and he said they were as good as *Piers Plowman*."

"He showed you some bits, did he?" asked Stephen, who had always thought it strange that so little was known about Dame Joanna if she were really deserving of a statue in the Pleasure Gardens.

"Yes. I can't say I *completely* understood them, although literature has always been my pet hobby, as you might say." Councillor Noakes sighed. "I wish I'd had more time for it; but we public men have to make our sacrifices. So I had to tell Gurney that the stuff was a bit beyond me. Shakespeare, yes. Gilbert and Sullivan, yes. Byron, Rupert

Brooke, yes. But Chaucer and Langland and those early people, definitely no. I can't even pronounce the stuff, though I can see it's good. However, Gurney's going to hunt up a few lines for me to quote at the unveiling, and I'll have to get them off pat by next week. Perhaps you wouldn't mind glancing at them and—er—*translating* them for me?"

" I'll try; but I'm afraid it isn't my period," Stephen said. " It's queer, though, that I'd never even *heard* of Dame Joanna till I saw Gurney's synopsis of the Pageant." The shadow of a horrid doubt was faintly stirring in his mind.

" Well, I must do my best." Noakes beamed. " Gurney promised he'd find something *really suitable* for the occasion. I must say he's taking a lot of trouble over it. As you know, I don't altogether get on with Gurney; but I'm a broad-minded man, and I won't belittle his scholarship."

" I've often wondered," Stephen dared to ask, " what was the cause of the trouble between you two."

" You'd hardly believe it: a young lady," said Councillor Noakes surprisingly. " Her name was Abigail. It's so long ago I can hardly remember; but the name sticks in my mind. The hot blood of youth, you know, the hot blood of youth! "

Stephen found it difficult to keep his face straight as he tried to picture that grotesque past in which Councillor Noakes and Mr. Gurney contended for the favours of a young lady called Abigail. Noakes went on solemnly:

" We've had our differences since then—in business, you know, in Public Life, and even at the Bowling Club;

but I always suspect that Abigail lies at the root of all. And I can't even remember the colour of her eyes! Ah, well . . . *Anno Domini*!" He glanced at his gold half-hunter. "Goodness, I must be off. I've got a meeting of the Sanitary Committee at twelve. From literature to sewage! What chequered lives we public men do lead! Now whatever you do, don't forget *Fanny Hill*."

Stephen showed him out through the front shop. At the door he paused to smile back at the sun which beamed from an immaculate sky.

"Everything hunky-dory!" said Councillor Noakes.

Stephen hurried back into his office, where two telephones were ringing, and dealt in turn with a press photographer who wanted to take pictures at the Dress Rehearsal, and with Sir Almeric, who complained that half the horses were suffering from galls on the withers. "Your precious performers don't know how to saddle 'em, Mr. Stephen Tasker." A moment later Faith came in, flushed with triumph because she had sold fifty pounds' worth of seats in a couple of hours. The inquest, as she brutally put it, had "gone off well." Virginia had testified with terrible precision that the late Mr. Micklethwaite had appeared to be in very ' hay ' spirits; indeed he had gone so far as to ask her out for a drink, whereupon she had been compelled to explain that she did not take drinks with strangers. The Coroner had pointed out that this evidence might have an important bearing upon the deceased's state of mind, since Virginia had been the last person to see him alive. The verdict was Accidental Death, and Virginia had her picture taken by a man who said it might come out in the *News of the World*.

" It's terribly exciting in the Booking Office," added Faith. " The telephones go all the time, and we've sold out completely for the first night except the ten bobs."

" Can Virginia manage? "

" She's given up knitting and she's got a girl to help her and she copes quite well. I rather like Virginia. I had a King Charles spaniel like her once, beautiful and silly and so good-natured."

She was picking up the newspapers on the desk one after another and studying the captions underneath the photographs of the tower.

" The *Mail* mentions us," she said; " but the *Express* doesn't. However, even the picture by itself helps. ' One-hundred-and-forty-foot death-fall.' "

" You are," said Stephen, " the most callous girl I have ever met in my life. May I ask, was Mr. Micklethwaite married? "

" With four children," said Faith, very wide-eyed. " Isn't it awful? "

" I think you are worse than Lady Macbeth."

Faith stretched out her hands and looked at them.

" My brother was in the Navy in the war," she said, " and one morning when he was in the middle of the Atlantic he woke up with an awful hangover. Gin, you know. He wanted a glass of water terribly badly, so he switched on the light beside his bunk. At the *very moment* he clicked the switch the ship was torpedoed. He said it was a most awe-inspiring thing, because for quite a long

time he thought he'd done it. I mean, he thought he'd
caused the bang. He was rescued all right, but in the end
they had to put him in hospital because he couldn't bring
himself to touch electric-light switches. They called it a
psychosis or something."

" What's all this got to do with Mr. Micklethwaite? "

" Don't you see? In the same way I feel as if *we'd done
it*. First the flying saucers and then poor Mr. M. We started
something when we sent off those balloons, Stephen."

" Frankenstein's monster? " said Stephen, remembering
that morning in the Red Lion when he had first played
with the notion that perhaps the Festival would run away
with its creators. Faith looked up sharply.

" You feel that too? "

" Sometimes."

" How funny. I do, *all* the time. And I keep on
wondering what's going to happen next."

What happened next was a knock on the door, accompanied by the scraping of large boots on the mat outside.
There entered a burly man in overalls and a cloth cap who
strode up to the desk with the purposeful air and owlishly
solemn expression of one who brings heavy tidings on to
the stage. Stephen was reminded of a Sergeant who had
played Seyton for him in a rest-camp production of
Macbeth. The man had stumped on to the boards as if he
were entering an orderly-room to report all present and
correct with the exception of one deserter. " The queen,
my lord, is dead."

Astonishingly enough, this was more or less what the
burly man did say. Touching his cap smartly, he announced:

" Beg pardon, sir. But her's jud."

" Dead? " echoed Faith. " But I saw her alive only this morning! "

" In the long grass her was, at the bottom of the orchard, stiff's a board."

" I can hardly believe it," said Faith.

" With her legs in the air," added the burly man.

Stephen, who had listened to this conversation with mounting horror, interjected at last:

" Who are you talking about? Who's dead? "

The man turned to him ponderously.

" Never seen a jud donkey before, sir, and that's a fact. They lives so long, you see, that you hardly ever *hears* of one dying. But when we went to fetch her, as Miss Pargetter told us to, there her was, lying in the long grass, stiff's a poker. At first I thought she was rolling, seeing her legs sticking up in the air; and I said to my mate: ' Don't you touch her lest her kick.' But there warn't a kick left in her, not a kick. Jud's a doornail."

" Well, that's that," said Stephen. " No donkey for the Holy Hermit."

" Afraid I'll have to charge you for the journey, sir. Ten shillings."

Faith paid him ten shillings out of the Petty Cash. When he had gone she sighed.

" Poor Mrs. Perks! She loved that old donkey. It was twenty-seven and it was called Toto."

" I expect it's too late to get another one in time for the Dress Rehearsal? "

" Too late? Good Lord, no." She jumped to her feet

and began to walk quickly up and down the room. Stephen had never seen her so animated.

" I've got it!" she said suddenly. "'The Donkey That Refused Fame.' You can write, I can't. Have a go at that."

" What *are* you talking about? "

" ' For twenty-seven years Toto had lived in Mrs. Perks' orchard, nibbling the moondaisies and the little red cider apples which fell from the trees in the autumn. Then, suddenly, stardom shone before her: all the glamour of a First Night. But Toto was modest.'" Under the stress of inspiration, Faith continued to stride to and fro and Stephen noticed that although she was so slight and trod so silently, her action was that of one who is accustomed to sticky ploughland. She planted her feet firmly and picked them up with decision. She had very long legs, which greatly attracted him.

" ' Toto was modest. Rather than face the bright lights and the what-d'you-callums, plaudits of the crowd, like Tom Pearse's grey mare she lay down and she died.' That's the line, I think; but you can write it while I get through on the telephone."

" Get through? "

" We want another donkey and we want some more pub.," explained Faith patiently, "and this will give us both. Now, you sit down and scribble. I think ' Scorned ' is better than ' Refused,' don't you? ' The Donkey that Scorned Fame.' Poor Toto. Poor Mrs. Perks. She's very frail. I shouldn't be surprised if the shock killed her." She sighed deeply as she picked up the telephone. " Trunks

Enquiries. . . . Give me, please, the number of the *Daily Mirror*."

II

WHAT FAITH would later describe as Donkey Saturday, in contradistinction to Balloon Monday, dawned bright and clear. There were no donkeys as yet, though there was a moving paragraph about the death of Toto in the *Daily Mirror*. Stephen glanced at it and promptly forgot about it. He had enough worries of his own.

The official opening of the Festival was due to take place in the Pleasure Gardens at three o'clock. There would be speeches by the Mayor and Councillors, followed by the choosing of the Beauty Queens. After that an immense Carnival Procession would perambulate the town. But the first night of the Pageant did not happen till Monday; one more rehearsal, therefore, lay before Stephen, the Dress Rehearsal at eight-thirty to which various bodies of school-children, Old Folks, and patients from a neighbouring mental institution would be admitted free. Beyond the power of words to express Stephen dreaded it.

Last night, from half-past six until nearly twelve, he had for the first time rehearsed the whole Pageant through from beginning to end: from the entry of Odo and Dodo leading their dismounted Hermit by the hand to the disastrous Grand Finale in which three hundred players, the band of the British Legion, and a pack of foxhounds tangled themselves into a confused insoluble *mêlée* which reminded him of the beaches of Dunkirk. As the lifeless episodes succeeded one another, it had seemed to Stephen that each was more excruciating than its predecessor. On leaden feet the Pageant went its doomed way like a procession of protracted death.

In his little producer's box at the back of the grandstand, which had draughty gaps between the floorboards and reminded Stephen of the penitentiary of a broody hen, he writhed in agony and sweated with shame. Even the loud-speaker installation had gone wrong, so that when he spoke into the microphone he could hear the echo of his own voice coming back to him, faint, distorted, a pitiful bleating like the plaint of a damned soul rising up from hell. There was no authority in it; and when, in an access of rage and frustration, he suddenly let himself go and shouted into the instrument, the only effect it had was to bring everybody to a standstill, in which situation they remained for a full thirty seconds, turning white faces in bewilderment up to the sky.

Even on the rare occasions when the actors went correctly through the motions assigned to them, Dionysus for some reason withheld his magic, so that there was no illusion that they were anything but themselves. Odo and Dodo, stepping out the ground-plan of their projected Abbey, were simply Mr. Oxford and Timms walking from pub to pub collecting betting-slips. William Shakespeare, with an open folio carried before him, was Councillor Noakes gloating over an old book with naughty pictures in it which he had picked up cheap. Queen Margaret watching

the battle was Sir Almeric's formidable mother, the
Dowager Lady Jukes, watching a Point-to-Point; and King
Edward the Fourth, in command of the Yorkist army, was
Sir Almeric himself, baulked at a gateway out hunting,
crying petulantly, " 'Ware heels! "

Lance's choruses, mouthed by young ladies who were
learning elocution and eurhythmics at a School of Dramatic
Art, sounded like the keening of widowed women in a
play of the Celtic Twilight. In remarkable contrast, the
folk-songs chanted to Bloody Mary by another class from
the same school were given with the terrible heartiness of
Girl Guides singing around a camp fire. The " skirmish
during the Civil War " was rendered farcical by the young
curate in charge of the Roundheads, who always spoke as
if he had a plum in his mouth and whose cry of " The
bottle, the bottle, On with the bottle," would undoubtedly
get the only predictable laugh in the whole Pageant. During
the next episode, when Charles was fleeing from his
pursuers after the Battle of Worcester, the dusk thickened
and Stephen called for the lights. But instead of helping to
create an illusion, they served only to illuminate and
emphasise the element of farce. Charles, who looked like
a pickpocket on the run, was hunted all over the arena by
a single wavering spotlight, which failed to catch up with
him until he had reached the exit and was peacefully lighting
a cigarette.

As for the Grand Finale, Shakespeare had a word for it;
and when, long past midnight, Stephen went back to the
shop, he took down from his shelves a grubby copy of *The
Tempest*—the reflection that almost all his books were in

that condition only slightly deepened his depression—and turned the pages until he came to the Masque of the Goddesses. Shakespeare, evidently as sick of Masques as Stephen himself was, had sensibly given the whole thing up and written:

"Enter certain NYMPHS. . . . Enter certain REAPERS, properly habited; they join with the NYMPHS in a graceful dance . . . after which, *to a strange and confused music, they heavily vanish.*"

Having underlined these words, and placed the book on Faith's desk because he thought it would amuse her, Stephen went to bed. For most of the night, half-sleeping, half-waking, he wove the Pageant into a dreadful fantasy in his mind. Odo and Dodo, mounted on donkeys, galloped across the field shouting "Five to one bar!" Cavaliers in plumed hats intruded into the Wars of the Roses; Dame Joanna wagged her finger at Bloody Mary and severely commanded her, "Get thee to a nunnery"; Councillor Noakes, still dressed as Shakespeare, declaimed bawdy passages from *The Memoirs of a Lady of Pleasure.* A little before dawn, as at last he composed himself to sleep, he thought rationally: "This is the consequence of being overtired; I shall feel better about it in the morning."

But in the morning he didn't. When Virginia rang up to say that she already had full houses for six performances out of seven, his only reaction was one of horror that so many people would witness his shame. Nor, for once, did Faith have any encouragement to offer him; she refrained from mentioning the rehearsal and made no comment upon the book he had put on her desk. In any case there was no time for talk this morning. A series of large and lesser crises filled the hours between nine and twelve. Inspector Heyhoe had discovered at the last moment an insoluble parking problem; for it was the day of the All Midlands Angling Competition, the car parks would be full of charabancs, the streets must be kept clear for the Carnival Procession, so where, therefore, would the visitors to the official opening put their cars? "Trouble, trouble, all around us trouble," said Inspector Heyhoe; and Stephen heartily agreed. For the chinchilla lady was complaining of a mass escape of rabbits from the hutches at her abominable Exhibition, and Sir Almeric brought a catalogue of eleven horses which were suffering from splints, spavins, thoroughpins, kicks on the hocks, and a complaint called the staggers which Stephen had never heard of. The lighting-man announced that the flood water had got into his main cable and caused a short which had blown all his lamps; and the programmes, needless to say, had not yet arrived from the printers. While Stephen dealt as best he could with all these troubles, what seemed to him a positive spate of telegrams arrived one after another in the office. Faith opened them, smiled, added them to the growing pile on her desk, but made no comment. There was one, however, which did not cause her to smile. She brought it across to Stephen and laid it in front of him. It was from the town's M.P. who had promised to judge the Beauty Competition. It said:

> *Deeply regret must fail you owing to pressing business in House.*

" Cold feet," said Faith. " He's got cold feet."

" I don't blame him," said Stephen. " What now? "

" No *local* person would dare to take it on."

" Better tell the Mayor. It's his affair more than ours."

But as Faith went back to her desk to telephone to the Mayor a new crisis arose. Followed by a number of her pupils, the lady from the School of Drama burst into the room. In the background, huge and fleshy, loomed Councillor Noakes. The Wardrobe Mistress, with a face of stone, followed. The Drama Lady explained incoherently that her Chorus had just put on for the first time the dresses which Robin had designed for them. They had then paraded on the Bloody Meadow before a Press photographer, and as they did so the sun had come out from behind a cloud. The muslin dresses had proved to be transparent. *But transparent!* said the Drama Lady. Everything showed through! *But everything!* And what, she asked, would be the effect of floodlights at night? *But unthinkable!* Her girls, she observed, were Ladies. They did not belong to a Pantomime. She had not understood that the Pageant was a branch of the *Folies Bergères*. Something would have to be done about it immediately.

" Slips," said Faith shortly.

The Wardrobe Mistress interposed:

" I always said there'd have to be slips. He doesn't understand materials. How can we make twelve slips in eight hours *and* do all the other last-minute jobs to the costumes? "

Everybody started talking at once. The girls who had

been taught verse-speaking enunciated with great clarity, "Pink knickers, my dear!" "And a most extra-ordinary bra!" The Drama Lady wailed "Indecent! *But indecent!*" The Wardrobe Mistress called heaven to witness that in the midst of this crisis the so-called Dress Designer had gone fishing. A post-office messenger pushed his way through the crush and handed Stephen a bundle of telegrams, which he unthinkingly stuffed into his pocket without opening them. One of the verse-speakers with beautiful elocution said: "My sweet, I felt like a Circassian in a slave-market being Eyed." Only Faith remained silent, a small oasis of quietude in a howling wilderness.

Councillor Noakes, steering himself through the crowd of girls with gentle but well-directed pushes and prods, reached Stephen's desk at last and stood before him.

"This is serious," he said.

How in the world had Noakes contrived to mix himself up in this? He had probably been hanging about on the Bloody Meadow waiting to see the young women have their photographs taken. The pink knickers must have pleased him, thought Stephen grimly.

"We must particularly guard against any scandal," Noakes went on, as if it had been Stephen's fault. "I rely on you, my boy. *Sans reproche*, remember. Our Festival must be *sans reproche*."

The telephone rang and Faith answered it.

"Bloody Mary's got a rash," she said shortly. "She thinks it's measles."

Nobody took any notice, and Councillor Noakes continued:

"These are young girls, Stephen. Young girls. We are, in a sense, *in loco parentis*. It is unthinkable that we should cause them to make an exhibition——"

Suddenly Stephen felt that he couldn't stand Councillor Noakes for one minute longer. A sense of the fatuous absurdity of the Festival and all its works utterly overwhelmed him. He had been subject, ever since he was a child, to such flurries of unreasonable panic. As a small boy he would sometimes rush out of the house and carry the burden of some secret fear or shame into the woods, desiring only to hide himself, running blindly until he tripped and fell. Later he had learned to rationalise and control these impulses. But to-day he was overtired and overworried, and when the sudden panic came it caught him off his balance.

So he fled: not precipately, as he had done in childhood, but with dignity and decorum. A bad headache and a touch of the heat, he explained; a few minutes in the fresh air and he would be all right again. He bowed to the Drama Lady, smiled at Faith, brushed aside Councillor Noakes' solicitous arm, and got himself to the door. He closed it gently behind him and set off up the street. He walked very fast, despite his lame leg, not caring which way he went, seeking only solitude; and as he walked he tried to calm himself with a childish formula that had lain half-buried in his memory for thirty years or so: "Whatever happens, they can't shoot me." As a boy of seven, reluctantly trudging towards the day-school which he loathed and feared, he had invented the formula and found it extremely effective. At sixteen, out first ball in his first

house-match, he had gleaned some crumbs of comfort from
it as he walked back seven leagues or so towards the
pavilion in which the prefects sat with pitiless faces. The
last time he had used it was in the air over Thessaly in the
moment before he dropped through the hole in the floor
of the aeroplane. "Whatever happens, they can't shoot
me." And then suddenly he had realised that they could,
and probably would. The joke seemed so funny that he
had laughed aloud, and with the laughter dying on his
lips had plunged into the dark night. Polly, who followed
him, had been immensely impressed by his laughter, and
Stephen had never told him the reason for it. "Of all the
crazy guys," said Polly. "Say, what were you laughing at?
Was it you thought maybe your chute wouldn't open, or
were you thinking of mine? Of all the crazy guys!"

But now the formula was valid once more. They
couldn't shoot him, whatever happened on Monday night.

Stephen was calm again when he encountered Mr.
Handiman: calm enough to wonder what had thrown
the little man into such a state of agitation and to notice
with surprise his haggard expression and tormented eyes.

"Oh, Mr. Tasker, please, can you help me? You haven't
seen Mr. Oxford anywhere? Or Mr. Timms? It's most
important."

"I haven't seen them," said Stephen. "But I can make
a pretty good guess where they'll be. The Ramping Cat
or the Lamb or the Red Lion."

"Oh, dear," said Mr. Handiman.

"The Lamb's likeliest, at this time of day."

"Oh, dear. You see I don't—well, to tell the truth I've never—never actually gone into a bar," said Mr. Handiman. "But it's urgent, so I suppose I'll have to. The Lamb, you think? Well, thank you very much."

"And if they're not there try the Lion."

"Thank you." Mr. Handiman toddled off towards the Lamb, which was just round the corner in a side street. Stephen, now quite recovered from his foolish panic, decided that he needed a drink before he risked any further discussion of young women's underwear with Councillor Noakes; so he turned into the cobbled courtyard of the Red Lion.

Florrie was decorating her bar with bunches of balloons, which John Handiman had given her, and with red and white roses, which she had paid for out of her own pocket. Her questing glance darted to and fro about the room as if she were a bird in spring-time examining an unpromising thicket to see where it could build a nest. Her actions were like a bird's too, as she plucked a spray of white rambler roses from the pile on the counter, fluttered round the room with it, and finally set it up behind the notice which said, THE PASSING OF BETTING-SLIPS IN THIS BAR IS STRICTLY FORBIDDEN. Timms, meanwhile, though not exactly passing betting-slips, was extracting them from his pockets and sorting them into neat little heaps on the counter, while Mr. Oxford leaned back in his corner and discoursed with Florrie on the subject of kindness to animals.

"One can become very attached to a dumb brute," he was saying, as Stephen came in; although, to tell the truth, the only dumb brutes he was attached to were exceedingly abstract, being represented by symbols such as " 5/- Doub. S.P. Urst Park 2.30 " in his little black notebook.

" I was real sorry for that poor old lady," said Florrie. " Good morning, Mr. Tasker. We was talking about that donkey in the paper this morning. ' Bashful Toto Scorned Fame,' it says. Real pathetic. Half-pint for you, sir? "

Stephen felt in need of something stronger than beer, so he ordered a large pink gin. As she mixed it, Florrie continued:

" My first husband, now, grew very fond of a lioness, but it turned treacherous, and one night at a circus it went for him and had to be destroyed. Believe it or not, Mr. Tasker, *although* it had tried to bite his head off, when they shot that lioness my husband cried like a little child. And though we was only just married by no means could I console him."

While she was speaking, Old Screwnose came slinking into the bar, and as a matter of form Timms concealed the betting-slips with his elbows. Screwnose looked at the balloons and sniffed. " Making the place look like a pally de dance," he said, and immediately began to cross-examine Florrie about the loss of a whole batch of ashtrays which, it appeared, had mysteriously and simultaneously disappeared from her bar a week ago.

" You don't tell me they had wings and flew," he said nastily.

" They was only little bits of tin, anyhow," said Florrie, as if this made them more airworthy.

" It was those Buffaloes," said Screwnose, edging towards

the door; for he always made certain of his line of retreat before risking an argument with Florrie. "I feel quite sure in my mind it was that Buffaloes' Outing which came in a charabanc last Wednesday. And to-day it's the fishermen, and all next week it's the Festival. Mark my words, by Saturday you won't have an ashtray left."

He withdrew, and Florrie, shrugging her shoulders at his departing back, observed with large tolerance:

"It takes all sorts to make a world. It's not drinking, I dare say, that makes him so miserable."

"Never a drop has passed his lips, they tell me," said Mr. Oxford, not without awe.

Florrie nodded gravely.

"None of my husbands were what you'd call moderate men," she said. "Ambrose—that was his professional name —slipped into the habit of fortifying himself against the lions, and George used to say he could understand horses and stars better when he'd had a few, and my last, Bertie, he used to punish the whisky something dreadful. And yet, if I had my time over again, I'd never marry a teetotaller. There's something slinky about teetotallers; you can't hear 'em coming upstairs."

She looked up from the glass she was polishing and it was clear from her expression that you could have knocked her down with a feather, for on the threshold of her bar, with the door just closing behind him, stood a notorious teetotaller indeed. The expression on Mr. Handiman's face was that of a city-dweller who finds himself by some strange chance set down in a savage jungle. He glanced to right and left as if he expected to be assailed by the arm'd rhinoceros

and the Hyrcan tiger; or at least as if he expected to witness
scenes of devilment and debauchery. The quiet decorum
of the place seemed to surprise him, and after a moment's
hesitation he advanced more confidently towards the
bar.

Florrie, meanwhile, stood ready with the brandy bottle;
for it was her experience that only in cases of severe and
indeed mortal sickness would such a strict teetotaller as
Mr. Handiman enter a public house. Mr. Handiman, however, when Stephen asked him what he'd have, timidly
requested a lemonade; and clutching the glass in a hand
that was obviously not much used to holding glasses, he
went across to Mr. Oxford, with whom he began a conversation in urgent whispers. Florrie tactfully raised her
voice as she discoursed to Stephen on the subject of her
last husband and his peculiar hobby.

"—And when he'd finished the bottle," she said; " well,
punished it, that was always his word, Florrie, he'd say,
looking quite ashamed like, 'I've been punishing the whisky
again'—then he'd ask for a kettle of boiling water and he'd
steam off the label ever so careful and stick it in his scrapbook."

Stephen, who was beginning to enjoy himself, bought
Florrie a port and himself another pink gin. Florrie went
on:

" But in the war there was too many brands, you see,
and he overdid it. They had gaudy labels such as I'd never
seen in fifty years in the Trade, all about dewy glens and
mountain mists and there was one with a picture of a dying
stag on it, called Twelve-Pointer. Now 'tis my belief as

that Twelve-Pointer killed my husband; for it was the last bottle of whisky he ever drank. Pleased as Punch he was to find it, because he said it made his hundredth brand. And when I came back from work that night he said quietly, ' I've been punishing the Twelve-Pointer, Florrie, I'm afraid.' But he didn't have the heart to steam the label off it. I got the doctor to him in the night, and next day he died."

Florrie heaved a tremulous sigh. Stephen observed a brief silence to the memory of Bertie and the bottle of Twelve-Pointer, and heard Mr. Oxford, whose whisper would in lesser men have been described as a hoarse shout, saying:

" Not a bet, not a *bet*, Mr. Handiman: what you mean is a little investment."

" That's it, investment," squeaked Timms.

There was the sound of notes being counted; and Mr. Oxford said to Timms out of the corner of his mouth: " Two hundred pounds to a fiver, Mr. H. Put that down careful, 'cause we'll have to lay it off." He turned to Mr. Handiman.

" Shake on it," he said; and Mr. Handiman, unaccustomed to these formalities, shyly put out his hand. A moment later he took his leave and scurried out of the bar like a bolted rabbit.

Mr. Oxford swallowed his whisky, licked his lips, and said at last:

" It will out. You cannot keep it down. It's like rubbub beneath a concrete floor; it always comes up in the end."

" What does? " asked Stephen.

" The Englishman's natural desire to 'ave a little flutter,"

M

said Mr. Oxford, beaming. "Spite of laws, spite of Ministers, spite of Methody. You cannot keep the Englishman down."

"Tradition!" exclaimed Timms, as one who had made a startling discovery.

"As you say, old man, tradition. 'Earts of hoak! And where should we be, I ask you, if we had not got that tradition? We'd never 'ave 'ad a little flutter at Mons; we'd never 'ave 'ad a little flutter at Dunkirk. Winnie'd never 'ave 'ad 'is bloody great gamble on invading Normandy. In other words, old man, if it weren't for the Englishman's 'abit of 'aving a little flutter, we'd be down the plug-'ole, all of us!"

Delighted with this logical conclusion to his argument, Mr. Oxford called for drinks all round; and although Stephen was well aware that he ought to go back to his office, where Faith was dealing single-handed with whatever fresh catastrophes the past half-hour had brought, he allowed himself to be persuaded to have a third glass of gin. He was already feeling the beneficial effect of the first two, for his panic had entirely vanished and in retrospect the affair of the transparent dresses seemed to have been very funny indeed. Councillor Noakes was no longer repellent, but was a figure of minor comedy; as dear old Florrie sensibly said, it took all sorts to make a world. Even last night's rehearsal had been funny, thought Stephen, if one looked at it in the right way; and to-night's promised to be funnier still. In a mood of unwonted devil-may-care he swigged his gin and, since it was now his turn, ordered another round. While he was doing so Lance came into the bar, followed shortly by Mr. Gurney, who as soon as he saw him playfully poked him in the stomach with his umbrella, crying, "Naughty! Naughty! I have found you out!"

"What have I done now?" said Lance.

"I went to the rehearsal last night. You can't pull the wool over my old eyes."

"Well?"

"Young man," said Mr. Gurney, "you *made up* those folk-songs."

Lance, in considerable embarrassment, gave Stephen a sideways look.

"Well, not exactly. Say if you like that I improvised on an old theme."

"Oh, don't imagine I'm blaming you," grinned Mr. Gurney. "A man who's been in the old furniture trade as long as I have knows that many a forgery is better than the original. And sometimes," he added thoughtfully, "the forgeries are harder to produce."

Stephen, who as producer should have been shocked by Lance's admission that the folk-songs weren't genuine, was surprised to discover that it merely endeared Lance to him by betraying a new, mischievous and original aspect of his character. For now, after four gins, he was aware of comedy stirring all round him, in the corvine croak of Mr. Gurney, in the rich pomposities of Mr. Oxford, in Timms' diminuendo squeak, in Florrie's tales about her three husbands. Surely, he thought, she is the Wife of Bath reincarnated! And there came into his mind the perfect motto for her:

> *And Jesu Crist us sende*
> *Housbondes meke, yonge, and fresshe-a-bedde,*
> *And grace to overbyde hem that we wedde.*

He was so pleased with the aptness of the quotation, and the accuracy of his memory, that his heart warmed to Florrie, and when in her old-fashioned way she said, "It's my turn to stand treat now," he felt that it would be discourteous, cavalierly, it would be downright un-chivalrous in the face of such a friendly gesture to refuse her; and since Florrie had been brought up in the Trade, in which the greatest sin is to be niggardly in hospi-tality, she poured him out a very large one, with which most daringly he drank a toast to her fourth marriage: "for you've done the hat-trick, my dear Florrie," he said in a voice that was curiously unlike his own, "and upon my word, I believe you'll bowl another man out yet!"

Florrie's large bosom heaved with pleasure, quivered and fluttered as if some eager bird were imprisoned in it. Stephen was now comfortably leaning on the bar in the attitude of one who had been there for a long time and proposed to remain there much longer, and she rose up before him like a mountain—no, there was a suggestion of cragginess about mountains, like a huge hill of Cotswold, Stephen thought, composed of the kindliest convexities which ran together towards the summit and suddenly fell away in a steep escarpment on the other side. Splendid and spendthrift she must have been in her youth, thought Stephen:

And I was yong and ful of ragerye,
Stiborn and strong, and joly as a pye.

He had a keen sense of history and of the continuity of English things; and perhaps this sense was sharpened by drink, for as Florrie turned away to serve him with another gin—Mr. Gurney had called for a round—and as he contemplated the steep scarp of her back, broad and rippling beneath the black lace dress, he said to himself, " She is the Wife of Bath indeed. In each generation she is born again. These are the true, the only immortals—she and Falstaff, Doll Tearsheet, Bottom, Shallow, Pistol, Nym, the Wellers, Mr. Micawber. They are omnipresent and ubiquitous. You could always find them, somewhere in England, if you knew where to look. They, and not poor little whimsy Peter Pan, are the ones that never grow old!" Into the midst of these confused but fascinating speculations burst the voice of Mr. Oxford booming, most aptly, the word "Tradition," and Stephen was struck by the percipience of Mr. Oxford, who through a haze of whisky was nevertheless able to distinguish eternal truth. A lovable fellow, thought Stephen; and Timms was only slightly less so. He moved across the bar towards them.

" Take Charles the First," said Mr. Oxford. " There's tradition for you!"

" They cut his bleeding head off," said Timms.

" Ah," Mr. Oxford sighed. " There was, indeed, a breach of tradition there. But take Charles the Second, 'iding in a hoak-tree. The hoak, symbolic, as they say, of

England. 'Earts of hoak, old man! There's tradition for
you!"

" 'Dition." Timms' squeak was becoming very faint
indeed; it must be getting late, thought Stephen, and
looking at the clock above Florrie's head, which was
decorated with a big bunch of balloons, he was horrified
to see that it was a quarter to two. And the official opening
was at three! Nevertheless, he decided he just had time to
smoke one cigarette and drink the gin which Mr. Gurney
had bought for him. He put his hand into his pocket,
searching for the cigarette packet, and discovered the
forgotten bundle of telegrams. He opened one, finding
unaccustomed difficulty in slitting the envelope, and read:

*Daisy delighted deputise Toto very quiet aged shall I send
road or rail Smythe.* . . .

He read it again, and it meant nothing to him. He
opened another telegram.

*Will gladly lend little girl's pet dark tan unusual markings
Railton.* . . .

Stephen took a third telegram at random. Fortunately
for his sanity this one was more explicit. It said:

*Am sending substitute donkey in horse-box no charge
Brown.* . . .

He finished his gin, and for an uncomfortable moment
the comical and extravagant world seemed to revolve about
him, nebulous as a dream. Then he heard Lance saying:
" Have one for the road, Stephen," and with a great effort
he collected his wits; though his voice, as he thanked
Lance, seemed even more alien to himself than it had done
before.

" Alas, no," he said gravely. " I have to see a girl about a donkey." And with no more difficulty than might have been ascribed to his wounded knee he contrived to make his way to the door.

A fleet of red charabancs was passing through the town. They were full of fishermen and the wives and intendeds of fishermen, but Stephen associated them vaguely with the Festival because most of the women were wearing comic paper-hats. They lent colour to the streets as they went by, matching the flags which had broken out all over the town like bunting on a ship's mast when she suddenly makes a long signal. How strange, thought Stephen, that he had not noticed those flags when he walked up the street on his way to the Red Lion, and that he had paid no attention to the roses either, which filled the window-boxes outside almost every house and shop. Why, the Town Hall, with red and white ramblers growing in tubs on each side of the door, and more ramblers hanging from mossy baskets, was a very bower, an arbour of roses. What a purblind miserable wretch he must have been not to see them; and by contrast what an impressionable, responsive, cheerful Matthew Merrygreek he felt now, as he daringly dodged the charabancs and waved his hat gaily in response to the banter of the paper-hatted women! He gazed about him like a sightseer, craning his neck to look at the flags of all the nations which were hung across the street. Remnants of old coronations and jubilees, they fluttered with a sad defiance in the wind, the blue, black and white of Esthonia, the black, white and red of Germany before Hitler, Albania's eagle, the forgotten flags of Latvia, Lithuania, Czecho-slovakia, Serbia, Hungary and Montenegro. They came out of the rag-bag of a dead Europe, they were the attic-rubbish of a departed age.

But certainly they brightened the town. It had been quite transformed by the flags and the roses; and Stephen was troubled by a sense of unfamiliarity with the street which he walked along every day: an odd feeling, dream-like and disconcerting. But here, at any rate, was a homely figure: that of Mr. Handiman with his fishing-rod over his shoulder and an old wicker creel on his back. Stephen remembered that he was responsible for the roses and hastened to congratulate him.

" Mr. Handiman," he said, shaking him warmly by the hand, " you are like the Goddess Flora ! "

" I beg your pardon," said Mr. Handiman, looking strangely at him.

" Roses and raptures ! " exclaimed Stephen, making a sweeping gesture towards the window-boxes and tubs outside the Town Hall; but Mr. Handiman had already fled, leaving Stephen with his arm upraised like a bishop giving a blessing. From time to time, as he hurried up the street, Mr. Handiman glanced back over his shoulder in a puzzled and rather furtive way, which made Stephen feel extremely uncomfortable; and he was also worried about the behaviour of his lame leg, for it seemed even stiffer than usual and caused him to walk with a sort of goose-step which felt quite as ridiculous as he was sure it must appear to the passers-by. After a few paces he paused to rest it, leaning upon his stick, and in that moment it was borne upon him that he was drunk. Drunk, by God, within less than an hour of the official opening! Simultaneously there emerged from the Town Hall the Mayor himself, in his robes and chain of office. He waved to Stephen and hastened towards him.

" My poor chap," said the Mayor kindly. " Your leg's giving you trouble, I'm afraid."

" A mere twinge," Stephen managed to say.

" Ah, you make light of it, I know." The Mayor put a hand upon his shoulder. He looked ridiculous in his robes, yet curiously engaging, like a well-loved uncle dressed up as Father Christmas. Eager as a schoolboy, he burst out:

" I've got some news for you, Stephen. *Foreign visitors* are beginning to arrive!"

Stephen thought it best to say nothing. He fixed his eyes upon the heavy medallion at the end of the Mayor's gold chain and orientated himself by that fixed point as by a star.

" To be precise," said Jno. Wilkes, " *one* foreign visitor; but we hope—like the first swallow, eh—that he's the fore-runner of many. I met him in the street as I came to the Town Hall to change: an obvious foreigner, you could tell by his clothes. And he was smoking a large cigar. I said to myself, as soon as I caught sight of him, ' Dollars,' I said. Even our little town is doing its bit!"

The Mayor chattered happily on, but Stephen was not listening. He was wondering how long it would take the Mayor to perceive what must be obvious to everybody: that his Festival Organiser was drunk at midday on the opening day.

" Stephen," said the Mayor, with sudden gravity. And

Stephen thought: He's twigged at last. He's going to tell me to go and lie down, and on no account to show myself till I am sober. He liked Jno. Wilkes and felt sorry that he had disgraced him.

"Stephen, have you ever considered taking any active part in public life?"

Stephen stared at him helplessly.

"You've done a great deal for this town in the last few months. I only want to assure you it hasn't passed unnoticed. Noakes and I were talking about you only yesterday. The Council will have to elect a new Alderman shortly." Becoming aware of Stephen's blank and bewildered look, he added:

"You mustn't think of Aldermen as city fathers with watch-chains stretching across their tummies. Not a bit of it! What the Council needs is a bit of young blood to liven it up. So if you'll allow us to put your name forward—well, there it is. Think about it, my boy, when your present anxieties are over, give it a little thought."

When the Mayor had gone, whisked off in a hired car to fetch the Mayoress to the opening ceremony, Stephen was able to collect himself sufficiently to walk the hundred yards or so from the Town Hall to his shop. A most improbable picture of himself as Alderman tickled his fancy and reawakened his feeling that the spirit of comedy was stirring, that some large jest was in the making, that Dionysus had mischievously chosen the town's little Festival as his theme for a piece of improvised sport. This feeling was fortified as he approached his shop and saw in the street

outside it that which at first he took to be a circus but which
resolved itself into a herd of donkeys, at least a dozen of
them, all sorts and sizes, little ones such as children ride at
the seaside, big raw-boned asses which hucksters drive in
carts, donkeys of every shade from pale beige to dark
brown! Thus was manifest the Power of the Press; but
Stephen with his head full of furious fancies preferred to
ascribe the whole thing to that ancient president of the
amphitheatre and the grape-gathering, the boisterous son of
Zeus and Semele whose immanent presence he had been
conscious of all the morning. The satyr's unexacting master,
the beloved of the nymphs, the charioteer of the swift
panthers, the wearer of the crown of vine—let him now
take charge. He who lords it alike over feast, fiesta, fête
and festival, thought Stephen—wildly rejoicing now in his
drunkenness which only a few minutes ago had appalled
him—he who presided long ago over the orgies of Thrace
and who now broods kindly over the Vicar in charge of
bowling for the pig—let him take as his tribute our balloons
and our donkeys, our flags and our roses, our Odo and
Dodo and even our chinchilla rabbits! Let him mix them
up together and make what he will of them!

Having performed this strange act of dedication, Stephen
patted the nearest donkey heartily on the rump and strode
somewhat unsteadily into his shop.

Faith came out into the front to meet him. Whatever
turmoils she had been through during the morning had
left her unmoved. Wherever she stood or sat, thought
Stephen, she carried about with her that oasis of quietude!

She regarded him now with calm and untroubled eyes and
gently took his arm. Thus had her mother and her grandmother, thus had some six generations of farmers' wives,
welcomed their wayward men back from market.

Leading Stephen towards the back room, she pronounced
the single word:

" Peart."

" What? "

" What we call market-peart," she explained, patiently
and without reproof. " We used to say father was peart
if he could just climb into the trap and let the old horse
bring him home after market; but nowadays with the
motor-car he has to be more careful. Hot black coffee'll
put you right."

She paused outside the door of the back shop.

" There's nothing to worry about. Bloody Mary hasn't
got measles, it was too many strawberries. The modesty
of the elocutionists will be preserved; we are running up
slips for them. The chinchilla rabbits have been found, all
except one which was eaten by a greyhound. We have
thirteen donkeys here at the moment and forty-three offers
of donkeys by phone and wire."

She put her hand on the door-knob.

" One more thing. Your many-seeded gentleman has
arrived. He's peart too."

She opened the door, and Stephen's heart gave a great
and glorious bound, for it seemed to him as if his prayer
had been miraculously answered. There sat at Faith's untidy
desk, with a steaming cup of coffee in front of him, if not
Dionysus, at any rate his emissary, his chief of staff, his

plenipotentiary upon earth. An enormous brick-red Westerner was balanced precariously on the back of his head. In his hand he clutched, as if it were a talisman, one of the balloons which had been sent off to advertise the Festival. He was gently snoring.

" Polly ! "

His eyes opened, those lazy laughing eyes, and for a moment he looked about him in bewilderment; then, as he jumped up, the whole office seemed to contract until it was about the size of a rabbit-hutch. The tall crown of his hat just touched the ceiling.

" Stevie ! "

He seized Stephen's hand in his great hairy one, and with his other hand bounced the balloon on Stephen's head. Thus they performed a foolish sort of jig together, while Faith quietly pulled the chairs out of their way. When they had stopped for lack of breath Polly said contritely:

" Oh, Stevie, your knee ! I forgot about your knee."

" It's all right when I'm sober," said Stephen.

" I feel kinda bad about that knee."

" Forget it," said Stephen. " You got my letter, then? "

" Sure I got your letter. It caught up with me in a place called Magnolia, Alabama. I was there with my circus. I've gotten a circus now, Stevie, five elephants, two lions, a grizzly bear called Theodore Roosevelt, the only duck-billed platypus in the United States, forty-eight horses, ten clowns, some performing fleas, and six ecdysiast dancers. Ecdysiast's strip-tease. And I left that circus in Magnolia, and came over in the Lizz. No more flying for me, Stevie ! And then I got your balloon."

" You got my balloon? "

" I-got-your-balloon. I went to see about a zebra at Clifton Zoo. That's Bristol—you know. I want to buy six zebras, Stevie, for the ecdysiasts, because they're kinda graceful things, the zebras, I mean (but you ought to see those dames), and I reckoned they'd match the dames just swell. Nobody's ever thought of teaming up a strip-tease act with riding on a zebra. Get this, Stevie—I'd have those girls in black and yellow striped dresses and as they cantered round the ring on the zebras they'd strip-tease. Can you beat it? Trouble is the man at Clifton says you can't really train a zebra so's to make it a nice quiet ride for a young lady. Anyhow, there I was looking at the sea-lions and suddenly a balloon comes down out of the sky and falls in the pond, and the sea-lions start poking it with their noses. I saw some writing on the balloon, so I hooked it out with a stick. And here it is, and here I am."

Faith had gone upstairs to fetch another cup of coffee. She put it on the desk and said to Stephen: " Drink that." Polly went on:

" I've had that balloon on my mind for a week. I went back to London and tried to find out how to feed a duck-billed platypus: ours is on hunger-strike. And all the time I was worrying about that goddam balloon. It dropped into the pond right at my feet; it was as if you'd sent it me. I didn't mean to come down before the end of the week; but I jest couldn't wait. So I got on a train which took me seven times round England before I got here. It's a swell little island, Stevie, but all the railway stations look alike and by the time I'd seen each of 'em seven times

I'd had enough. There was no diner and no bar; but luckily I had a flask."

"He had a flask," said Faith softly. "You two had better drink your coffee. It's half-past two."

"My God!" said Stephen suddenly. "The Beauty Competition! Did you tell the Mayor?"

For once Faith was startled out of her customary calm.

"Oh, Stephen! How awful. I meant to ring him up and I put the M.P.'s telegram on my desk, but I suppose it got mixed up with the donkeys. How *awful*. What shall we do now?"

Stephen glanced at Polly. The spirit of comedy was on the march. Let Dionysus have his head!

"Polly."

"Yes, Stevie?"

"Do you think you'd be capable of judging the final of a Beauty Competition?"

Polly threw back his great head and laughed.

"Could I judge a Beauty Contest? *Could* I? Stevie, I've been judging Beauty Contests all my life. I started when I was about fourteen. There were ten little girls in my class at school and I placed them one, two, three, four, all the way down to number ten. I've been judging my private Beauty Contest ever since. *Could I* judge?" He gulped his coffee. "Let's go."

PART FIVE

I

A SMALL boy, one of those numerous alley ragamuffins who obtained hooks from Mr. Handiman on indefinite tick, had taken it upon himself to give an unofficial commentary upon the Fishing Match. He trotted along the banks of the Bloody Meadow shrilly crying the latest catches; and now for the third time he returned to Mr. Handiman's peg and announced:

"Number Two-eight-nine's got another roach. That makes seven. 'E pulls 'em out as easy as shellin' peas."

This didn't mean, of course, that Number Two-eight-nine was necessarily winning; for nearly a thousand competitors lined both banks of the river for several miles. Who could say but that downstream or upstream someone beloved of fortune had drawn out Leviathan with an hook? However, if Number Two-eight-nine had really caught seven roach already it was probable that he had been lucky enough to find a whole shoal on the feed, and would catch a good many more before the contest was over. Mr. Handiman's chances began to look very slight indeed; for he had caught nothing at all. He hadn't even had a bite.

The positions, marked by numbered pegs, had been drawn for some days ago; and it happened that Mr. Handiman's peg was close to the spot where Lance and Edna had been lying on that Sunday afternoon. Even before he put his tackle together his hopes had begun to fade, for a gravelly ledge ran far out into the river and he could see that he would have to make a long and difficult cast to reach the deeper water. Moreover, immediately downstream was a big patch of yellow brandy-bottles; and it was clear that the current would carry his line towards them and that at the end of every cast their stems would entangle his hook. There was no shade or cover where a good fish might lie save for a single willow-tree twenty yards away; and besides being practically out of reach, this tree was guarded by a phalanx of brandy-bottles. Mr. Handiman, who was accustomed to wandering along the bank in search of likely eddies—who stalked his fish, indeed, like a big-game hunter—felt helpless and frustrated because the rules compelled him to remain in this one unpromising spot. He felt as if he were tethered to his peg, like a gipsy's pony on a common which sees delectable grazing all around but cannot reach it.

His sense of constriction, of lacking elbow-room for his fishing, was increased by the proximity of the competitors on either side of him. His immediate neighbour upstream was accompanied by a girl, and the one downstream had brought no less than three women to give him encouragement. From time to time these women cried loudly:

"Eow, 'e's got a boite!"

"'Is float's gone deown!"

N

" Neow, it in't a boite. 'E's caught up on the bottom! "

Mr. Handiman, dragging up a long water-lily stem every few minutes, was conscious of a feeling of malicious satisfaction each time he heard of his neighbours' misfortune; but he sternly reproved himself for an emotion so unbecoming to a follower of gentle Izaak Walton, who had written that all anglers were brothers. This, he reflected, was what fishing competitions did to you; they engendered jealousy and envy. Never would Mr. Handiman take part in one again!

His brother of the angle on the upstream side seemed less interested in fishing than in the interminable discourse of his girl-friend, who related with the minimum of modesty her experiences at the hands of another young man, presumably her present squire's rival, with whom she had gone to a dance in a Works' Canteen.

" Eow I said stop your squeezin', you needn't think you can treat me like one of your sixpennies at the pally. I'm only tryin' to 'old you up, 'e said sharp-like; so I says to 'im, D'you mean that nasty, I says; and 'e says wistful, Them sixpennies is as light as a fevver. . . ."

The small boy had trotted off, but soon he was back with tidings of two more roach hauled out by Number Two-eight-nine.

" 'E's caught a bloody little yale as well," said the boy. " 'Ad to cut its yud off to get the 'ook out."

" You shouldn't swear, Jimmy," said Mr. Handiman primly. " At your age! "

" You calls this the Bloody Meadow," said Jimmy. " Don't you? "

" That's different. It's to do with the battle. It means the meadow was once covered with blood."

" Well, so was the little yale," said Jimmy triumphantly. " When 'e cut its yud off." He set off upon another tour of inspection.

Mr. Handiman landed his twentieth water-lily stem.

" 'E's caught up in the wades," said the woman downstream, who from her position on the high bank was able to observe Mr. Handiman's activities as well as those of her own champion.

" I says to 'im," went on the girl upstream, continuing her epic of the Works' Canteen, " stop fiddling, I says; and 'e says, real nasty now, You'd fiddle if you was tryin' to git 'olt of a sack of titers wivart nothin' to git 'olt of it by."

Mr. Handiman disentangled the slimy lily stem and re-baited his hook. (" 'E's puttin' on a wairm now," said the woman downstream.) He cast it out as far as he could, followed the quill float with his rod-point as it sailed down on the stream, checked it just short of the brandy-bottles, and cast out once more. He summoned all his skill of hand and eye, and all the experience of nearly fifty years to his aid; but in his heart he knew that he had no chance. A dove-grey cloud suddenly obscured the sun and the wind got up, making the long cast more difficult than ever, blowing in his line towards the shore, and laying the float flat on the water where little wavelets broke over it. The yellow lanceolate leaves of last season spun down off the single willow-tree, formed a scum on the slack water, or

swirled in the eddies until they were drowned. Sinking,
they flashed dull-bronze like the sides of a shoal of phantom
fishes, mocking him. It began to rain.

That short sharp thunderstorm was the weather's last
prank of all; but it struck the town, like a whiplash of the
departing devil's tail, at the very moment when the Mayor
was opening the Festival and when the semi-finalist Beauty
Queens, ten minutes late, were getting out of the car which
had brought them from the Town Hall. Only Mr. Gurney's
umbrella, the only umbrella in the Pleasure Gardens, saved
them from a drenching. As he conducted them on to the
platform their Maids of Honour, looking very uncourtly
with borrowed mackintoshes over their heads, hinted in
whispers at terrible happenings on the Town Hall stairs:
Virginia had accidentally trodden on Edna's dress, practically
tearing it off her back, Edna had called her a clumsy bitch,
Virginia had slapped Edna's face, and Edna, provoked
beyond endurance, had seized Virginia by the hair. Whatever truth there was in these stories, there could be no
doubt that both girls were extremely angry; and they
looked correspondingly beautiful. As they reached the
platform and stood before Polly the scud passed and the
sun came out again; and Stephen, not yet quite sober,
thought they looked like Pallas and Aphrodite called before
the Cloud-Gatherer to account for a dispute between them.
Edna, a sweet disorder in her dress, her long yellow hair
in disarray, might indeed have risen shining from the foam;
Virginia, usually so placid, was animated by ill-temper, she
was Athene of the flashing eyes. If he had not known that

nothing went on inside her head but an endless repetition of the names of film-stars alternating with P1 (fig.) K2 tog., Stephen could easily have imagined an owl sitting upon her shoulder.

The Mayor, by a stroke of genius, had just introduced Polly as " Mr. Polycarpos Gabrielides, the well-known impresario from the United States "; nor was this very far from the truth, for did he not own six strip-tease dancers and a duck-billed platypus? Wearing his extraordinary hat, he looked as if he might possess a controlling interest in half the theatres of New York and all the studios of Hollywood as well. In considerable awe, therefore, Virginia and Edna ranged themselves on either side of the Mayor and heard him say: " Our distinguished visitor will now perform the judgment of Paris."

And Polly, confronted by those flushed and dishevelled goddesses, confused as much by their beauty as by the half-bottle of Bourbon he had drunk in the train, nevertheless rose to the occasion to make a better and wiser judgment than the son of Priam had done. He said nothing, but bent down and plucked from the bank of flowers which decorated the platform a red rose; then, from the other side of the platform, he took a white one. He held them both up before the expectant crowd.

" Mr. Mayor," he said, " I've been hearing from Mr. Tasker about your little old battle, which happened in 1471; I sure don't want to start another in 1951, so I guess you gotta have two Beauty Queens."

He handed the red rose to Edna and the white rose to Virginia.

"The Queen of Lancaster," he said, "and the Queen of York."

The crowd cheered so loudly that the fishermen three miles up the river could hear them, and wondered what it was all about.

The cheering reminded Mr. Handiman that he was playing truant from the opening ceremony; and he wondered if anybody had noticed that the Festival Treasurer was missing. It didn't matter much if they had; for the whole story of his embezzlement was bound to be known by Monday. John had told him last night that the Argentine man had failed to pay and that the balloon factory would probably have to go into liquidation; and in his innocence John had offered to pay back the hundred and fifty pounds at the rate of five pounds a week. He still didn't know where the money had come from; he supposed, no doubt, that it was part of Mr. Handiman's private hoard, or the accumulated takings of the shop—though if the shop took ten pounds in a week it was lucky! To-morrow after chapel, thought Mr. Handiman wretchedly, he would go and see the Mayor. He would make his confession, and then they could do what they liked with him. All last week, like a fish on a hook, he had felt his panic gradually draining away as a sort of hopeless resignation took its place. His entry for the Fishing Match had been, as it were, a final desperate wriggle; but it could not save him from the consequences of his folly. Number Two-eight-nine had filled a whole basket with roach; and Mr. Handiman's creel was still empty. There was only a quarter of an hour to go.

He still cast out his line more or less automatically, let the float go downstream as far as the lilies, wound in, and cast again; but he no longer had the slightest hope of catching anything, and he was concerned less with fishing than with a detailed examination of his sins.

Not the least of these, he decided, was his lack of humility in entering for the competition at all. Why should he imagine that he was a better fisherman than these thousand-odd experts from all over the Midlands, and why should he think that he could achieve more with his cheap coarse tackle than they with their dressed silk lines and gut-casts as fine as hairs, with their beautifully-balanced rods and their reels of shining aluminium? Conceit, just wicked conceit. He had set himself above other people and that was a terrible sin, almost as bad as embezzlement; and he was being very properly punished for it now. He had set himself above Mr. Lance and Edna, when he found them in the grass, thinking their dalliance wicked, whereas his own wickedness was so much greater; he set himself above the people who drank in pubs and the people who gambled; and he set himself above these men from Birmingham who worked in factories and perhaps lived in slums, and looked forward to their single day's outing for months on end. It positively served him right, thought Mr. Handiman, to have drawn one of the worst positions on the river; and he hung his head in shame.

As he did so his attention was attracted by a tiny commotion in the muddy water at his feet; and peering down he saw a very small frog hopping about there. Now *The Compleat Angler*, which he knew by heart, has a famous passage about the use of frogs as bait; and it jumped at once into Mr. Handiman's memory.

"Put your hook into his mouth, which you may easily do from the middle of April till August, and then the frog's mouth grows up, and he continues so for at least six months without eating, but is sustained none but He whose name is Wonderful knows how: I say, put your hook through his mouth and out at his gills; and then with a fine needle and silk sew the upper part of his leg to the arming-wire of your hook; and in so doing use him as if you loved him, that he may live the longer."

Glancing downstream at the single willow-tree, it occurred to Mr. Handiman that if by any chance a chub *did* lie beneath it, a frog, dapped down on the swift current, would be the most tempting bait for it; and this frog, being about two inches long and the colour of a yellowing leaf, was one which he felt sure no chub could resist. He therefore bent down and scooped it up in his hand, and using it as if he loved it gently ran the hook through its lips. (" 'E's puttin' on another wairm," announced the lady downstream.) Then he pulled a dozen yards of line off his clicking wooden reel, coiled them carefully at his feet, swung the rod two or three times to get the feel of it, and let go. The frog shot out over the river, beyond the gravelly ledge, beyond the first patch of brandy-bottles, beyond the second, and fell with a little plop into the very place he had aimed at, where the longest branch of the willow-tree dipped towards the water. There it swam and flopped about on the surface, while an eddy, as Mr. Handiman had foreseen, carried it in towards the bank, right underneath the overhanging bough.

" 'E in't got no float," said the downstream lady. " 'Is float must of come off in the ay-er."

Very gently, with small sharp flicks of his rod-point, Mr. Handiman began to draw in the frog towards him. It was now or never, because soon it would be caught up among the brandy-bottles, when he would almost certainly lose it.

He had forgotten all about his sins; he had even forgotten that he was taking part in a fishing match. The only things he thought about were the eddies under the willow-tree, the little splashes made by the frog, the situation of his line so precariously resting on the flat leaves of the water-lilies.

The voice of the girl upstream came to him very shrill and clear.

" And then 'e pinched me on the arse. Right through my dress 'e did, you can see the bruises neow."

Unmoved apparently by this extraordinary confession, her young man said cheerfully:

" Pinched you on the arse, did 'e? Toss us down that tin of wairms."

At that moment three things happened to Mr. Handiman; he would never know which of them happened first. He heard a tremendous splash; he saw, between the leaves on the overhanging bough, a sudden swirl with a cavernous open mouth in the middle of it; he felt a kind of electric shock in the butt of his rod. He tightened, and the old greenheart top of the bamboo rod bent into the shape of a bow.

" 'E's muxt up in the fleowers," said the downstream lady. " I thought 'e'd get muxt up in them fleowers."

But Mr. Handiman knew better. He had seen that great mouth, greyish-white, rather like an open oyster shell, which vanished from view as it closed; and now his line was jerkily cutting through the water and leaving an arrow-shaped wake behind it. *Click-click-click* like a deathwatch beetle went his wooden reel as the line was pulled off it, five yards, ten yards, fifteen, and then Mr. Handiman could see the brown spool of the reel showing, so he put his finger on the rim to check the fish's headlong run. He could feel the whole rod *kick* as he did so, the butt jabbed itself into his round little belly and remained cushioned there. But the chub's first rush was checked, and the taut line swung round in a half-circle, just missing the brandy-bottles, while Mr. Handiman reeled in a few yards of slack.

The woman downstream had at last realised that there was a fish on the end of Mr. Handiman's line; and she jigged up and down on the bank, yelling encouragement. Her cries brought Jimmy helter-skelter from his latest tour of inspection, and several of the nearby fishermen, who had already given up hope of catching anything themselves, came running to see what the commotion was about. Now they all began to give Mr. Handiman contrary advice: " Let 'im 'ave 'is 'ead! " " Kape a toight loine on 'im! " " Tike care of them wades! Moind 'e don't git into them wades! " and so on. But Mr. Handiman, who had once landed a salmon, foul-hooked in the back fin, on his old bamboo rod, took no notice of them. He knew that he

had hooked the chub well and truly—and had not Izaak
Walton said, "He is one of the leather-mouthed fishes, of
which a hook does scarce ever lose its hold"? He knew
that his stout water-cord line would stand the strain, and he
knew that after the first two or three plunges the fish would
quickly tire. Only one thing was worrying him, the
inadequacy of his landing-net; for the chub was the biggest
he had ever seen, it must surely weigh about seven pounds
and his net was neither deep nor wide enough to contain it.
Nor were his neighbours' nets, which they hurried to fetch
for him, any better designed to cope with this whale, this
Triton, this Behemoth among chub; they were neat little
collapsible things, with folding handles, and Mr. Handiman
suspected that they would indeed collapse beneath the
weight of his monster. So when at last he had played it
out, and its steely-grey hammer-head broke the surface and
was easily held there, the great mouth opening and shutting,
the dorsal fin cutting through the water like a torpedo-
boat's bow—then Mr. Handiman decided that the time
had come for heroic measures. Raising the point of his
rod, and so dragging the exhausted fish over the ledge of
gravel, Mr. Handiman stepped into the water, where
immediately he sank up to his knees. At that moment the
fish gave a flick of its tail and a last plunge towards the
brandy-bottles; and Mr. Handiman, plunging after it,
seized it behind the gills. In doing so he simultaneously
dropped his rod and lost his footing, but no matter, he had
his fish. With the water up to his middle, he cradled it in
his arms as if it were a baby; and indeed it weighed as
much as most babies do when they are born. And so in

triumph Mr. Handiman waded ashore, while Jimmy performed a war-dance on the bank, the downstream woman
shouted, "It's a salmon! It's a salmon! It's a bloody
great salmon!" and all his rivals waved their landing-nets
and cheered. They stretched down their hands to help him
up the slippery bank, they fetched him a stout stick with
which to crack the monster on the head, they used their
own expensive rods to hook out his cheap one. In short,
they were his brothers of the angle indeed—brothers and
sisters of the angle, for even she whose arse had been pinched
offered Mr. Handiman a thermos of hot tea to keep out the
cold.

"You wants to git 'ome quick, dearie," she said
solicitously. "At your age with them wet trarsiz."

Beaming from one to another of his new-found friends,
Mr. Handiman loved them all.

II

WITH HIS notebook on his knee, Lance sat on the river
bank just above the weir, and tried to compose on
behalf of the Beauty Queens an address to their Loyal
Subjects. "Such a lark!" Edna had said. "It's going to be
printed in the *Intelligencer*. Do let Lance make it up,
Virginia; he'll do it ever so nice." And Virginia, whose
literary accomplishments were limited to knitting-patterns,
gladly agreed, only reminding Lance that the purpose of the

Address was to ask people to donate to various local charities. Lance had protested:

"Don't you think 'give' would sound better?"

Virginia shook her head.

"'Donate' is nacer, Ay think." And Edna, to Lance's distress, had agreed. "'Donate' sounds more *grand* somehow. And Virginia works in the *Intelligencer* office. She ought to know."

So Lance scribbled, with a little smile: "And we appeal to our faithful subjects to donate generously to the Hospital Comforts, the Old Folks' Golden Hour, and the Vicar's Organ Fund. . . ." There didn't seem to be much more to say, so he chewed his pencil and stared at the river below the weir, where every now and then a salmon leapt or wriggled up through the white foam at the edge of the waterfall. When the Dress Rehearsal was over Robin would surely be out here with his illicit gaff, poised stock-still like a heron at the edge of the salmon-ladder. Lance strongly suspected that Robin made more money by poaching salmon than he earned by selling his pictures.

After the Carnival Procession he and Robin had taken the two Beauty Queens to the Red Lion for a drink, to celebrate their joint accession to the Throne. "Thank you, Ay will hev a half paint," Virginia had said; and she had turned to Edna who sat beside her in the corner of the bar and added precisely: "Ay think, don't you, that paints are rather vulgar?" But Edna obviously didn't think so, for she accepted from Robin a big pewter tankard of beer, behind which she giggled irrepressibly. Watching Virginia

sipping her shandy, as daintily as a sparrow drinking from
a puddle, Lance was reminded of a curious phrase used by
a monk of Gloucester many hundreds of years ago. He had
discovered it in one of those calf-bound books of sermons
in his father's library. The jovial priest, preaching apparently
at Christmas-time, had accused certain members of his
congregation of being " covetous of unbuxomness." That,
thought Lance, described Virginia exactly. She raised her
head after every little sip, just like a bird, to let the fizzy
shandy trickle down her delicate throat, and meanwhile
she glanced with disapproval at the tankard of beer which
Edna cuddled to her bosom as if she cherished it. Poor,
dear Virginia: she couldn't help it, but she was covetous
of unbuxomness, and that was why Robin had given her
such a perfunctory kiss on the cheek when they said good
night in the empty courtyard of the Red Lion—for Robin
had to go to the Dress Rehearsal, and the Beauty Queens,
like all royalty, had now become the slaves of their people,
and were about to set out on a three-hours' tour of all the
surrounding villages. Left alone, Lance had wandered along
the bank of the Bloody Meadow until he came to the weir,
where he sat down to watch the sunset and the jumping
salmon.

" May the sun shine upon our brief reign . . ." he wrote;
but already his mind was wandering away from the Beauty
Queens' Address, and the elusive rhythms which were
always tormenting him began to play through it like the
wind in an aspen-tree. Dusk was falling over the river,
inexpressibly beautiful, inexpressibly sad, bringing with
it those intimations of mortality to which only the very

young can afford to give heed. It will still be here, all this, he thought, in a hundred years' time: the murmurous water, the white mist swirling over it, the greeny-blue sky, Sirius blinking over the distant hills, the small moon coming up behind the melancholy willows; and I shall not be aware of it. The midge-hunting bats will dart and squeal, and the lovely bright salmon leap like spears thrown by Poseidon; and I shall not see them. On this very bank, young girls like Edna will walk beside young men like me; and I shall know nothing of their heart-beats and their heart-aches. O tenuous, transient, beautiful world, thought Lance, how brief, how brief, and how it will hurt to leave it!

Ah, yes! But perhaps it only hurt if you were young when you left it. For delight faded with the passing of the years, as the colours in the landscape were fading now. A sunset was just another day gone; a new moon was just another month beginning. "The grasshopper shall be a burden, and desire shall fail." Even at thirty, Lance had read somewhere, a man's ears could no longer pick up the bats' slate-pencil squealing; and although the sound was not in itself beautiful, it seemed to Lance a very tragic thought that in eight years' time he would not be able to hear it. If the physical senses were so quickly blunted, what of the emotions, the passions, the quick dreams? Did one look back from thirty with a shrug of the shoulders at the torment of twenty-two: "I had an affair with a factory girl once. . . . I actually wrote verses about her. How odd!"

The whole of Lance's spirit cried out against such a blasphemy; the whole of his reason told him it was true.

" Then I must write it all down *now*," he thought. " Now, before it is too late—the sunset sky, the crescent moon, the bat's swiftness, the salmon's leap, my own heart's leap every time I see her." The wind of words blew through Lance's head, and their rhythms sang to him like the wind in an aspen-tree; and with a sense of terrible urgency he began to write. It was becoming so dark that he could hardly see what he was writing, and he scribbled his adolescent poetry all over the Beauty Queens' Address. He had no eyes now for the salmon which showed themselves among the white waters, like molten ingots of silver; he had no ears for the trumpet which summoned York and Lancaster to battle in the arena less than half a mile away. The beauty and the terror of the words possessed him; and as he wrote there ran down his spine a little shiver of the most exquisite sadness: " Sorrow that is not sorrow, but delight."

III

OUT OF the darkness a trumpet sounded its querulous challenge, and that was a signal for the lights. The floods, for once obedient to their cue, poured broad white beams upon one half of the arena, leaving the other half in deep shadow; and the Yorkist line of battle, thus suddenly revealed, looked like a flower-border at midsummer. The heralds and trumpeters in the forefront were golden marigolds, blue lobelias, fire-red salvias; the tabards of the knights behind them made a low hedge of scarlet and gold; and the pennons were long-stemmed blossoms waving in the wind.

"Why, Stevie," said Polly softly, "it's *beautiful*." And then the floods faded and a dim green spotlight like a will-o'-the-wisp in a marsh picked out the Lancastrian ambuscade, ghostly bowmen crouching behind a clump of bushes, motionless horsemen drawn up among the trees. A horse neighed, a bit jangled, and Stephen felt Polly's hand tightening on his elbow. "Oh, Stevie, d'you remember that night near Larissa? When we lay in wait for the convoy at the edge of the cork-forest? And how I had to take the bridle off my mule, because of the noise it made chewing its bit?" The pale glimmer, creeping between the willows, just touched the silvery helmets of the knights, gleamed dully on their chainmail, and in its turn faded. Now the other half of the field was floodlit; and on a great chestnut horse, groomed so that the muscles of its shoulders seemed etched like an anatomical drawing, Robin rode into the brightness. There was a rose as red as blood on the banner borne before him, and all the knights of Lancaster trotted at his heels.

Again the trumpet wailed its brazen cry into the darkness; all the lights came on at once; and the Yorkists with Sir Almeric at their head broke into a hand gallop.

Even Stephen caught his breath. Thus he had imagined it, months ago, when he had begun work on Mr. Gurney's synopsis and read for the first time an account of the battle in Fleetwood's *Chronicler*:

" Edward apparailed hymselfe and all his hoost set in good array; ordeined three wards, displayed his bannars; dyd blow up the trompets; committed his caws and qwarrel to Almighty God, to our blessed Lady his Mothar, Vyrgyn Mary, the glorious Martyr Seint George and all the Saynts, and avaunced directly upon his enemyes."

Thus he had imagined it, stirred by those old words and by a picture in his mind of the sunlight on the helmets and the pennons waving like a border of tall flowers. But during the long weeks of preparation and rehearsal the pristine vision had faded; indeed he had lost it altogether, and now, when it so unexpectedly unfolded itself before his eyes, it almost startled him, he could scarcely believe that it had been his. " Did *I* imagine this pattern of a whole garden on the move? Did *I* dream that shadowy ambush, half-seen, half-hinted at, like the Third Murderer in *Macbeth*? " In wonder and delight he watched the pattern changing and breaking up as bright splinters flew off to right and left of the Yorkist lines, the King's party with herald and pursuivant, the horsemen moving out to cover the flanks. And then suddenly it was as if a great wind had blown through the garden of flowers, scattering them and laying them low, as all the waving pennons dropped and the knights of York spurred their horses to the charge.

When the Dress Rehearsal was over, Stephen and Polly walked back across the arena, dimly lit now that the big floods were out, in which Roundheads rubbed shoulders with Lancastrians, plumed Cavaliers strolled arm-in-arm with nuns, the girls from the Drama School fluttered about like ghost-moths in their white muslin dresses, the bandsmen of the British Legion noisily packed up their instruments, and Sir Almeric's huntsman cracked his whip with a sound like a pistol-shot as he called together his hounds.

"It was fine, Stevie, fine!" said Polly, as excited as a schoolboy. "Three hundred actors—gee, and I boasted of six ecdysiasts!"

Even the Grand Finale, which Stephen had so much dreaded, had gone off without a hitch—instead of "heavily vanishing" the various groups had wheeled like trained soldiers to their separate exits. Indeed there had been scarcely a flaw in the whole performance; and the scenes which yesterday had seemed quite moribund had suddenly and miraculously come alive. Perhaps Robin's costumes, worn for the first time, had something to do with it; perhaps the lights, working properly at last, had helped to effect the transformation. But Stephen, most absurdly, was inclined to put it down to the presence of Polly. He was a sort of talisman, he had arrived out of the blue like a sign from Dionysus; and Stephen felt as he had done in Greece, that nothing could go wrong when Polly was there.

"They wanna *hold* that ambush," he was saying eagerly. "Like we did at Larissa—they wanna take 'em in the flank and the rear and give 'em the works!"

"Right you are! I'll polish it up on Monday." Polly was a born soldier, so he ought to know! But he was a born showman too, and he went on:

"Those kings or princes or whatever they was—when they're scrapping together you wanna cut your floods and just catch 'em in a spotlight, all by themselves——"

" By God, you're right again ! " said Stephen. " I ought to have thought of that——"

" And, Stevie——"

" Yes? "

" You wanna put in a *bang* somewhere."

" A bang? "

" You wanna blow something up."

Stephen laughed. " You and your bangs ! "

" Why, Stevie, you're limping ! " Polly seemed to have noticed it for the first time. " I sure do feel bad about your knee. But I mean what I was saying. We gotta have a good-big-bang. That skirmish—Roundheads and Cavaliers, I never could figure out which was which—it just tails off; but if we could blow up a mine, or maybe build a little bridge across the river and send it sky-high, that'd kinda finish the scene off neat and tidy. Say, did Roundheads and Cavaliers have gunpowder? "

" Guy Fawkes tried to blow up Parliament with it long before that ! "

" Well, there you are; sure they had gunpowder; sure they could blow up a bridge. If we could get hold of two or three sticks of dynamite——"

Stephen was smiling to himself at the " we " which kept creeping into Polly's discourse—for Polly was never content to remain a mere spectator of anything—when they reached the main exit, where a single floodlight pointed the way to the turnstiles. Through them streamed a motley crowd of players on their way home, Sir Almeric in shining armour, Bloody Mary with her folk-dancers, Dame Joanna, a bunch of assorted Elizabethans, Odo and Dodo with their eremite mounted on a donkey chosen at random from Faith's innumerable herd. In the midst of this hotch-potch from the past stood a small stiff figure in a shabby mackintosh, looking curiously out of place and unaccountably pathetic. With the air of a Salvation Army lass in a pub, an air of heroic disapprobation, Miss Foulkes parted the crowd with her banner held up before her as if it were a shield:

WE DON'T WANT FESTIVALS
WE WANT HOUSES, WORK AND WAGES
FORGET THE DEAD PAST
JOIN THE C.P. AND LOOK TO THE
LIVING FUTURE

"Well!" said Polly, stopping dead in his tracks.

"Miss Foulkes, our only local Communist," said Stephen.

"Stevie," said Polly, "that sorta makes me feel home-sick."

"Homesick?"

"The little Red schoolteacher I stole from Elas was the living spit of her."

"She works in the balloon factory."

"Funny," said Polly, staring hard at Miss Foulkes, who had just caught sight of him and stared stonily back, "that Reds and redheads, in the case of dames, always seem to go together. That Elas dame was a redhead; and had she got guts? I carried her half a mile slung over my shoulder, going at a smart trot, with the Elas guys taking pot-shots at my backside, and all the time she was tearing my hair

out by the roots. You'd got to hand it to her; I hid
three nights in a cave, and it was like teaming up with a
tigress. But when she'd worked the poison out of her
system we kinda settled down; and could she cook!
Stevie, I reckon I've gotten a special sort of soft spot for
Red redheads. You gotta let me meet this Miss Foulkes
of yours."

"She doesn't approve of Americans," said Stephen.
" She'll probably snap your head off."

" That's just the way I like it," said Polly simply. " Give
me a dame with spirit every time. My little Red schoolteacher in Thessaly——"

Just then, as Stephen was wondering what excuse he
could find for the introduction, Sir Almeric bore down
upon Miss Foulkes. Possibly he hadn't noticed her, for his
tall grey steeplechaser was throwing its head about and
trying to break into a trot, while Sir Almeric reined it in
with hands as light as a sailor's on the sheet. More likely,
however, he thought that the Communist rat deserved to
be taught a lesson and rode his horse at her deliberately.
White-faced, trembling, and obviously terrified of horses,
Miss Foulkes stood her ground, defying the Fascist Beast
with her frail banner. The horse was almost on top of her
when Polly stretched out his arm, caught her firmly by the
waist, and lifted her out of its way almost as casually as a
man would pluck a flower.

" Seems the Knights around these parts ain't got much
chivalry," said Polly, so loudly that Sir Almeric turned
and glared at him.

Stephen seized his opportunity.

" Miss Foulkes," he said, " this is Mr. Gabrielides, a friend of mine from America."

Miss Foulkes wore the expression which a good Communist should who is saved from the brutalities of British Fascism only to find herself in the arms of Uncle Sam. She detached her waist from Polly's grasp, and asserted her independence by taking two steps backwards.

" Glad to meet you, Miss Foulkes," said Polly gaily.

" How do you do? " said Miss Foulkes, in a tone which implied that she was far from glad. She took a very small handkerchief out of her mackintosh pocket and wiped off some foam which had fallen from the horse's mouth on to her forehead.

" You sure got guts," said Polly, " standing there all alone with that banner."

" This is a free country," replied Miss Foulkes surprisingly, for she frequently asserted the opposite. " Unlike some other nations I could name, we do not yet throw our political opponents into prison. I suppose," she added deliberately, " that you've come over here to buy us up with your almighty dollars? "

Polly grinned.

" Well, I don't exactly know about that, but I do want to buy six zebras if you know where I can find them."

" Six *zebras*? "

" Yeah. And I'm open to buy some balloons too, if you could make them in the shape of a duck-billed platypus."

Miss Foulkes gazed at him wide-eyed but without resentment; clearly he was no longer to be blamed for being an American, but to be pitied for being mad. She therefore made no protest when he took her in the friendliest way by her thin, knobbly elbow and drew her confidentially towards him.

"See here," he said, "I got a circus in Louisiana; five elephants, two lions, a grizzly bear called Theodore Roosevelt, forty-eight piebald horses, ten clowns, some performing fleas, six strip-tease dancers, and the only duck-billed platypus in America. I thought maybe I could advertise my circus with balloons like Mr. Tasker did his Pageant. So I'm asking whether your factory could make me a balloon in the shape of a duck-billed platypus, see?"

"We could make a balloon in the shape of anything," said Miss Foulkes. "It's just a matter of the shape of the formas. Unless it had a very long thin tail."

"Well, that's fine! It has a very short, fat tail. And how much would it cost, d'you reckon, to make a balloon like that, supposing I ordered a hundred thousand?"

"Twelve and six a gross," replied Miss Foulkes promptly, quoting *verbatim* from the stock letter which she typed almost every day. "Two and a half per cent discount for cash on delivery. There would be a small extra charge for the special forma, and, of course, an additional charge for anything fancy, such as a squeak."

"Duck-billed platypuses don't squeak."

"Don't they?" she said gravely, looking up at Polly who towered immensely above her. Equally gravely he shook his head; and suddenly there flickered about Miss Foulkes' thin little mouth the shadow of a smile. Stephen had never seen her smile before, and it transformed her. He had the impression of a tight-budded flower opening to the sun. While he was watching this phenomenon, he became aware of another. Polly was saying " No, lady, there ain't no squeak in platypuses," when he began to search his pockets frantically for a handkerchief. Long before he found one he was shaken by a huge and explosive sneeze. It was followed rapidly by a second and a third, and Miss Foulkes kindly proffered her tiny piece of pale-blue lawn. Speechless with sneezing, Polly shook his head; and indeed if he had put Miss Foulkes' handkerchief to his nose it would have been like placing a car's windscreen in the path of an armour-piercing shell. Finding his own handkerchief at last, he shook it in the air to open it, displaying about two square yards of bright yellow silk decorated with a design representing the Dance of the Seven Veils. With the aid of this flag of truce, as it seemed when he waved it, he smothered the next sneeze and achieved a moment's respite, during which he had time to gasp:

" Hay fever. It's a Nallergy," before the next paroxysm overtook him and shook his enormous frame as if he were a great oak defying the equinoctial gales.

Miss Foulkes stared up at him with the astonishment of one who gazes for the first time upon Niagara, Vesuvius or the Victoria Falls.

IV

Next morning was Sunday, and the Mayor and Corporation in their robes of office processed from the Town Hall to the Abbey beneath a cloudless sky. The Vicar preached his Festival Sermon on a text from Ecclesiastes: " A pleasant thing it is for the eyes to behold the sun." Having endured this discourse on meteorology, which lasted for three-quarters of an hour, Stephen went back to his office, where he found Faith trying to get " Trunks " on the telephone.

" What's the trouble now? " he asked her.

" Prevalence of donkeys. They broke out of their paddock in the night and ate *all* the flowers in the Pleasure Gardens! Isn't it awful! And they've been grazing on the snapdragons in the Vicar's border; and they've eaten down all the Bishop delphiniums and the Russell lupins *to the quick*, his wife says. But I thought we might as well turn it to good account and get some pub. out of it; and it'll make a good story for the *Daily Mirror*."

Stephen had promised to meet Polly at the Red Lion where he was putting up, so he left Faith to her telephoning and made his way up the street. He got to the Red Lion ten minutes before opening time, but Florrie was already tidying up the bar, so he went in and sat down to wait for the stroke of twelve.

"You can have a pint now if you like," said Florrie surprisingly, for the Red Lion, under the management of Old Screwnose, was usually very strict about Licensing Hours.

"Is that all right?" said Stephen. "What about Mr. Hawker?"

"To tell the truth, he's not very well. He isn't up yet," Florrie said. "And it's all the fault of that American friend of yours. By the way, he left a message for you; he's gone to the factory to see about buying some balloons. A nice mess he got me into last night," she added.

"Goodness, what's he been up to now?"

"You may well ask. He came back at half-past eleven, just as I was finishing washing up, and before I knew where I was he'd started mixing drinks behind the counter. I should never have allowed it, Mr. Tasker; but you must admit he has a way with him."

"He has indeed."

"He concocted something he called a snakebite cocktail. There was rum and gin and goodness knows what else in it; but it was mostly whisky. I had a little one myself, just to be friendly, and it fairly made my head go round! Then we got talking about circuses and animals, my first husband having been in the lion-taming profession, as you know. So I had another of those snakebites; but your Mr. Polly-something, he had about half a dozen; and then, Mr. Tasker, he started singing."

"He would," said Stephen, remembering VE-day in Greece.

"I should never have allowed it; I don't know what come over us, except that he has such a way with him. And although they were in a foreign language, I could tell they were improper songs, from the expression on his face. Well, before long, of course, down comes Mr. Hawker in his dressing-gown. He pokes his little whiskers round the door, just like a weasel, you know, and there was Mr. Polly swinging his long legs as he sat on the counter, and there was I—well, I must tell you the truth—I'd got the giggles, Mr. Tasker; just like a schoolgirl, I was, laughing till the tears ran down my face."

"So Mr. Hawker wasn't very pleased?"

"He carried on about the police, and the place being respectable—you couldn't blame him, Mr. Tasker, I'm not blaming him at all—and then, all of a sudden I come over swimmy, owing to that snakebite, and I had to leave the room. Just then Mr. Hawker was saying it was a shame the way we'd woken him up, he being under the weather and all, and your friend was telling him that if he was under the weather he ought to have a drop of snakebite to put him on top of the world again. 'Even if you was bitten by a rattlesnake,' he was saying, 'this stuff would fix you in no time.' But I never thought he'd allow himself to be persuaded, him being a teetotaller as you might say from the cradle."

"And did he?"

Florrie nodded her head gravely.

"Nobody could have done it but your friend. *Nobody.* But when I came back, Mr. Tasker—as soon as the swimminess had gone—believe it or not, they was *both* singing.

They was sitting on the bar like two birds on a perch and
they was singing:

> " ' *Here's to the good old snakebite,*
> *Put it down, put it down!* '

They was, Mr. Tasker. Yes, they was." She nodded her
head again and went on:

" But of course, it couldn't last. As soon as Mr. Hawker
began to twiddle his thumbs I guessed what was coming.
None of my husbands was what you'd call moderate men,
Mr. Tasker; so whenever I sees a gentleman with his eyes
half-shut, and his chin on his chest, and his hands clasped
across his stomach, *and* his thumbs twiddling, I know that
I shan't get any more sense out of him till morning. Your
friend was singing away, and I don't suppose he even
noticed; but Mr. Hawker slid off the counter like a sack of
potatoes into my arms, and I—" finished Florrie with
pardonable pride—" *I* carried him up to bed."

It was a splendid picture which rose up in Stephen's mind,
of Florrie's broad back rippling like the withers of a great
Percheron mare of Normandy as she lifted up the little
man and enveloped him within her strong arms and
generous bosom. She would know the way to do it; for
had she not carried to bed the lion-tamer and the astrologer
and the punisher of whisky, those fabulous immoderate
husbands of hers?

But just then, as Florrie took a deep breath and prepared
to continue her story, the porter came in to tell Stephen
that he was wanted on the telephone. He went into the

stuffy little box in the hall on the walls of which somebody
—perhaps Mr. Oxford—had scribbled the names of innumerable race-horses, and heard Faith's voice saying:

" The Mayor wants you in the office, please. There's an
awful crisis on."

" What is it? "

" Mr. Gurney——" She broke off suddenly, there was
a scrabbling sound, and instead of her clear young voice a
throaty whisper filled the telephone-box. It could belong
to none but Councillor Noakes.

" Walls have ears."

PART SIX

I

DAME JOANNA'S statue was still draped in readiness for its unveiling at the end of the week, for it had been deemed indecorous to associate this solemn ceremony with the choosing of the Beauty Queens. Amorphous in its draperies, it appeared to be almost headless, like a piece of sculpture by Mr. Henry Moore. Portentous, brooding, it looked across the river from the Pleasure Gardens towards the grandstands on the Bloody Meadow with an air that was curiously and indefinably sinister; and well it might.

"If that ain't jest too bad," said Polly. "And you're telling me that there never was no such dame as this Joanna?"

"There never was," said Stephen, still awe-stricken by the revelation.

"Well, if that ain't jest too bad."

It was Monday morning, and the sun beamed its blessing upon the festive town, the flags and the roses, the purple loosestrife on the river-bank, the Bloody Meadow bedecked already with the favours of Lancaster and York. Forecasts more reliable than the Vicar's promised a week of fine weather. But all was overshadowed, darkened, blighted, by yesterday's shocking discovery. As the Mayor had pathetically said: "It somehow spoils everything." He seemed to have shrunk and withered, so that he looked even more unimportant than usual, and his kindly face wore an expression of hopeless bewilderment. "If we unveil her," he had sighed, "we lay ourselves open to ridicule; but if we do not unveil her, people will want to know why. We are in a cleft stick, Stephen." As for Councillor Noakes, he seemed capable of no positive action at all, but strode up and down in Stephen's office like a caged animal, exclaiming in hollow tones: "Figures of fun. That's what we shall be. Figures of fun, laughing stocks, butts, to the end of our days." It was mainly to escape from him that Stephen had sought out Polly in the Pleasure Gardens, where with the aid of some of the grandstand carpenters he was building an improvised bridge over the narrow neck of the river just below the mill-pool. Stephen called him up the bank and confided in him the appalling problem of Dame Joanna.

A professor on holiday had started the trouble. The voice-pipe in Mr. Runcorn's office, wailing like a bird of doom, had announced him late on Saturday afternoon. He was something of a specialist, he said, in Middle English literature. He was therefore interested in Dame Joanna, and he proceeded to ask some awkward questions about the local poetess. When he had departed Mr. Runcorn sighed deeply and put through a telephone call to the Bodleian. Its Librarian promised to make inquiries and on Sunday morning he rang up the Mayor. He disclaimed the possession of any manuscripts by Dame Joanna. He had never heard of such a poet. Mr. Gurney, in fact, had invented her.

But Mr. Gurney, when the Mayor rang him up to ask for an explanation, had uttered a bird-like squawk and put down the receiver. Later, when Stephen accompanied the Mayor to his shop, they had received no answer to their urgent knocking on the door. The familiar notice *Back in half an hour* had been removed from the window and replaced by another which bore the single word *Wait*.

So Joanna turned out to be as mythical as the unicorn and the roc and the great sea serpent; an airy nothing, a creature of Mr. Gurney's mischievous imagination, an ingenious fraud like the Chippendale and Hepplewhite chairs in his shop window, and, like them, faked up with infinite pains, to feed fat his ancient grudge against Councillor Noakes. But her statue remained, as pointless as the pyramids, six feet six inches from the base of the pedestal to the top of her head, seven hundredweight (as Councillor Noakes put it) of hoax. She whom it com-memorated no longer had any substance; but its formidable solidity would mock the town for ever. And it had cost the ratepayers four hundred pounds.

"I'm real sorry for your little Mayor," said Polly. He lifted the draperies about Joanna's skirt and stared at her reflectively. "And I'm sorry for you too, Stevie. Let's go to the Red Lion and have a drink."

He waved to the carpenters, who were laying wooden crosspieces upon the framework of the little bridge, and took Stephen's arm as they walked down the back lane

P

which led past the balloon factory towards the main street.

"Those planks," he said, "will blow clean out, see, so we can collect 'em up and use 'em again for each performance. I've gotten some dynamite, Stevie. We can have a real big bang."

How on earth, Stephen wondered, does a stranger in a strange land get hold of some dynamite? But that was all of a piece with the numinosity of Polly, it was another demonstration of his Dionysiac quality: he could do things which were impossible to ordinary men.

"And I dated up that redhead," he observed casually, as they came opposite the balloon factory from all the windows of which, like smoke from a crowded room, there streamed a thin haze of french chalk. "And I bought a hundred thousand balloons to advertise my circus."

Dionysiac indeed! Within less than forty-eight hours he had caused Old Screwnose to sing *Here's to the good old snakebite*, he had persuaded the carpenters to work all Sunday afternoon, he had mysteriously obtained some dynamite, he had dated up Miss Foulkes, he had bought a hundred thousand balloons. And now, at the corner where the lane entered the street, he suddenly paused and exclaimed excitedly:

"Stevie, I got an idea!"

"Yes? What is it this time?"

"I been thinking. If you could have those Pleasure Gardens closed to the public for an hour or two this afternoon, and the gates locked during the performance——"

"Yes—why?"

"I could fix that Dame Joanna of yours."

"You're rather good at fixing dames, aren't you?" laughed Stephen. "But what exactly do you mean?"

"Well, are you sure your little old Mayor would be glad to be rid of her, Stevie? Are you quite sure of that?"

"I should think he'd give his right arm if she could just magically disappear."

"That's fine. Then I'll fix her. I reckon," said Polly thoughtfully, wrinkling his forehead, "that the narrowest part of a dame is somewhere round about her waist."

II

BECAUSE EDNA had gone up to London for her film-test, Mrs. Greening had taken her place at the end of the long bench, and was testing the new batch of beach-balls which were being turned out in a hurry to fulfil an unexpected repeat order from Australia. When they were done the factory was going to start on Polly's platypuses. There was enough work on hand for nearly a month, and all the arrears of wages had been paid that morning.

"What would they be like, these platy pusses?" said Mrs. Greening to Jim, as he brought her another dozen beach-balls which he had just peeled off the formas.

"Dunno. They make some pretty funny things in this line of business, but I can't say I've ever 'eard of a platy puss. But good luck to 'em. Means we keeps our jobs, anyway." Then, as he went back to his oven, he resumed his description of the things which would happen to Edna if her film-test were successful.

"Fust thing," he said, "they takes out all your teef."

"They never!"

"They does. I read it in the *Worker*. Nobody's natural teef ain't good enough for them B. plutocrats what owns the fillums. Then they pulls out your eyebrows 'air by 'air, 'cause you 'as to 'ave new ones painted on special. Just the same wiv your mouf. Maybe it's the wrong shape; not what the plutocrats calls kissable. Maybe it ain't big enough. So they paints you on another."

"They never!" said Mrs. Greening again.

"Read it in the paper. 'Sides, you can see it's right every time you goes to the fillums. Those lushus great mouvs wiv the paint dripping off of 'em like strawberry jam ain't *real*, don't you kid yourself. Nor's the eyelashes. They'll pull out Edna's eyelashes wiv the tweezers, and stick on artificial ones about an inch long. But mark my words, Mrs. Grinnin," croaked Jim solemnly, "it's ten to one that when they're done wiv 'er they won't like the result. They'll fiddle about wiv 'er face till they've made a muck of it, and then they'll say they don't like 'er figure or something. Maybe she ain't got enough uplift or maybe she's got too much—uplift's bosoms, it said so in the *Worker* —and then they'll just send 'er back to store. Girls is just cannon-fodder to them."

"Who'd have thought it?" exclaimed Mrs. Greening in amazement. "I'd rather 'ave me pendix out meself. Now what'd them long eyelashes be made of, d'you suppose?"

" Pigs' bristles, I dessay," improvised Jim on the spur of the moment.

" But what for do they do it, like? "

" So's they lie flat on 'er cheek and she looks like she's swoonin' when she's being made love to by James Mason or some such chap. When she looks like a dyin' duck in a thunderstorm it means she's enjoyin' of it special. I often seen it 'appen on the fillums."

" Does your old 'oman swoon when you makes love to 'er? " inquired Mrs. Greening tartly.

" She'd be that took back, she would if I tried," said Jim; and all the women at the long bench set up such a cackle of laughter that it sounded as if a fox had got in among a lot of old hens. Even John Handiman in his office could hear it, and he looked across the room at Miss Foulkes and smiled.

" What kind of a tail did you say it had? " said John, who was making the rough drawing for the matrix of the formas from an engraving of a duck-billed platypus in an old Encyclopædia. " This picture doesn't show it."

" Short and fat," said Miss Foulkes promptly.

" All the book says about it is that it's oviparous," said John. " What's oviparous, Enid? "

" Lays eggs, instead of bringing forth its young alive."

" You seem to know a lot about the beast," said John. He glanced up from his drawing and was astonished to see Miss Foulkes smiling at him quite composedly. This was a rare phenomenon anyhow, but what particularly struck him was that it was a peculiarly *contented* smile. He found

himself staring at her, wondering why she looked so different
this morning. There were lights in her hair which he had
never noticed before; in the sunlight which came through
the small window over her head it burned with a slow-
smouldering flame. And somehow—John couldn't explain
it—her manner was changed too. Some of the sharp edges
seemed to have been rubbed away. Aware that he was
looking at her, she returned his glance quite calmly, without
any of the awkward defensiveness which so often embarrassed him. Then there was a knock at the door, and
in came the messenger-boy from the florist's.

Miss Foulkes did not immediately look round; and
John had said, "Put them on the filing-cabinet," before she
noticed the messenger. The flowers this time were gladioli,
an enormous bunch of salmon-pink ones which must have
cost, John thought, at least a pound. He was horrified at
the thought of her spending so much of her wages on such
nonsense. Then he became aware that Miss Foulkes had
got up from her desk and was staring in amazement at the
gladioli. He expected that her blush would match the
flowers themselves, and prepared as usual to avert his glance.
But this time Enid Foulkes did not even blush. Instead the
blood drained away from her pale skin so that it looked
quite transparent.

" But—but I didn't order them!" she gasped, and
slumped back in her chair.

III

STEPHEN AND POLLY had just ordered their drinks, and inquired after the health of Mr. Hawker—"He's getting up now; but shaky as an aspen-leaf," said Florrie—when the clock in the hall began to strike twelve, and as if at a signal Mr. Oxford entered the bar. He was followed by Timms, bearing like an acolyte a large silver trophy which he set down upon the counter. Mr. Oxford, who had a strong sense of the dramatic, stood before it in silence while he deliberately counted out five pound notes.

"Fill that," he commanded, handing them to Florrie, "with a mixture of equal parts of brandy and champagne!"

"Why, Mr. Oxford, whatever has come over you?" Florrie fluttered. "Have you won the Irish Sweep or something?"

Mr. Oxford took a step back from the counter and looked about him. He nodded to Stephen, who introduced Polly. "Welcome to our ancient borough!" said Mr. Oxford, taking off his hat. Then he waved his hand towards the trophy, and Florrie dutifully reached up for a bottle of Martell Three-Star on the shelf over her head.

"That cup," said Mr. Oxford, "is presented every year to the champion angler of all the Midlands, and it was won on Saturday by Mr. Handiman senior of this town with a chub weighing eight pounds two and a half ounces. Am I right, Timms?"

"Two and three-quarter," squeaked Timms.

"Two and three-quarter to be precise. Now, Mr. Handiman, flying as you might say in the face of all his prejudices and principles, backed himself with me to win two hundred pounds, and fortunately I had the good sense to lay off that bet among my confrères. It cost me, personally, a mere matter of twenty smackers, which I was very pleased to part with in a good cause."

"Well, fancy that! And Mr. Handiman so strict!" said Florrie.

"You know my motto," Mr. Oxford went on. "'Pay up with a smile and pay on the nile,' as they say in Brummagem. So first thing on Sunday morning I says to Timms, 'Timms,' I says, 'the better the day the better the deed.' So off we go to Mr. Handiman to pay him his two hundred pounds. It was a moving moment, gentlemen! I have paid out a great deal of money in my time—it is always a pleasure—but I can honestly say I have never been so touched in all my professional career. 'Praise the Lord!' he said; and there were tears in his eyes as he said it. 'But if you don't mind,' he said, 'I'd rather not actually *handle* the money on the Sabbath. May I have it to-morrow instead?' Then 'Praise the Lord!' he cries again; and he puts on his bowler hat and hurries off to chapel like a man in a dream."

Mr. Oxford's discourse was interrupted by the pop of the cork coming out of the champagne. He continued:

"So this morning Timms and I return first thing to Mr.

Handiman's ironmongery. Timms counts out two hundred
smackers; and once again Mr. Handiman's eyes are moist
with tears. Then he hands me this cup, and these five
pound notes, and 'Take that to the Red Lion,' he says,
'and fill it up with what's proper.' 'Horse's neck,' says
I, 'or dog's nose?' But he being teetotal don't understand.
It being so hot a day, I thought a dog's nose would be too
heavy; so horse's neck it is."

By now Florrie had filled the cup, and at Mr. Oxford's
request she took the first sip of it.

"Here's to Mr. Handiman!" she said. "I still can't get
over *him* having a bet."

"Ah, but it's bred in the bone!" boomed Mr. Oxford.
"Ingrained, as you might say, in the British Race!
Tradition, that's what it is! You can't keep it down any
more than you can keep rubbub down. Here, for instance,
comes Sir Halmeric, who 'as 'ad a little flutter with me
every week day, barring the war years, since he was
sixteen." Sir Almeric lounged up to the bar and leaned upon
it, glancing curiously at Polly, who was wiping his mouth
after taking a long swig from the cup. Mr. Oxford hastened
to introduce him.

"Let me present you, sir, to Sir Halmeric Jukes, Bart.,
a representative of our ancient squirearchy!"

"Glad to meet you, Sir Jukes," said Polly, extending his
hand. "My name's Polycarpos Gabrielides. Known as
Polly."

Sir Almeric took his hand lazily and stared hard at his
big hat.

"Yeah. I guess we both go in for crazy headgear," said

Polly cheerfully. "Where d'you buy yours?" Sir Almeric
was wearing his little tweed cap with the button on top of
it. "I'll maybe get one like it."

"It is made specially for me," drawled Sir Almeric, "by
a man called Lock. If you *really* want to know," he added
nastily, "Mr. Pollywhatsit Gabrielides." With that he
turned his back on Polly and handed a betting-slip to Mr.
Oxford. There was a short uncomfortable silence, which
was broken by a faint scrabbling sound at the door behind
the bar. At last the door opened, and Mr. Hawker appeared.
It was apparent that the effects of the snakebite had not yet
worn off. He came sidling in, not with his usual weasel-
like air of questing furtiveness, but like a puppy that has
made a mess. As Florrie had said, he was as shaky as an
aspen; and his face was the colour of carbide which has
been used. He carried two bottles of whisky, which he set
down on the counter.

"Your Allocation," he said to Florrie in a faint voice.

"Say, buddy," grinned Polly, "you don't look too good.
Better take a pull at this." He held out the silver cup, and
Mr. Hawker retreated in terror before it. And then an
extraordinary thing happened. Florrie put her arm about
Mr. Hawker's shoulder and impelled him forward. With
her other hand she took the cup from Polly.

"*Go on, dearie,*" she said, "*a little drop of the hair of the
dog won't do you any harm.*"

Stephen could scarcely believe his ears; Mr. Oxford
stared at her in astonishment; even Sir Almeric had lifted
his elbows off the counter. And then Florrie drew herself
up and announced with dignity:

" Mr. Hawker and I, you see, are shortly going to be married."

Behind the enormous cup, which he now raised to his mouth with trembling hands, Mr. Hawker nodded. He tipped the cup, and his face disappeared behind it, until only the eyes with their rimless glasses like the goggle eyes of some deep-sea fish remained visible. Florrie said to Stephen in a compassionate whisper: " He wanted looking after, you see," and there ran through his mind another couplet from the Wife of Bath:

Of remedies of love she knew parchance
For she coude of that art the olde dance.

And then Mr. Oxford loudly thumped upon the counter and called for the cup to be topped up with another bottle of champagne.

IV

IN THE cubicle at the end of the long dressing-tent, which was curtained off from the rest and labelled BEAUTY QUEENS, Virginia waited, while Edna, still in her brassière and knickers, fiddled with her make-up in front of the only mirror. Edna was always late for everything, whereas Virginia invariably saw to it that she was made-up, dressed, groomed and ready about half an hour before she was due to appear. She dreaded last-minute rushes; and she was quite content as a rule to sit about and close her eyes and dream her dreams.

But to-night it was different, because she was aware that if she shut her eyes and tried to perform her private conjuring trick with the whirling lights and the names in technicolor *there would be nothing there*. In the car on the way back from the film-test she had tried it; and instead of the flickering credit titles there was a frightening vacancy, her secret cinema screen was blank and empty, the words "Starring Virginia Vance" failed to appear. Virginia Vance was dead. The kindly apologetic man in the studio had killed her with the single word "but." "You photograph awfully well, but . . ." Virginia hadn't really listened any more; but she remembered him saying something about "There's a lot of money in modelling nowadays," and adding, in a half-jocular embarrassed tone, "and as a matter of fact, there's quite a career, I believe, for Beauty Queens." Virginia hadn't got much imagination, but she knew what he meant, and the pages of a sort of mental photograph album flicked over in her brain, Miss Brighton 1951, Miss Holiday Camp, a strictly regulation bathing-dress lettered BUTLIN BELLE 1952; and then you faded out, though you still got a free perm for a year or two; and in the end you married the sort of man who marries Beauty Queens.

Virginia Vance was dead; and that being so, it seemed strange that Virginia Smith should continue to exist, should make-up her face, do her hair, get ready to parade across the arena and sit at the Mayor's right hand at the opening performance. For without Vance, Smith was nothing. Smith had *been* Vance, night and day, for two years. If the guy-ropes of this tent were cut away, thought Virginia, it would surely tumble down upon our heads. Yet without visible support Virginia Smith carried on.

She glanced at Edna, half in and half out of her dress, wriggling it down over her wide hips in a casual and uncaring way and not bothering, not thinking about her body, as Virginia would have done, who even before a girl was self-conscious and shy. Perhaps that was what they called " having personality," " being yourself." The film-man had said very kindly: " It isn't a question of good looks, exactly; it's a question of being able to project *yourself* beyond that photograph, beyond the screen." Perhaps that was what Edna could do, for Virginia felt quite certain in her mind that Edna's test had been successful. Yet she hadn't asked Edna; nor had Edna asked her. A queer sort of mutual courtesy had prevented them. Virginia wondered if she would hate Edna, if Edna had been offered a trial; and was rather surprised to discover that in the void and vacuum of her existence there was no room for hate. Only, she thought, it might be a little bit easier to bear if Edna also had failed.

As she did her hair, Edna was thinking: She's much better-looking than I am, and much more refined. It was my voice that did it, I bet, though he didn't exactly say so. But she speaks ever so lady-like. I do hope she got it, because she wants it so much. It would have been a lark if I'd been chosen, but I only went in for a lark anyhow, so who cares?

I wish I could ask her, but I don't like to in case she was turned down. Then she might cry. And we've got to be in our seats in ten minutes.

It'll be fun, she thought, telling Lance all about it, in our secret hiding-place up on the hill, after the show.

The call-boy flapped with his fists on the curtain of the cubicle.

"Beauty Queens!" he called. "Five minutes to go!"

Edna gave her hair a last casual dab with the brush.

"Come along, ducks," she said, "and be nice to the Mayor. I wonder who'll be on the other side of us. I hope it isn't that Councillor Noakes; him and his fiddling!"

Virginia got up slowly. She was so tall and dignified, and she moved so beautifully, that Edna felt quite sure the film-man must have chosen her. "Oh, you look lovely!" she said spontaneously; and then Virginia turned towards her and made a queer little gesture, half-grateful, half-despairing, which told her better than words that Virginia had failed. It told her so much that she didn't need to ask for confirmation. She just put her arm round Virginia's waist, and said:

"Me too."

"You too?" Virginia almost whispered.

"I've got a common voice, ducks. Can't help it. Anyhow, it was only for a lark. But you—oh, Virginia, you speaks so nice, I'm that *sorry*!"

Virginia discovered somewhere a small, still, secret reservoir of courage and said quite calmly:

"Ay don't maind."

V

ROBIN, WHO rather fancied himself on horseback, was riding round the Performers' Enclosure, which lay between the dressing-tents and the main arena, where the British Legion band was just beginning to play the overture. It would be at least an hour before he led his Lancastrians out to battle, and Sir Almeric, in command of the Yorkists, had not yet changed out of his yellow polo jumper into his suit of mail. He was watching a groom saddling up his splendid grey when Robin rode up to him. He drawled: "What does it feel like on that old camel?" For he despised all riding-school hacks, and Robin's was a tall raw-boned chestnut with a slight wheeze and the marks of firing on both its forelegs: the sort of beast which appears in the sale catalogue as:

Chestnut mare, aged, with all faults

and which neither vendor nor purchaser asks the vet to examine.

"Oh, she's not so bad," said Robin, who resented Sir Almeric's air of superiority. "I shouldn't mind a day's hunting on her, anyhow."

Sir Almeric laughed.

"My dear fellow, you'd never get farther than the first fence."

" Rot," said Robin. " Look at her quarters. She'd jump a house." Less than a fortnight ago Sir Almeric had called him " a bloody poacher " and he was still smarting under this perfectly just accusation. " It isn't everybody," he said, " who can afford to swank about at a Pageant on a five-hundred-guinea 'chaser.'"

Sir Almeric regarded him with lazy insolence.

" I'll bet you five to one in pounds," he said, " that your fleabitten old crock won't lepp the post and rails round this enclosure; if you've got the guts to try."

At this opportune moment Mr. Oxford and Timms appeared, in the guise of Odo and Dodo, and leading a donkey. They were due to go on in five minutes; and it was clear that Mr. Oxford had been fortifying himself against this ordeal with whisky.

" Fife to one bar none! " he cried thickly. " Fife to one bar none."

" I'm betting him," said Sir Almeric, " that his seventeen hands of knacker's meat won't jump those rails."

" That's England! " said Mr. Oxford obscurely. " 'Earts of hoak! Good old England. Good old tradition. Good old instink to have a little flutter. Like rubbub it comes up. Never let it be said that Oxford hangs back. Some says good old Oxford, some says beggar old Oxford; but all says Oxford is a sport. I'll double it. I'll offer him tens. Ten smackers to one he doesn't jump the rails! "

Robin hadn't bargained for this. He glanced at the rails and noticed that they were four feet high, and extremely solid. But Mr. Oxford was shouting " Ten to one the chestnut! " and a crowd of performers was beginning to

collect round him; there was no escape now from the
foolish adventure, so he kicked his old mare in the ribs and
trotted back to a position from which he could get a clear
run at the fence. As he turned towards it he noticed Edna
and Virginia making their way through the crush towards
the entrance to the arena, and waved to them, thinking
how lovely they looked and how well they wore the dresses
he had designed for them. They waved back, and then
stopped beside the fence to watch him as he cantered up
to it.

"Ten to one bar none!" bawled Mr. Oxford, as the
chestnut gathered itself for the jump.

Robin felt her shoulders rising beneath him, he felt the
heave and lift of her quarters and he thought, "She's done
it. We're over. Hurray!" But he hadn't reckoned with
the slippery take-off, for the ground was baked on the
surface and still sodden underneath from last week's flood.
The mare seemed for a fraction of a second to twist in the
air, and he was aware of the whistle in her wind as she
strained to clear the rails. Then he heard the crash as she
hit them sideways, and while he still somersaulted on the
ground he saw the glint of the sunset on her shoes as she
rolled over on top of him.

Kneeling beside Robin, Virginia said coolly:
"Fetch an ambulance man, somebody. He's broken his
arm."

She looked up at the crowd pressing round her, and there
was Sir Almeric fumbling in his pocket for a handkerchief
to wipe Robin's bloody face; and Mr. Oxford with his

Q

mouth wide open; and Timms shuffling helplessly from
one foot to another; and a Norman knight, who represented
Robert Fitzhamon, leaning on his battleaxe. None of them
seemed to be capable of *doing* anything except Sir Almeric,
who gave her his handkerchief, thus acknowledging that
she was in charge, and his groom, who had caught the
chestnut and was entirely preoccupied with feeling its legs
one by one; for he held the stableyard view that horses
were more important than people.

She dabbed gently at Robin's face with the handkerchief,
while the crowd watched her.

" Bleeding something awful," observed Mr. Oxford.

" Fair turns me up, it does," said Timms.

But nobody offered to help her, and Virginia despised
them, failing to realise that it was her own unexpected
authority which caused them to hold back. Then two
ambulance men arrived with a stretcher and knelt down
beside her.

" Cor, look at 'is face! " exclaimed one of the ambulance
men.

" Don't be silly," snapped Virginia. " That's only nose-
bleed. But take care how you move him in case he's
concussed. And I think he's broken his right arm just
above the elbow."

She helped them lift Robin on to the stretcher, and as
she bent over him he opened his eyes. He stared at her for
a moment in bewilderment and suddenly grinned. " Hello,
Virgie."

" Hello, Robin. They're just going to take you to
hospital."

"What have I done?"

"Nothing much. You'll soon be all right."

"Funny girl," said Robin dreamily. He shut his eyes again. "Funny girl. Remember that cat in the trap? Good at this sort of thing." The ambulance men carried him away.

Virginia stood up, and as she did so Edna came out of the crowd towards her. "Oh, Virginia, your dress!" she cried. "Your beautiful dress!" And Virginia looked down and saw the red smears all over the front of the maize taffeta which Robin had designed for her that evening on the hill. Glancing up again, she stared with amazement at Edna's face, which was so white in contrast with her lipstick and eyeblack that she looked like a clown. Virginia caught her as she swayed forward.

"I'm sorry, ducks," breathed Edna. "I just can't bear the sight of blood."

"Sit down there with your head between your knees." Standing behind Edna to prop her up, Virginia strove with a queer sense of triumph which she knew she ought not to be feeling. Edna's frailty, which seemed to her so absurd, gave her a new self-confidence, an advantage over Edna which was momentary but complete; and because of this she experienced an unexpected tenderness towards her, a kind of affectionate and possessive pity, and as she leaned down and whispered, "You'll be all right in a minute, dear," she let her fingers run gently through Edna's yellow hair.

"Better now," said Edna. "Virginia, you were *brave*!"

"Stay where you are for a minute. They're still playing the overture." And as she listened to the band, wondering how much time there was to spare before the parade of the Beauty Queens, Virginia day-dreamed. For a fraction of a second she closed her eyes, and saw, not Virginia Vance in gorgeous technicolor, but a humbler though by no means unglamorous figure, whose very ordinary name was Nurse Smith.

VI

WHEN STEPHEN was told of the accident he did not hesitate for a moment but asked Polly to take Robin's part and lead the Lancastrians on to the field. He was a horseman, he was a soldier, he was the beloved of Dionysus; and Stephen still cherished the unreasonable faith that nothing could go wrong when Polly was there. Moreover, Polly had watched the Dress Rehearsal at Stephen's side and therefore had a pretty good idea of what he was expected to do; and any mistakes he might make would probably pass unnoticed in the confusion of the battle.

But Faith was shocked at Stephen's decision. "How do you know he can ride?" she objected.

Stephen smiled. "He was wonderful on a mule in Greece!" He didn't tell her that Polly had spent two years of his youth as a cowboy in the West. Faith shook her head.

" Something awful is bound to happen," she sighed.

" Why? "

" I can't explain. He's got a dæmon, that man. He's dangerous. You see."

" Don't flap," said Stephen, who was secretly rather pleased to discover that he was quite calm whereas Faith was agitated; it was generally the other way round. " Go and find him in the dressing-tent, and run through his part with him and find him a horse from somewhere. I've got to stay up here and watch the show."

So Faith met Polly as he came out of the tent, huge and heroic indeed in all the panoply of Prince Edward of Wales; she made him memorise a whole lot of last-minute instructions, and then took him into the paddock in search of the chestnut mare. When they found it, tethered to the railings, she ran her hand professionally down its fetlocks and declared that it was none the worse for its fall.

" D'you want a leg up? " she said doubtfully. " It's rather a tall animal."

" I guess I can manage." And Polly put one hand on the mare's withers and another on the saddle and vaulted up as if the great beast had been a child's rocking-horse. Faith said:

" You'll want to tighten the girths before you start. They blow out their tummies, you know."

" Sure, they blow out their tummies." Faith looked up at him and saw him laughing at her. He was lengthening his stirrup-leathers, and Faith watched with astonishment as he put the buckle in the lowest hole of all, so that he was sitting straight-legged as an old-fashioned dragoon.

"Guess you British have all gotten very small bottoms," observed Polly to the world at large. "This little saddle feels about the size of a postage stamp."

At that moment Sir Almeric went by on his grey, with his knees tucked up under him as if he were going to ride a race.

"What d'you want?" he drawled, "an armchair?" And as he led his Yorkist knights out through the paddock gate, on his way to take up his position at the farther entrance, he caught sight of Mr. Oxford, who had just come out of the arena, and called:

"Bet you a level quid that dago falls off."

Polly made no comment, and Faith hoped he hadn't heard; but when she glanced up at him she saw a slow grin spreading slowly across his face. Somehow that grin disquieted her.

From his little box at the top of the grandstand Stephen watched the border of flowers come suddenly to life again as the floods lit up the Yorkist array, herald, page, trumpeter, pursuivant, making a moving frieze of scarlet and blue and gold, the pennons of the knights fluttering like moon-daisies in a meadow. He watched the floods fade out, leaving a blacker darkness than there had been before, while the pale green spotlight like a finger of doom sought out the bosky corner where the ambush lurked and revealed spectral knights, faintly luminescent, like horsemen of the apocalypse. Faith crept into the box, breathless from running up the steps, and stood beside him. Darkness again, and the torment of the trumpet crying in the void;

and then the cold white lights shining upon Polly and his Lancastrians, freezing them like a lightning flash, more and more floods throwing down their brightness upon the field until even the green grass seemed silvery-white.

Stock-still for a moment the cohorts stood, frozen in the ice-cold light; and then as the pinks and ambers came up there was a sudden warmth generated and the whole scene glowed like a summer garden bathed in noonday sun. Like an anthill stirred with a stick the whole mass was set in turbulent motion. Rose-red pennons of Lancaster and white ones of York fluttered in a mazy dance. Fiery particles broke off here and there and shot away in different directions. A great shout went up from Lancaster, and as York bayed back in defiance all the lances dropped as if before a wind, and the thudding of the horse-hoofs became menacing and loud.

This was the moment, the split second before the ambush, when Stephen always experienced an almost unbearable tension. From the dark patch of bushes came neither sign nor sound as the Yorkist knights cantered past it; and Stephen wanted to cry out loud: " Fall on them now, fall on them *now* ! " He heard Faith catch her breath, and he was suddenly aware of the pressure of her body against his and in the darkness of the box he sought for her hand. Then, like the explosion of a many-coloured firework, the ambush burst out. Stephen heard himself shouting " Hurray ! " Sparking fragments of red, yellow and white whirled about each other, coalesced and broke apart. For a minute the whole arena was in turmoil; but gradually a new pattern emerged, and the middle of the field was left clear as the

wheeling groups of knights and soldiers spun away as if
impelled by centrifugal force towards the edges. Nobody
had eyes for them any more; so the floods faded, and the
scrimmaging knots and clusters melted into the darkness
while a grey horse and a chestnut galloped hell-for-leather
towards each other, and in a small and lonely pool of light
at the field's centre Sir Almeric and Polly met face-to-face
and lance-to-lance, and began to do battle.

"He's managing beautifully," said Stephen. "I knew it
would be all right. As the spotlight moves across the field,
he moves with it." Faith had particularly impressed upon
Polly that he must keep within the pool of light and retire
gradually before Sir Almeric's fury; thus he would be
forced back into the ranks of his own Lancastrians, whom
he would then rally in a last hopeless stand before they
were driven in headlong rout from the battlefield.
Polly was obeying these instructions perfectly, and
allowing Sir Almeric to chivvy him yard by yard towards
the exit.

"I knew it would be all right," said Stephen again.

"I wonder! He's got a dæmon."

"Now the floods come on again. Look!" The lights
revealed the broken ranks of Lancaster still raggedly
fighting in Polly's rear. Two score of casualties lay where
they had fallen and three riderless horses gave an extra touch
of verisimilitude to the stricken field as they galloped about
the arena. Already the Yorkist knights were re-forming for
their final charge; in a moment Lancaster would be swept
away. But for a little longer the scene was one of wild and

splendid turbulence, and Stephen wished it would never come to an end.

As he fell back before Sir Almeric's onslaught, Polly became aware for the first time that his foe was actually trying to unseat him. Three times he had charged straight at him, and once Polly had had to lie flat on his horse's neck to avoid the padded lance. Sir Almeric accompanied these charges with bloodthirsty shouts of "Yoicks!" and "Tally-ho!"

In evading them, Polly had lost more ground than he had meant to, and now he found himself unexpectedly in the middle of a fight between some of his own foot-soldiers and those of the enemy. Into this *mêlée* galloped Sir Almeric, regardless of whether he knocked anybody down, waving his lance wildly and shouting, most ridiculously it seemed to Polly, his strange hunting-cries:

"Whoy, rip 'im and tear 'im! Worry, worry, worry!"

Naturally enough the foot-soldiers scattered before him, and the carefully planned movement which Stephen had intended to represent a rout became a rout indeed, with a score of bowmen fleeing from Sir Almeric's charge towards a narrow exit which was already blocked by the milling knights of Lancaster who were trying to guide their horses through it. Polly heard at his back a murmur of genuine anger as one of the foot-soldiers tripped and fell, and Sir Almeric continued his mad career with yells of "Worry worry, worry!"

Perhaps it was this murmur of indignation from his own side which inspired Polly to do what he did. Perhaps it was the recollection that he had been described as a dago. Or perhaps—who knows?—ancestral memories stirred him, stemming from Spartan forebears who held against the host of Xerxes the pass between Mount Oeta and the sea. Not Leonidas himself, surely, rallied his immortal three hundred with such a great cry as Polly uttered when he turned in sudden fury upon the foe; nor did the weary defenders of Thermopylæ respond to it more gallantly. For as Polly turned his horse and charged full pelt at Sir Almeric the Lancastrian knights, either in anger or bewilderment, with one accord galloped away from the exit and joined the battle again. The foot-soldiers, whom Sir Almeric had chased like rabbits, took heart once more and began to revenge themselves most unjustly upon their opposite numbers of York, whom they belaboured unmercifully with their wooden battleaxes. Meanwhile the knights, whose horses were frightened by the cries of the wretched Yorkists and the enthusiastic shouts of the suddenly awakened crowd, were carried by the impetus of their charge into the flank of the opposing horsemen, whose formation they sliced in two as a knife cuts butter. Taken off their guard, and utterly dumbfounded by an emergency for which the rehearsals had not prepared them, the Yorkist knights lost their heads altogether and scattered all over the arena. The Lancastrians, whose terrified horses were now in complete charge, continued to sweep all before them.

Polly, galloping as if he meant to head off the cattle-rustlers in Dead Man's Gulch, met Sir Almeric head-on in what might have been a fatal collision had not Sir Almeric's steeplechaser, which was unaccustomed to meeting horses

going in the opposite direction, reared sideways out of the
way. This manœuvre nearly unseated Sir Almeric, who
lost his stirrups and clung on only by his horse's mane. His
horse whipped round and galloped towards the only exit
it knew, and Sir Almeric, with his arms round its neck,
was powerless to stop it. Polly, whose blood was up,
thundered at its heels, turning the tables on his foe with
shouts of "Yoicks!" and "Worry!"

Elsewhere on the field strange things began to happen.
As if at the cry "*Debout les morts!*" dead men rose up and
joined in the fray. A whole company of fallen bowmen
seized their bows again, discovered some unused arrows in
their quivers, and shot them at the backs of the routed
Yorkists, adding to the confusion. The knights who had
taken part in the ambush, and were supposed to have been
slain, remounted their tethered horses and swelled the
victorious ranks of Lancaster. Even the lighting-man seemed
to have thrown in his lot with the victors; for a single spot,
deftly manipulated, illuminated the inglorious exit of Sir
Almeric, hanging upside down upon his horse's neck and
clinging on, as Mr. Oxford put it, "by his eyebrows."
Then the partisan spotlight swept into the middle of the
field to discover Polly in triumph with his knights and foot-
soldiers gathered about him. There was hardly a Yorkist
in sight ; Lancaster possessed the field, and shamelessly
cheered its victory.

And there might have been seen, against the rails, a small
angular figure in a dirty mackintosh at whose feet a trampled
banner lay: WE DON'T WANT FEST—— But it was

impossible to read the remainder, because Miss Foulkes
had inadvertently been jumping up and down on it. Like
a football fan on the touchline, Miss Foulkes rooted for
Lancaster; and as the knights acclaimed their triumph she
added her little cheer to theirs.

VII

DIONYSUS IS a choosy god, and fickle in his favours.
The most expensive and elaborate show we can devise
in his honour, with ten thousand pounds' worth of dresses,
a revolving stage, a cyclorama, and a chorus of sixty
ravishing blondes, may yet fail to delight him; and should
he withhold from it his blessing, that show will be no more
than an empty charade, a vain wailing in the wilderness, a
pointless stamping upon the stage. Yet some poor wandering players performing *Maria Marten* in a windy barn on
a platform lit by naphtha-flares may tickle his fancy with
their devotion or their innocence, and lo! his unmistakable
glory shines about their heads. He may glance aside with a
yawn of boredom from the smooth competent West-End
actors in a drawing-room comedy to bestow his immortal
laughter upon a clumsy schoolboy wearing the ass's head
of Bottom at a speech-day entertainment. There is no
saying where the benison of Dionysus may fall nor whom
his magic may inspire; but we must suppose that only
those who are truly dedicated to his service may receive it.

When he gives, however, he gives without stint; and without stint his measureless bounty descended like fire from heaven upon Stephen's little pageant. What matter if Virginia's new dress was spoiled with bloodstains, and Edna was as pale as a ghost when they paraded across the arena to take their seats at the Mayor's side? To the crowd they seemed like two young goddesses. What matter if Mr. Oxford and Timms were drunk when they made their entrance, and even drunker, on account of the action of the cool air upon their hot heads, when they walked with cautious deliberation towards the exits? For their drunkenness gave to their gait a strange and unwonted dignity. Like sleep-walkers they perambulated the ground-plan of the church; like zombies stolen from their graves they performed the act of dedication; but so powerful was Dionysus' magic that the spectators were impressed with their air of reverent humility. What matter if Lance's folk-songs had been made up out of his head? Sung to Bloody Mary in her barge on the opalescent river they had sounded more authentic than any genuine ones. What matter if the disgruntled captain of the Cricket Club had bowled the professional who represented Dr. Grace with his first ball, a vicious yorker, instead of tossing up a half-volley which could be hit for six, as he had been instructed to? What matter if Polly's big bang, which blew up the bridge behind the retreating cavaliers, blew sky-high also in a thousand shattered fragments the statue of Dame Joanna, to whose waist he had ingeniously affixed a sizeable stick of dynamite? The crowd had yelled their approval of such prodigious fireworks, and the only people who regretted the dis-

integration of Joanna were those few dwellers by the riverside whose windows were broken and Inspector Heyhoe,
who padded about murmuring, " Trouble, more trouble,"
and gravely suspected Miss Foulkes of Communist sabotage.

And above all, what matter if the wrong side had won
the battle and the whole course of the Wars of the Roses
had been altered by Polly's heroic defiance of Sir Almeric?
It had been the best battle, the spectators agreed, that they
had ever witnessed in their lives; and they had cheered
it wildly for fully five minutes, not caring a fig whether
the winter of their discontent was made glorious summer
by the sun of Lancaster or York. And at the end of the
show they had stood up on their seats and cheered again,
yelling themselves hoarse when two aeroplanes swooped
out of the dark sky, to the astonishment of everybody except
Faith, who had arranged the matter secretly with her
Group-Captain, and showered upon the arena and the
crowd a miraculous rain of red and white roses.

" I'm afraid," said the Mayor half-ruefully, as he walked
with Stephen and Polly across the hoof-scarred turf, while
the crowd with strange reluctance began to make its way
towards the exits, " I'm afraid, Mr. Gabrielides, that the
'istory wasn't quite right." And Polly, gigantic and glorious
in his armour, with his helmet pushed on to the back of
his head, smiled down at him, and said gallantly:

" But, Mr. Mayor, *you* are history."

As he said this, he made a large and comprehensive
gesture which might have included not only the Mayor
and his ancient office, but the little town behind him, the

Abbey tower looming over it, the struggling balloon factory making duck-billed platypuses to earn dollars; Mr. Handiman gazing proudly at his silver trophy; Mr. Oxford and Timms discussing Tradition; Florrie, like the Wife of Bath come to life again; Mr. Runcorn in his dusty office sitting down to write a leader dyed in imperial purple: " Only the pyrotechnics, perhaps, were a trifle excessive . . ." and it might have included too, the trampled and broken banner of Miss Foulkes: WE DON'T WANT FEST——

The Mayor pondered Polly's remark; and Stephen watched the crowd streaming through the turnstiles, and the players in their oddly assorted costumes, roundhead and cavalier, folk-dancer, foot-soldier, knight and nun, Councillor Noakes who despite his beard looked less like Shakespeare than anybody Stephen had ever seen, the Vicar bustling along in his threadbare cassock, Virginia going gravely towards the dressing-tent, and Lance with his arm round Edna's waist as they scampered away into the shadows. Polly is right, he thought. These are the particles that make us what we are; out of such particles is our history made.

The Mayor gravely and gratefully shook Polly's hand and went off to disrobe himself. Stephen as he walked with Polly in the direction of the men's dressing-tent caught sight of Faith coming down off the grandstand and for a moment hesitated. Polly gave him a push. " Go on," he said, with a great grin. " Go on. You're in love with her, Steve ! "

So Stephen ran to the bottom of the grandstand steps and met Faith there; and somehow it seemed quite natural now to take her by the hand, and quite natural too that their steps should lead them, not back towards the town, but away from it into the misty darkness. As they passed out of range of the last dimmed floodlight a small scurrying figure rather like a brown moth passed through its beam. The shabby old mackintosh was unmistakable; and so Stephen was not unduly surprised when a few moments later there came from out of the shadows behind the dressing-tent, shattering the night's sweet stillness, the sound of a minor explosion: a gigantic, a gargantuan, a superhuman sneeze.

Kemerton, July, 1950